## THE WAY OF THE BEAR

"An intriguing plot matches the well-developed, reflective leads. As always, the real strength of this series lies in its authentic atmosphere, evocative descriptions of the landscape, and fascinating details of Navajo life. Hillerman consistently satisfies."

—*Publishers Weekly*

"Besides offering an involving mystery, Hillerman delivers meaty insights on the natural world, paleontology, ancient and enduring Navajo customs and traditions, and the role of Indigenous people in preserving the land and nature's bounty."

—*Booklist*

## THE SACRED BRIDGE

"Captivating. . . . Series fans will be well satisfied."

—*Publishers Weekly*

"Gripping."                    —Bookreporter.com

## STARGAZER

"Tony Hillerman fans will appreciate her keeping his fictional creations, Jim Chee and Joe Leaphorn, alive and thriving. The storytelling gene has been proudly passed on from father to daughter."

—Bookreporter.com

## THE TALE TELLER

"Hillerman's writing becomes stronger with every new installment in the series, deepening the development of each character. . . . The picturesque Southwest, as well as the history of the Navajo, come through on each page."

—*Library Journal* (starred review)

"*The Tale Teller* is more than just a police procedural set in the Southwest, it's a reading experience not to be missed. Anne Hillerman has reached a new level of storytelling in this one, and she deserves recognition as one of the finest mystery authors currently working in the genre."

—New York Journal of Books

## SONG OF THE LION

"Hillerman seamlessly blends tribal lore and custom into a well-directed plot, continuing in the spirit of her late father, Tony, by keeping his characters (like Chee) in the mix, but still establishing Manuelito as the main player in what has become a fine legacy series."

—*Booklist*

"The latest from Hillerman continues worldbuilding in a tale that will reward long-term readers."

—*Kirkus Reviews*

"Fans of Leaphorn, Chee, and Manuelito, characters created by the author's father, Tony Hillerman, will savor this multilayered story of suspense, with its background of contemporary environmental versus development issues."

—*Library Journal*

# ROCK WITH WINGS

# SPIDER WOMAN'S DAUGHTER

# THE WAY
# OF THE BEAR

**Also by Anne Hillerman**

# ANNE
# HILLERMAN

# THE WAY
# OF THE BEAR

## A LEAPHORN, CHEE & MANUELITO NOVEL

**HARPER**

*An Imprint of HarperCollinsPublishers*

THE WAY OF THE BEAR. Copyright © 2023 by Anne Hillerman. All rights reserved. Printed in the United States of America. No part of this book may be used or reproduced in any manner whatsoever without written permission except in the case of brief quotations embodied in critical articles and reviews. For information, address HarperCollins Publishers, 195 Broadway, New York, NY 10007.

First Harper premium printing: August 2024
First Harper paperback printing: January 2024
First Harper hardcover printing: April 2023

Print Edition ISBN: 978-0-06-290840-7
Digital Edition ISBN: 978-0-06-290841-4

*Cover design by Jarrod Taylor*
*Cover photographs © Nick Fox/Alamy Stock Photo*

Harper and HarperCollins are registered trademarks of HarperCollins Publishers in the United States of America and other countries.

24 25 26 27 28  BVGM  10 9 8 7 6 5 4 3 2 1

# THE WAY
# OF THE BEAR

# 1

An unexpected noise, the *crack-crack* of gunshots, stopped Bernadette Manuelito where she stood and put her instantly on alert.

She lowered her hand to her weapon and felt her body begin to flood with adrenaline. Instinctively, she flattened herself against the red sandstone cliff face. Her breath came in shallow bursts as she waited for more shots or whatever else came next.

It was December, Nítch'itsoh, a season when nature rested, calmly settling in for the challenge of deep winter's long nights. The surprise of the gunshots shattered Bernie's peace, but the winter evening rolled on as if the blast had never happened.

The more intently Bernie listened, the more the desert seemed to grow silent. Nítch'itsoh could be the time of great winds, but this evening was windless. She could barely make out the sound of a vehicle moving in the distance. She knew a powerful snowstorm was in the twenty-four-hour forecast. The dry earth would welcome the moisture. For now, anticipation hung heavily in the still air and a frigid, fierce winter loomed ahead.

Through the darkness a few feet from where she stood, she saw an owl's slow, gliding flight, its swooping descent, and then the quick ascent with a struggling mouse in its talons.

The né'èshjaà landed on a rock that jutted from the cliff face, and after a moment she heard its call. The sound reminded her of something Jim Chee's uncle had told her and Chee years before. He had explained to them that Owl was an envoy of the Holy People. She also knew that many considered owls to be omens of death, and she'd encountered more than enough of that recently in her job as a police officer. For a Navajo raised with abiding respect for the traditional ways, seeing an owl meant it was time to offer a prayer for protection. Bernie took a moment to do that.

She leaned against the cold stone and reflected on the word *Nílch'itsoh* and the meaning of the season. For her and Chee, her husband, the days had been filled with strong winds of change, a tornado of turmoil on the job and off. She had come to this special place, the Valley of the Gods in the shadow of the sacred Bears Ears Buttes, in search of a few hours of winter peace.

Relax, she told herself. She filled her lungs with the dry, frigid air, straightened her spine, ordered her shoulders down from her ears, and rolled her head from right to left and back again to release the tension in her neck. She stepped away from the rock face to look out over the expansive landscape. She took another soothing breath.

Finally, the stillness that had seemed threatening reassured her. The shots weren't close and she reminded herself that in rural areas such as this, occasional gunshots were part of the human soundtrack.

Bernie had never visited the Bears Ears National Monument, so last week when Chee invited her to join him, she'd eagerly accepted. Because Chee had an assignment in Bluff, he had arranged a time to speak with Desmond Grayhair. The hatááłii and leader from the Navajo Mountain community had suggested a spot at the southern edge of Bears Ears, and asked Chee to invite his wife so they could get acquainted. Chee had urged Bernie to go with him to meet the medicine man, gently mentioning that her energy could use some recharging and that Bears Ears was the perfect spot for that. Indeed, the power of Bears Ears as a place to heal was deeply embedded in Diné tradition.

When they had spoken earlier that afternoon, the old hatááłii had sensed her sadness and, instead of more conversation or a sweat lodge with the women, suggested she take a quiet walk among the imposing red stone monoliths of Valley of the Gods. Bernie agreed. She wanted a heart-stirring place to watch the sun set, to hike, to think, to begin to figure out what came next for her. She needed a new plan, a map for the future, because what she thought would work clearly hadn't.

Earlier that afternoon she had left their motel in Bluff, wanting plenty of light for her explorations, and driven herself to the beautiful Valley of the Gods while the medicine man, Chee, and other men participated in a sweat lodge ceremony. The valley sat at the edge of the expansive Bears Ears landscape—more than a million acres in south-eastern Utah's San Juan County. Bernie welcomed the opportunity to have some time alone and to see this special place, an area some people called a miniature Monument Valley, a reference to the Navajo Nation geological park forty-five min-utes to the south. The area's beautiful sandstone buttes and forms were similar to those of Monu-ment Valley, each uniquely eroded. The formation called Lady in the Bathtub made Bernie smile; it didn't take much imagination to see the profile of a woman with her hair piled atop her head sitting in the stone tub with a towel supporting her neck. It looked to Bernie as though the person in stone was enjoying a book along with her soak.

She had read that the valley was rich with ar-chaeological and paleontological artifacts, and hoped she might find an arrowhead or find the outlines of an ancient bone in the eroded sand-stone. She spotted a potsherd and then another, and began to search more closely. Abandoned dwellings of ancestral southwestern people dot-ted the Colorado Plateau and Bears Ears National Monument, but something triggered her suspi-cion. The potsherds lay everywhere on the bare ground, as though someone had scattered them from a bucket.

Then she saw the tools. Modern tools, not those used by the ancient ones. The sunset's soft light reflected on the metal of picks, shovels, chisels, and hammers, and made the wooden handles of trowels and brushes glow. Someone had left sieves and buckets on the red sandstone. Teams looking for pots and yucca sandals could use these tools, but she sensed that something else was happening here. She moved closer to investigate and, with one final step, lost her balance.

The tumble left her breathless, lying on her back in the dirt below ground level. The fall had come so fast that it took a moment for her to process what had happened. Had she stepped into an open grave?

No, she realized; it was shallower than a grave, but just as narrow. It was a trench, probably part of whatever sort of excavation was going on here. But a trench like this should have been marked.

She lay still a moment, assessing herself for possible injury. Her hip and back might be bruised, but nothing was broken. Bernie was grateful for two things: she'd come to no major harm, and Chee hadn't witnessed her clumsiness.

She sat up. Then, using her embarrassment as a prod, she boosted herself to standing and climbed back to ground level. As she brushed the dirt from her jeans and coat, she noticed that she had scraped the palms of her hands on her climb out of the hole. She readjusted her red knit cap. She'd gathered her hair in a high ponytail; it provided good insulation on this chilly late afternoon.

Bernie surveyed her surroundings more closely. Tall, smooth sandstone walls towered above the trenching. She saw what seemed to be a panel of petroglyphs carved into the sandstone. The ancient images banded the rock about five feet from the cliff base, but as far away as she was, she couldn't clearly identify the symbols. Because of their unique beauty, she knew petroglyphs were sometimes referred to as rock art. She wasn't surprised to see them, given the area's long history of human occupation.

She realized that these images painstakingly created by pecking or carving directly on the rock surface were more than just pretty pictures. As symbols, some might silently speak to the cultural and spiritual beliefs of the ancient ones who created them. Other petroglyphs represented tribal, clan, kiva, or society markers, perhaps the people's equivalent of a logo. Some might have been messages to those who passed by, or symbols that referred to traditional stories perhaps now forgotten.

Bernie's Diné ancestors had considered Bears Ears a sacred place, and modern Navajos continued that practice. Ute, Paiute, Zuni, Hopi, and other Indigenous people also came here to pray, to hunt, to gather firewood, and to harvest plants and seeds for meals and for ceremonial uses.

She looked away from the rock art toward the huge natural structures of stone that gave the valley its name, the earth's creations to which American newcomers had given descriptive titles: Seven Sailors, Rooster Butte, and more. The early sunset gilded the desert with a gentle pink glow, warm hues reflected in the sky as well as in the rocks. The full moon had risen, adding another element to the beauty that surrounded her.

Bernie told herself she could enjoy being here a bit longer. She had just enough light, before the first star appeared, to hike up to the cliff base for a closer look at the rock carvings. Then she would head back to Bluff and her cozy motel room. The trench and misplaced sherds left her uneasy.

She slipped into a rhythm as she climbed toward the hillside and thought about the things she'd been avoiding: how to move forward with her career after being rejected for a job as detective; what to do to help Darleen and Mama; and, of course, the experience she was too sad to name. But instead, she told herself to take it easy as she hiked toward the ancient figures, noticing that they were well shielded from the elements by their position on a wall beneath a protective overhang. She turned on her phone's flashlight—the only thing the device was good for out here, with no service—to penetrate the shadows. Its bright beam found human-like figures the old ones had left here.

She felt a chill up her spine and stepped away, averting her eyes.

The faces of the images had been scratched off, destroyed. White people called that defacement vandalism, but it was something bigger to the Diné. For them, the now-faceless people etched into the sandstone spoke of witchcraft. She didn't want to look at the images, but she was a good cop. She forced herself to take some photos so she could report the damage to the Bureau of Land Management tomorrow when she got cell coverage. She would send the pictures along with her report of the disfigurement, the unmarked pit, and the seemingly abandoned tools. The BLM and the Forest Service cooperated in providing law enforcement to the area, and she knew this part of the monument was BLM territory.

Bernie had earned a college degree in botany and then, inspired by a family heritage of service, went on to practical, no-nonsense law enforcement training. But she had grown up listening to the stories of mysterious evil, of witches and skin walkers and chindis. The damaged images made her uneasy; time to head back to Bluff. Darkness came quickly after sunset in December, and she had underestimated how long it would take her to return to the vehicle.

She climbed down carefully and took pictures of the excavation trench and shovels before beginning the hike toward Chee's truck—their truck now, because her Tercel was parked in Shiprock. She zipped her jacket up to the soft fake-fur collar. The white coat was new, a color impractical for the desert, but she loved how warm and cocooned she felt inside it. As she walked, she listened for the rhythmic bleat of a nighthawk or the occasional rustle of an unknown creature moving earth to create a burrow, or perhaps a place from which to ambush passing prey.

Long after she had convinced herself that the gun blasts amounted to nothing more than a distant rancher shooting at a coyote, with the sandstone cliffs providing acoustic resonance, a different, fainter sound captured her attention. Engine noise again. As it grew louder, she categorized it as a pickup truck heading in her direction. A minute later she saw the flicker of headlights.

The lights paused when they came to the area where she had parked, perhaps two miles from where she'd seen the petroglyphs. Then the illumination proceeded along the rough dirt road, at a speed that reflected the confidence of someone who knew where the ruts and rocks lay. She reminded herself that Diné families lived out this way as she watched the lights bounce over the empty road, approaching her and the excavation site. As the vehicle grew nearer, she could see in the moonlight that it was a dark pickup with something shaped like a thick, elongated cylinder on the grille.

Her training and experience in law enforcement flashed a warning about standing alone in the dark in a white coat far from civilization at a place where she'd already heard shots and a petroglyph had been vandalized. She used the moonlight to navigate as she moved away from the easy walking terrain the road provided and started jogging into the rougher mesa country.

The truck also turned off the road, the headlights now shining on the open sand, shrubs, and rocks. It was coming toward her, almost as if on purpose.

Stay calm, she ordered herself, and she began a survival checklist. She put her hand on her loaded gun and estimated the distance it would take to get to the relative safety of her and Chee's truck. Too far. She looked around for a place she could hide, but could see none.

She started to run.

The truck headed directly for her. There was no mistaking it now.

She swerved as quickly as she could, glad that she'd worn boots instead of her jogging shoes. She stumbled over a dead tree limb, recovered her balance at the last possible moment, and kept

moving, looking for cover. The truck was gaining.
Her legs felt like rubber. Her heart pounded, and
her lungs burned. She was sweating despite the
cold air.

The truck was still gaining.

In the growing darkness, she could make out
an indentation in the earth that looked like an
arroyo, with cliffs on the other side. She sped
toward it, hoping the rougher terrain would de-
ter the truck. The vehicle lost ground, looking
for a smoother path. Bernie struggled out of her
beloved new white coat, which now made her a
perfect target. She stripped down to her red tur-
tleneck sweater and tossed the jacket as far from
her path as she could. Then she zagged away from
the truck's headlights, staying low in the arroyo.
She cataloged her advantages: she could hide in
places the truck couldn't go, could change directions faster, and she was an experienced, fit run-
ner. And, of course, she had a gun.

The truck slowed, inching through the arroyo.
Bernie held her breath until it had rolled past her
and then raced away from the lights toward some
larger rocks that offered the only possibility of a
gap that would hide her. Seeing a dark crevice that
might work, she took the chance and sprinted toward the cliff face. She pressed herself between
two sandstone slabs almost large enough to conceal her, but as cold as death.

Her breath now came in gasps. The truck's
lights shone near her feet but moved on. She kept
the truck in sight, hoping to catch the license
plate number, but the dim light and distance made
it impossible.

Then, in the moonlight, the truck changed course, again heading in her direction. An arm extended from the passenger window. An arm holding a rifle. She heard a shot.

The shooter had aimed for the white spot in the dark landscape, the brightness of her jacket, snagged on a bush. The cab light came on as the passenger-side door opened and the shooter climbed out, but Bernie couldn't discern any details. The person picked up the coat and stood holding it a moment, then shook it, dropped it, and stomped on it before heading back to the truck.

She smelled the dust in the air as the truck and its people rumbled away from the jacket she'd loved, away from her hiding place.

When Bernie could no longer see the taillights and her heart had stopped pounding so fiercely, she began to hike back to her vehicle, hoping no harm had come to it. She was cold and shaken, but as she neared her truck, anger replaced her fear. Whoever had been driving and whoever had shot the rifle had messed with the wrong woman.

Officer Bernadette Manuelito did not make a good crime victim.

She reached the truck, climbed in, started the engine, and put on an old coat Chee kept for emergencies. She had miles to drive before she found cell service to make her 911 call, then to reach Chee to explain why she was later than she'd expected, and then, finally, to get to bed. Her hip ached from the fall, and she was uncomfortably chilly. And when the truck started to warm up, she realized she was bone-tired.

As she drove, she thought about the attack and watched for the lights of the truck that had threatened her. It could be on the road in front of her, or it might have pulled over to a side road to wait in case she drove past. Perhaps the people in it were drunk or crazy. She'd been hiking on public land, so they couldn't claim she was in the wrong place at the wrong time. The fact that neither the shot nor the truck itself had struck her seemed to be a blessing from the sacred bears that protected this place—Shash Jáá, Bears Ears.

Bernie knew that in her culture's tradition, the bear was not only a guardian but also a spiritual guide that represents strength and self-knowledge. The spirit animal Shash, the bear, stands as a symbol of deliberate action, introspection, soul searching, and insight. Many believe that bears have great healing power, and she was in need of all of that now.

As fatigue gained ground, Bernie turned off the heater, lowered the window, and focused on the horizon, searching for different lights, the subtle glow that indicated the small town where they were staying.

Bluff, now a community of about four hundred hardy souls founded by Mormon pioneers in 1880, sustained itself with tourism and outdoor recreation. It and nearby Blanding and Monticello offered the most convenient supply stops for hikers, explorers, and campers on their way to Bears Ears.

Even though she'd never been here before, Bernie knew that Shash Jáá was a place of both blessings and controversy. The Bears Ears themselves, twin buttes that jut into the horizon, guarded federal land rich in resources, nature largely untouched by human interference. Local conservationists had excitedly welcomed President Barack Obama's decision to create Bears Ears National Monument in 2016, only to have their hopes crushed when the subsequent president had slashed the monument's more than a million acres to a fifth of its original size. She and Chee had been relieved when President Joe Biden restored the original boundaries.

Bernie knew that the return to the larger allotment had received broad support from a coalition of Native American groups. But others, including many Diné who lived in the area, opposed the national monument. Some Navajo healers who came to gather native plants and certain items essential for specific traditional practices worried that their work could be restricted by new federal regulations. Area families had long collected firewood for winter warmth in the Bears Ears forests, a legacy that could be ended under the national monument status. And she knew Utah Navajos who firmly believed that too much of their state was already under federal control. But now that a coalition of five tribes—Navajo, Hopi, Zuni, the Ute Mountain Ute, and the Ute Indian Tribe—was part of the management, Bernie had more confidence that the monument designation would help protect this sacred place.

She looked at the clock on the truck's dashboard. If all went well, she'd get back to the motel in another twenty minutes, much later than she'd planned. Chee would be worried about her. She decided she would tell him about the truck and the person with the rifle in the morning. She didn't want to deal with his protective side tonight, even as she realized this would be yet another secret withheld from the man she loved.

Her phone seemed to ring the moment she had service again.

"Hey, you. Everything OK?" Chee sounded tired.

"I'm fine. On my way back. I'll be there soon. How was your evening?"

"Oh, OK." The flatness in his voice surprised her, but that could have been the exhaustion talking. "See you soon. Wake me up if I'm asleep."

"OK."

"I'll be counting on it. I need to know you're here safely."

"No problem."

But a few minutes later, a problem arose. She noticed the vehicle ahead of her—not the dark pickup but a sedan—weaving dangerously on and off the pavement. It was the only car she'd encountered on this route, and it pulled her back to reality.

# 2

Not only was the old sedan with a burned-out taillight in front of Bernie veering, it sped up and slowed down erratically. Watching it drift onto the sandy shoulder, she tapped her brakes and flashed her lights. The car slowed down, crossed the center of the road, briefly returned to the correct side of the highway, then went off the road again. This time, the sedan stopped.

She pulled her truck onto the shoulder a safe distance behind the car and turned on her emergency flashers. Another drunk driver, she assumed as she took off her seat belt. They were lucky no one had been driving in the other lane. After everything that had already happened, an ugly collision was the last thing she needed.

The driver's door of the sedan opened, and a young Navajo man raced toward her, leaving his car's lights on and his vehicle running.

She lowered her window. "Yá'át'ééh. Everything OK with you?"

"No, ma'am, not OK. We've got a situation." She read the distress in his face as he rushed to the truck. She was glad she didn't smell beer on his breath.

"What's up?"

"My wife, she's having a baby."

"Right now?"

He nodded. "That's why I pulled over. We were on the way to the awéé' hayiinílí, the midwife, you know." His voice vibrated with tension. "Can you help us? Hannah says the baby won't wait."

She nodded. Chee always kept a first-aid kit in the truck, and she reached for it, along with her flashlight, the hand sanitizer they had stocked up on during the pandemic, and an all-purpose tool that included a knife and scissors. She grabbed the supplies and closed the truck's door. "What's your name?"

"Roper."

"I'm Bernie."

"Are you a nurse or a doctor or something?"

"No. I'm a cop. But don't worry. I've had training for situations like this." She felt anxiety rising in her gut, and ordered it to go away. She needed to project confidence for this man.

She expected him to ask if she'd ever delivered a baby, but to her relief, he just said, "Let's go."

Hannah, the mother-to-be, seemed too young and too small to be having a baby. But being petite worked in her favor tonight. It gave her room to be more comfortable in the front seat.

"Roper, turn on your emergency flashers. We don't want anyone running into us." Then Bernie introduced herself to the woman.

Hannah seemed strong, fit, and surprisingly calm. "The contractions are really close and strong. I figure the baby will be here soon. What do you think?"

"I know you will both do fine, and I'm here to help. Is this your first baby?"

"Yes. Roper and I just finished our birthing classes. Even though our little one's due date isn't for another two weeks, they said the baby could come anytime."

"We weren't expecting to be parents tonight, though." Roper put his hand on his wife's forehead as he spoke. "I'm glad you were driving out here."

Hannah nodded. "My auntie, my shimá yazhí, is our awééʼ hayiiníłí. We called her when my water broke. But this baby must be like its dad, an impatient . . ."

Then a contraction came, and Hannah groaned.

Bernie took her hand. "I know you will ace this. You were smart to take those classes. Everything will go well." She said it as much for herself as for the couple. "We'll all get through this." Although the front seat of a sedan parked on the shoulder of a deserted highway on a freezing winter night didn't make the ideal situation for delivering an infant, the three of them would do the best with what they had.

Roper said, "We packed an emergency bag. It's in the trunk. I can . . ."

"Not now." Bernie turned to him. "Stay here. I need your help with the light. I have to see what's happening."

She rubbed the sanitizer on her hands and arms

and instructed Roper to do the same. She was fast, but he moved like lightning. Then she handed him the flashlight and showed him where to aim it. In the expectant father's shaking hands the light became a strobe. Hannah began to moan more often and with greater intensity.

Bernie had heard from colleagues who had become volunteer emergency birth attendants that in the ideal situation, babies almost delivered themselves. In those fortunate situations the babies only needed tender, supporting hands to catch them when uterine contractions slid them from the birth canal into their big new world. She hoped that would be the case tonight.

With the help of the light, Bernie was relieved to see what she assumed was a bit of the baby's scalp. She didn't know what she would have done if the baby was in the breech position. Thankfully, Hannah remembered how to breathe with the contractions and knew to push when the time came. First the head, then a pause for the next contraction, then the shoulders slipped free. Bernie supported the tiny body as it slid out. Roper stood close by to hold the child. It was a girl, and she acknowledged her presence in the car with a healthy wail.

"Oh, darling baby, welcome to the world." Calmer now, he gently placed his daughter on her mother's chest beneath her shirt for skin-to-skin contact on this frigid evening. "Hannah, you did it. What a night. What a miracle."

Bernie looked for something to wipe the baby's nose and mouth and to wrap her in to keep her warm. As if reading Bernie's mind, Roper removed his jacket and then slipped off his long-sleeved T-shirt, printed with the image of a dinosaur. He handed it to her and she looked at it quizzically.

"That's a picture of a *Utahraptor*, Utah's official state dinosaur." He handed the shirt to her. "Amazing, right?"

"Yes. This whole thing is amazing."

He put his jacket back on and zipped it up against the evening's cold. Bernie gently picked up the newborn and used her father's soft T-shirt, warmed by his body heat, to dry and stimulate the baby. Then she gave the little one back to her mother. Hannah smiled and pulled her coat around them both.

Roper put his hand on Hannah's arm. "Honey, you did great. I'm glad Officer Bernie was the one in that truck. I don't know what would have happened otherwise."

Bernie felt a wave of embarrassment.

"Enough of that. We need to cut the umbilical cord and tie it off when it stops pulsing. Can you handle the job?"

"Yes. I'd like to. We have some yarn from Hannah's mother we can use to tie it with. I watched that in the birthing class."

When the time came, Roper rubbed more sanitizer on his hands and his knife, and cut the cord that linked Hannah to her daughter. Bernie saw tears in his eyes.

She snugged the shirt around the small body again, wishing she had a blanket or an extra coat or something to keep mother and infant warm.

Roper seemed to read her mind.

"I'll be right back. I'll get the bag we brought now."

She heard the trunk release, and then Roper returned with a duffel bag. He unzipped it on the back seat and handed Bernie a large towel. She placed it on top of mother and daughter for more warmth.

"Your wife could use a blanket, if you've got one somewhere."

"Sure."

He brought one from the bag and with touching gentleness spread it over Hannah and the baby. Hannah's face relaxed into a huge smile. Then she started to sob. Roper was weeping, too, weeping and grinning. Bernie felt teary-eyed herself, and enormously grateful that things had gone so well.

"What now?"

Bernie remembered her training. "We need to make sure the placenta will be delivered."

Hannah said, "Will you stay with us until then? I'm starting to feel shaky."

"Of course, I'm right here. Shaky is normal, perfectly normal." Bernie put her hand on the new dad's shoulder. "I'll let you know when you can start to get these two—and yourself—someplace warm. How far away is the midwife's house?"

Hannah never took her eyes off her daughter. "I'm not sure."

Roper said, "It's only twenty minutes at the most. She has delivered dozens of babies. We'll be in good hands."

Bernie finished her job as emergency baby

catcher, happy and somewhat amazed that all had gone smoothly.

"You guys are all set."

Hannah squeezed her hand.

Bernie left the new parents alone in the car with their precious one. She stood by the side of the road, looking up at the December sky. A shooting star flared overhead, stunningly brilliant before it faded to nothingness. She considered the irony of the situation. After all the thinking and hoping she and Chee had done over the decision to have a baby themselves, she, of all the people in the world, happened to be on hand to help bring this new life into the world.

Then she heard footsteps and turned to see Roper smiling from ear to ear.

"*Thank you* isn't a big enough word."

"Glad to help." She meant it, too.

"What are you doing out here at night anyway?"

"Oh, someone suggested I come to look at Valley of the Gods, and next thing I knew it was dark, and you and the mother-to-be were swerving all over the road in front of me."

"You know, Bernie, some places out here aren't safe at night. They say there might be some drawings on the rocks the old ones made, pictures that aren't right. And there's crazies out here. You be careful." He gave her a serious look. "I'm in the security business, Officer, so I know about this stuff."

"Well, talk your boss into giving you the day off tomorrow so you can help Hannah and get to know your baby."

"He better, otherwise I'll have to kill him or get a new job, or maybe both." Roper chuckled.

"Enjoy your daughter. I know you'll be great parents."

"I hope so."

"Were you expecting a girl?"

"We didn't know what to expect, but we were hoping for a daughter."

Bernie climbed into the truck and followed Roper and Hannah and their little one until the sedan pulled off at a junction with a dirt road and she saw the lights of a house ahead. Roper turned his emergency flashers back on and motioned to her with his arm out the window. She drove up next to him.

"What's wrong?"

Hannah said, "I forgot to thank you." She sounded happy and exhausted. "Ahéhee. We'd like to send you a photo of our girl. Would that be OK?"

"Better than OK. Of course. Text it, that's easiest." Bernie quickly gave them her cell number.

She watched their car disappear down the track heading to the building. She pictured the auntie's surprise at seeing the couple and then her relief and delight at the new child. As an experienced midwife, she would examine the infant and check Hannah and advise the couple on what to do from here. They should be in good hands.

As Bernie headed for Bluff, she felt energized and happier than she had felt for weeks. The reaction surprised her. She knew many things could have gone wrong with the baby or the mother.

She deeply appreciated the way the situation had worked out. She realized that she'd been focused on her own losses so totally that she hadn't allowed herself to share in someone else's joy.

She adjusted the truck's heater for more warmth and, as she grew closer to Bluff, considered pulling her phone from her backpack to call Chee. But then the lights of a patrol car flashed behind her. She didn't know what the speed limit was, so she slowed and pulled onto the shoulder, hoping the vehicle would sail past. Instead, the unit closed in directly behind her. She stopped and extracted her police ID.

The officer identified himself as sheriff's deputy Douglas Dayton, gave her a long silent stare, then asked to see her driver's license. She expected a scolding and maybe a ticket, depending on how the officer felt about professional courtesy.

"So you're Officer Bernadette Manuelito?"

"I am." She waited for him to explain why he had pulled her over.

"A Navajo Nation police lieutenant, a guy named Chee, thought your vehicle might have broken down out here. He called to ask for help looking for you, you know, making sure you were safe. He said he called and called your cell but no answer."

"Oh." The idea that her husband would contact a stranger to find her made her angry—did he think she couldn't take care of herself? But it also touched her heart. She was more than an hour overdue from the time she'd told him she'd be back at the lodge. "I'm fine. The problem is lack of cell service out there."

She saw the officer frown as he looked at the blood on her coat and jeans, a result of the delivery.

"You sure you're OK? You aren't injured?"

"I just helped a mom have a baby in a car on the side of the road. Kind of messy."

"What about her?"

"Oh, she and the baby seem to be fine."

A grin spread across his face. "Good. Glad to hear that. And welcome to one of the gateways to Bears Ears National Monument. I'd say see you later, but I'm starting vacation as soon as my shift ends. Heading to California before the blizzard gets here."

"There's something else before you go." She described the encounter with the truck and the rifle.

"I'll tell the sheriff about it so he can follow up."

She was surprised that he seemed so unconcerned, but attributed the attitude to his pending vacation, a variation of short-timer syndrome.

"Will you call Chee and tell him you are OK?"

"Of course."

She waited until the deputy left. Her phone had two bars, enough service for a staticky call.

Chee answered immediately. "Honey, I've been worried sick. I thought you would be back a lot sooner. What happened?"

"Complicated story, and I don't want to start it now." The narratives would take time, and so would his questions. She'd save it for when they were together. "And before you ask, I'm fine. FINE." She said it again for emphasis. "We'll talk when I see you. I'm on my way."

"But why are you so late? You're never—"

"It's been a long day. See you soon. Bye."

She'd tell him about Hannah and her husband, happy news first, and then about the encounter with people in a truck shooting at her with a rifle. She took a deep breath, grateful to be alive and to have a good man waiting for her.

3

Jim Chee had noticed a change in his wife ever since the department passed her over for the detective position the month before. They both realized that the chosen candidate had not only more seniority but also political and family connections to the chief of police, the man who made the call. But the rejection still hurt. For the past month Bernie had been quieter than usual, more distracted, and barely had laughed at all.

It didn't help her mood that the new captain at the Shiprock substation—the acting replacement for Captain Largo, who had retired—had accepted Largo's recommendation to promote Chee to lieutenant. Chee had negotiated a job description that enabled him to have hands-on involvement in cases that demanded extra attention, as an offset to too much bureaucracy. The extra income would make it easier for Bernie if she decided to take a break from working with Navajo Nation law enforcement. But the contrast between his luck and hers had created some tension between them.

Besides the professional disappointment, something else had happened to Bernie. Something personal, a deep grief. Until she could speak its name, he held it as her secret.

Bernie teased him about worrying over her, but she was precious to him. After she ended the phone call, he got out of the chair where he had been pretending to watch television and went outside. He stood on the portal of the Bluff Inn, looking out toward the cars that guests had parked and unloaded, as if somehow being there, waiting for her to approach in the truck, would bring her back sooner.

He watched a woman walk from the Bluff Inn office toward a blue van in the motel parking area. Under the lights, he could see that the vehicle was covered in dust and looked as though it had been rolled at least once and been repaired. The woman was slim, athletic, and attractive for a middle-aged bilagáana.

She looked his way. "Hey, handsome. Excuse me, but could you give me a hand?" He could hear the smile in her voice.

The question surprised him. "With what?"

"I've got a big cooler packed with supplies I need to bring inside. It's awkward. And a lot easier to carry with two people."

"Sure."

Chee approached her van. The cooler had handles on both ends. It was heavy even with the two of them lifting it. Luckily, they didn't have far to go.

"Hold on. I'll get the door to my room so we can lug it in."

She opened the motel room next door to his and Bernie's and clicked on the lights.

"Let's put it here." She tossed her head toward an empty space beneath the window, and they lowered it.

She rolled her shoulders. "I'm Jessica Johnson."

"Jim Chee."

"Thanks for your help. That thing was heavy."

Chee stepped back outside. "What's in the cooler?"

"Mostly beer. Some soft drinks and bottled water. It's for our celebration with the crew tomorrow, my last day on the site. A little party to thank them for their help. I remember those college days of never having quite enough to eat." She shook her head. "College? High school, elementary school. Our family never had enough of anything except bills and problems. I like to treat these young people with some respect." She smiled at him. "Wanna relax a minute and have a beer or something with me?"

"No, thank you. You mentioned the site. So, are you and your husband archaeologists?"

"I am. My husband, Kyle, is a paleontologist who does a lot of work out here too, and this time he's been my crew supervisor. I've been focusing on Pueblo ceramics. Just finishing up for the year."

"Where is your site?"

"Near Comb Ridge."

Chee knew that the Comb Ridge area had a rich heritage of early habitation. Known as Tséyík'áán, "the Big Snake," in the Navajo language, it was a

sacred place near another sacred place, Valley of
the Gods, where Bernie had gone hiking.

"How about you, Jim Chee? Are you a paleontologist too? Bears Ears attracts lots of you guys.
Or maybe an archaeologist?"

He shook his head. "Not me. I had a class on
geology in college that covered a little about fossils.
I enjoyed it, but when I took archaeology, I liked
that a whole lot better. In the end, I went a different
direction."

"Are you here on vacation?"

"No. I'm on an assignment. My wife, Bernie,
just got off a big job, so she's here with me."

"Work, huh? I get that totally."

They heard a vehicle approach and turned toward the noise.

Jessica said, "That might be Kyle. He went to
Blanding to get some more things for the celebration tomorrow. I took advantage of his absence to
play a game of chess with Walter. You've probably
met that guy. He manages the motel."

Chee recognized the sound as their truck and
saw Bernie signal her turn into the motel parking lot.

Jessica was still talking. "So, what kind of job
brings you to the Bears Ears area?"

He thought of the simplest way to answer her
question.

"I'm in law enforcement. So is my wife. She just
pulled in."

"That sounds fascinating." Jessica pulled out her
phone and fiddled with it a moment as she spoke.
"Do you have a specialty that draws you out here?"

"It's an assignment for the Navajo chief of police." He ignored her tell-me-more look. "I've got to go. Good luck with your party tomorrow."

Bernie knew how to tell a good story, and the evening had given her an abundance of material. As she shared her adventure of assisting at the birth, Chee noticed how she carefully added details such as the car's erratic driving, the chill of the evening, the father's sweet willingness to give the baby the shirt off his back, and that first welcome cry. Good details, and not too many.

Then she snuggled in closer and told him about the abandoned tools, the trench that surprised her, the vandalized petroglyphs, and the gunshots. She told him how the driver had tried to run her down, and how the passenger shot and struck the jacket she'd hurled onto a bush as she ran.

Bernie relayed the story with matter-of-fact calmness, as though it had happened to someone else. Like a good investigator, she covered all the obvious questions: Yes, she was sure it was intentional. No, she couldn't identify the people in the vehicle. Even with the full moon, she'd lacked enough light to make out the truck's color except to know it was dark, perhaps black or deep blue. She had seen something strange on the grille, some kind of cylinder.

Chee barely maintained his composure, growing angrier with each new detail. When he was sure that she had finished her narration, the details all in place, he had questions.

"Did you get the plate number?"

"I couldn't see it."

"Did you call the sheriff?"

"I called 911 when I had a signal. And I told Deputy Dayton about it when he stopped me."

Then he said, for the third time at least, "I'm glad nothing worse happened. I'm relieved you're not hurt." And they lay together quietly.

They had been talking in bed, and he felt her stretch her legs against his. He enjoyed the warmth of her sweet body against his skin.

After a few moments of relaxing Bernie said, "Do you have a theory about the petroglyphs?"

He shifted away from her to better concentrate on the conversation. "No. Not yet. How about you?"

A few weeks ago, Bernie would have teased him about avoiding her. Now, her silent acceptance of it saddened him.

She stuck to business. "The vandalism was odd and obviously focused. By design. I've been thinking about it quite a bit. I'm calling the BLM in the morning to report it and send the photos."

"I'll be interested to hear what they have to say about the petroglyphs. I think Ajax Becenti is still the guy who works out here."

"You know everyone."

He put his arm around her. "That's what happens when you've been around a while, beautiful. I think I still have his cell phone number."

"I haven't heard about your day. How did the sweat with Hosteen Grayhair go?"

Chee moved his hand to the small of her back and pressed her closer. "Let's talk about that later."

"OK, but—"

A knock on the motel door interrupted them. Then they heard a woman's voice laced with panic.

"Jim Chee? It's Jessica. I need your help."

Chee sat up and spoke softly. "Bernie, honey, Jessica is the archaeologist in the next unit. I moved a cooler from her van."

"You better see what's going on."

He yelled toward the voice. "Hold on. I'll be there in a minute or two." They jumped up, quickly dressed, and Chee went to the door while Bernie straightened the covers on the bed. He answered the door wearing his shirt and pants, but still barefoot.

Jessica got right to the point. "Kyle isn't back yet. I can't reach him on the phone; it goes right to message. The grocery is closed, so I can't check there. I'm frantic with worry. I called 911, and the lady who answered took the information about him and the car and told me to call again if he didn't get back to the motel in twenty-four hours."

"Come in. It's too cold to stand out there. This is my wife, Officer Bernadette Manuelito."

"Have a seat." Bernie motioned toward a stuffed green chair. She and Chee sat on the remade bed.

Chee said, "Does your husband have any friends out here he could be with?"

She shook her head. "I called the guys on our crew we know best on the off chance he'd stopped there. No luck. Nothing."

Jessica looked tired, Bernie thought, like a woman running on fumes. "Does he have any major health issues?"

"Not at all. Kyle might be a touch overweight, but who isn't?"

"Was something bothering him?"

"Like what?"

"Oh, something recently that could have left him depressed, restless, unsettled, some reason he might need some time by himself?"

The woman shrugged. Bernie knew it wasn't uncommon for a person feeling overwhelmed by life to want time alone. That's why she'd gone for the hike that got out of control that night.

"Could his car have broken down?" Chee asked.

"I wondered about that. He's got his old Land Cruiser. Ugly as sin but reliable, because he's always tinkering with it. I drove to the grocery myself and back, looking for him all along the route, just in case, you know? Nothing." Jessica stood and started to pace. "It's so unlike Kyle. I'm worried, and I remembered that you said you were in law enforcement, so I thought you might have some ideas. I don't know what to do."

Chee stood too. "My best idea is for you to go to bed and keep your phone on. We'll wait until morning. If he's still not back, contact us, and Bernie and I will go with you to the sheriff's office. You've already searched his likely route and called people who might have seen him. That was really smart. There's nothing else we can do at the moment."

"But there must be something else I could try."

"Lieutenant Chee has dealt with a lot of missing persons." Bernie kept her tone calm. "He knows what he's talking about."

"Yes, but it just doesn't seem right to go back to

bed when I don't know why he's not here yet. I feel terrible, and I need—"

"I know, but you have to trust Chee's judgment on this. He understands how to handle these situations."

Jessica nodded. "I'm sorry I interrupted your evening, but this is very much out of character for Kyle. You probably think I'm crazy."

"No, not at all." Chee empathized with the woman's state of mind. Just hours ago, he had asked the sheriff to keep a lookout for his wife.

Bernie's voice was softer now. "If Chee failed to come home, I'd worry too. But you've done all you can. Let us know if he isn't back by morning, and we can talk again then. How does that sound?"

Jessica seemed to lighten up. She looked at them. "Do you think I'm overreacting?"

Bernie searched for a tactful response. While Jessica was showing clear concern for her husband, Bernie worried that she would work herself even deeper into a panic. "I think you really care about him."

"I do."

"We've all had a long day," Chee said. "We should get some rest."

"OK. I just—"

Bernie extended her hands, damaged palms toward the woman, a signal to stop talking.

Jessica left the sentence unfinished, and focused on Bernie's hands. "Bernie, what happened to you?"

"I was hiking in the dark at Valley of the Gods, and I fell into a trench."

"That's terrible. I'm glad you didn't break anything."

"Me too. We can talk tomorrow."

Jessica left, and Chee locked the door.

"What do you think?"

"I don't have enough information to have a solid opinion, but off the top of my head, I wonder if he could have been bored with driving the same route, decided to take a different way back, and got lost. Or maybe he has a sweetie on the side." She paused. "Maybe he needed a break from Jessica. That woman seems pretty intense."

Chee sat next to her on the bed. "Maybe he is one of those outspoken Protect Bears Ears guys and upset the wrong people."

"Or maybe he's on the other side of the issue, someone opposed to the national monument."

"Why?"

"He's a paleontologist, and I read that a few of them thought the expanded designation would make it harder to get a permit for exploration."

"There are always two sides to everything, right?" Chee yawned. "Just like a bed has two sides, you know. I'm ready for horizontal."

She agreed, both with the dichotomy of life and with the need for sleep. The ongoing dance between good and evil, positive and negative, was a deeply held Navajo cultural tenet. Some Navajos, including families who lived closest to Bears Ears, objected to the larger federal land designation because they dreaded new government regulations. Goodness knows, Indigenous people were familiar with how government rules could go against them.

"When I talked to the hataałii before my hike, he sounded nervous about the national monument designation."

"I know. He had some misinformation, and I tried to set him straight, but I don't know if he believed me. We discussed that a little before the sweat lodge." Chee looked at the ceiling for a moment. "I'm betting Jessica's husband shows up unharmed. He'll be embarrassed that he took what he thought would be a shortcut, lost his bearings out there in the dark. Or ran out of gas. It happens."

"I hope you're right." She yawned.

"Let's get some sleep. We didn't come out here so we could worry about someone's missing husband, right?"

"Right. We came to celebrate your promotion, Lieutenant Chee." She smiled at him. "And to give us time to catch our breath after those last cases. And for you to talk with Hosteen Grayhair about that apprenticeship and to meet with Mr. Moneybags at the request of the chief."

The time away from work also gave her space to consider her own future. She'd sought the detective job because she wanted a new challenge and because her most recent assignment had taken a toll on her and her husband. She'd been drugged and her mother targeted for death by the criminals she was investigating. Jeopardizing her own life to solve a case was one thing, but endangering Mama took worry to a whole new level. As much as she loved daily police work, she hated putting her family at risk, and she couldn't assure herself that it wouldn't happen again.

And she was haunted by the other thing, the incident she couldn't talk about, not even with Chee, because it would break his heart.

She was about to climb into bed when her phone chimed to announce several photos of Roper, Hannah, and their baby girl, now wrapped in a pink blanket instead of in Daddy's dinosaur shirt. She texted them back a thank-you, then handed Chee her phone. "Take a look."

"That's wonderful." He squeezed her tighter and felt her tears on his shoulder. "You've had quite a night. A near-death experience and then watching new life arrive in the world. You wanna talk some more about all that?"

"No."

He kissed her gently.

Chee lay in bed next to Bernie, holding her hand, thinking about his own day as her breath gradually slipped into a deeper, slower rhythm. She drifted to sleep as his brain spun with unease. He had learned to use sleeplessness as the gift of time with nothing to do except review the twenty-four hours that had ended and to plan for the day ahead.

He had come to this beautiful landscape and booked a room at the Bluff Inn for four reasons: to give Bernie a change of scenery that might lift her spirits; to do a sweat lodge with Hosteen Grayhair; to represent the Navajo Police at a thank-you ceremony arranged by a coalition of Native activists; and to handle a fundraising job for his new captain and the new chief of police. Bernie, of course, would not have agreed to a trip for her mental health, so he recast it as a celebration of his promotion to lieutenant.

Usually, time in the sweat lodge left him at peace. He had hoped that sitting in the crowded, hot, dark, and prayerful space would melt away the self-doubt that plagued him. Bernie's disappointment at not getting the job she wanted left him heartbroken too. Before that, he had watched helplessly as a good but troubled man committed suicide. But even after the sweat, peace remained beyond his grasp. Hózhó eluded him.

The journey to Bears Ears had begun weeks before. He'd called Hosteen Grayhair, curious to know if the elder had made a decision on accepting him as an apprentice. He reached Grayhair at his house in Navajo Mountain. The old gentleman chuckled at Chee's discontent and told him not to be impatient.

The advice made him grumpy and even more impatient.

"I can't help being in a hurry," Chee said, first in Navajo and then in English. "I'm getting older, and I have some big decisions to make."

"You've been getting older from the day you were born." Grayhair chuckled again.

Chee understood the futility of argument. He realized the medicine man was right.

"My friend, you know more than you imagine," Grayhair had said. "You haven't made time to appreciate it yet. Cultivate patience. Come to Bears Ears, and do a sweat with me and some others."

As he waited for sleep, Chee thought about the

ta'chééh, the sweat lodge structure, and how it had been part of his life for decades. The Diyin Diné, the Holy Ones, taught First Man how to build a sweat lodge, and it became the inaugural part of the new Diné world. Chee could picture First Man crafting it as the Holy Ones specified, with fifty stripped cedar logs and bark and mud to seal the structure, always working consciously and with great respect.

In addition to the cleanse, Diné men and women would use the sweat lodge as a place to learn to pray and to sing, to discover their roots, ponder their goals, and consider the meaning of life. With purified bodies, minds, and souls and confidence to believe in themselves, they would be protected from harm, danger, and evil, and not forgotten by the Holy People. The Diyin Diné gave the people the ta'chééh during the time of emergence into the fourth world, the Glittering World in which we humans currently live. The songs and prayers for the sweat ceremony came from the Holy People themselves as a gift to their five-fingered creatures.

Chee had strongly felt the presence of the Holy People, the ones Hosteen Grayhair called the Grandfathers, today in the ta'chééh with the hatáálii and the other men. He was grateful for that comfort, a gift he rarely received. He closed his eyes and took a deep breath and said some silent prayers. He thought about the power of gratitude and the wisdom of saying thank you for what he had. The repetition of the language soothed him.

He had reached a welcome state of calm when

a flashing light danced across his closed eyelids. Again, again. It came from his phone, he realized, alerting him to a text message. He ignored it until a voice inside him told him, then ordered him, to pay attention.

Reluctantly, he got up, careful not to awaken Bernie, and walked across the room to the desk.

The message came from the group he had driven to Utah to meet with as a representative of the Navajo Police. The organization, Utah Diné Bikéyah, had wanted a representative of the Navajo Nation to come to receive a certificate of gratitude for the way the police had worked with all parties to keep the situation peaceful. This was the group of activists who had fought hard to restore Bears Ears National Monument to its original size. They were letting him and his new boss, Captain Texas Adakai, know they had canceled the next day's session due to both a health crisis in the family of one of the leaders and the National Weather Service's prediction of a heavy snowstorm over the next twenty-four hours. They promised to reschedule.

Chee didn't mind missing the hoopla, but the cancellation—and especially the predicted storm— could have ramifications for the rest of the day. His boss had asked, actually ordered, him to meet with a man named Chapman Dulles, a scientist who had decided that he wanted to support the Navajo Nation's Fallen Officers Memorial Fund. But before Dulles wrote the check—and he had hinted it would be a big one—he had questions. He lived near Bluff. Would it be possible for an officer to meet with him? The job overlapped with the Bears Ears Inter-Tribal Coalition meeting, so Chee was the chosen delegate for the funding questions.

When Chee hesitated, explaining that fund-raising was not in his nature, his boss made him an offer. Captain Adakai, acting head of the sub-station until the chief of police could name a replacement for newly retired captain Howard Largo, said he'd toss in an extra day off. So Chee agreed to put on a fundraiser cap and schedule the meeting with Hosteen Grayhair too.

He and Bernie had enjoyed the drive from Shiprock, stopping at Teec Nos Pos to visit friends. She'd met the healer and gone for her hike while he'd done the sweat. If things had been different, she would have joined him, but Navajo tradition al-lowed only men or only women in the sweat lodge at one time.

Thanks to the text and the thoughts it stirred, Chee was now wide awake. He crawled out of bed quietly, slipped into his shoes, zipped on his coat over the sweatpants that served as winter paja-mas, and stepped outside to check the weather. Earlier, the sky had shone with stars, but now clouds hung low and heavy with unfallen snow. The desert air smelled wonderfully moist. He walked until the cold encouraged him to go back inside. When he turned toward the motel, he no-ticed that Jessica had pulled the curtains closed, and her room seemed dark behind them. But light shone through the windows where he and Bernie were staying. His lovely wife never talked about what now awakened her at night except to say it was na'iidzeeł, a dream.

When he opened the door, Bernie looked up and put her book on the bed next to her. "I missed you. I woke up, and you were gone. Is everything OK?"

"Fine." He gave her a quick hug. "I got a text telling me that the tribal coalition event tomorrow was canceled because of weather. I went outside to see if the storm was here. Just cloudy out there." He slipped off his jacket and turned up the heat in the little room. The wall unit made a racket as it put out a welcome blast of warm air.

"I'm glad that's all it was. I'm not sleeping well either."

He had planned on trying to go back to sleep, but Bernie's tone of voice persuaded him to change his mind. "Want to talk?"

"No. See if you can find a movie to watch."

"You seem worried about something."

She shrugged. "I keep thinking about those darn petroglyphs. Of course, I know that creeps damage them for spite, but I can't help wondering if they were destroyed for another reason. If that is a site for witchcraft. Or if someone wants people to think that and keep their distance."

"Witches, vandals, or drunks. Is that all that's bothering you?"

She shrugged again. "The job I didn't get. Mama's forgetfulness. Darleen being Darleen. All that."

And there was something else, too, he knew. It was something she couldn't talk about. When he asked what bothered her, she simply replied that she couldn't speak of it yet. He worried about her but understood that continuing to probe would not make things better.

He turned on the TV and found something mindless for them to share.

Morning arrived too early. He awoke to find Bernie gone, but that didn't surprise him. Ever since he had known her, she'd liked to run before dawn, returning as the sky lightened. He dressed and made some in-room coffee. When she came back to the motel, she looked more peaceful than she had in a while.

She sipped the coffee without commenting that it could have been hotter and stronger. "Last night you told me your event was canceled. Did I hear that right?"

"Yes. The Bears Ears Inter-Tribal Coalition that wanted to thank us at their meeting, the one where I was representing the captain. I still have to talk to the funding guy." He finished his coffee, wishing it had been tastier.

"Was it snowing when you were out there last night?" Bernie went to the window and wiped off the fog that blocked her view.

"No."

"Well, it snowed a bit overnight. There's some accumulation, maybe a quarter inch, and it looks cloudy and cold." She put her cup on the table and turned back to him. "I have a favor to ask you. Would you come back to that vandalized site with me? I keep picturing those damaged petroglyphs and the tools. It bugs me."

"Sure." Thinking about Bernie's close call

reminded him of the panicked woman last night. "Since we haven't heard from Jessica about her missing husband, I'm assuming everything is OK."

Bernie nodded. "She's probably embarrassed that she made such a fuss."

"See if you can get the BLM ranger to meet you at the site this morning. I'll go with you. My appointment with the rich guy isn't until later."

"Ranger Ajax Becenti, right?" She frowned. "I'm disappointed he hasn't called to follow up on my complaint."

"Becenti is a good guy. Maybe he wasn't on duty. Or maybe the deputy you talked to didn't refer the call to the BLM."

She called the Bureau of Land Management office and left a concise message, including the availability of photos she'd taken and a description of the truck that tried to kill her.

They ate the sandwiches she'd packed, and when Becenti hadn't called back half an hour later, Bernie called again. This time a woman ranger, Cassidy Kingsley, answered and let her know that Becenti was involved in another case. Bernie identified herself as an officer with the Navajo Police and repeated the information she had left in the message to Becenti. She put the call on speaker so Chee could hear, too.

Kingsley sounded young. "Where's this at? I'm new out here."

Bernie described the location in several ways, each time adding more details. By her last attempt, Chee could practically see the site, but Ranger Kingsley still seemed confused. Finally Bernie suggested they meet at the place where she had parked last night and gave clear directions. "You can find that easily."

"OK." Ranger Kingsley mentioned the blizzard in the forecast. "Let's do this tomorrow. The weather today is supposed to include snow, and whatever damage they did will still be obvious."

Bernie scowled. "Ranger, if you want my help on this, I need to do it in the next hour." The sharpness in her voice was followed by silence, and then Kingsley said, "Whatever." She named a time. "See you there."

"Good." Bernie ended the call and closed her eyes, a technique Chee knew she used to gather her thoughts. "That woman sounded clueless. We're meeting her in forty-five minutes. If she can find the parking area."

Chee looked out the window at the clouds. "Do you think this will take long? I'm nervous about talking to this bilagáana who wants to be a donor. I don't want to get there late."

"You could talk to Dulles on the phone, you know. Then we could leave for home after we show the BLM ranger the vandalism."

"I could. But in person, face-to-face is always better. That's what he asked for." Chee grinned at her. "I wonder what the weather is like where Ranger Kingsley comes from? How many times have big storms been forecast out here, and they pass by without a snowflake to their name?"

"And how many times have we been walloped by a storm that wasn't forecast? It doesn't hurt to take this seriously. Maybe the tiny snowfall last night will be it. Let's go to the petroglyph area."

Chee nodded. "You know, if I come across

those slimeballs, the guy driving that truck and the one who shot at you, I'll give them what for. No one should threaten a person like that."

"I'm sure they're long gone. As for the vandalism, I bet all those losers get is a ticket for defacing public property. But it's not right. I'm glad to go back there and show the BLM woman the damage." She sighed. "But first I need to call Mama."

Bernie tried to talk to her mother every day on the phone, in addition to her regular in-person visits. She called Darleen's cell phone, and her sister answered on the second ring.

"Are you still in Utah?" Darleen sounded perky.

"Yes. A big storm is on the way, according to the forecast. Cloudy this morning."

"Well, it's beautiful here. Sunny, not too cold. If Mama was out there, you could ask her to double-check that forecast. Have you ever noticed how she can look at the sky and tell you it will snow before dark? And it does, even if the morning is clear." Darleen chuckled. "She's amazing that way."

"Have you and Mama had coffee?"

"Coffee and breakfast. We're ready to start raising a ruckus."

"Thanks for all you do for her, Sister. I think you're great."

"That's right. I am pretty darn wonderful." Darleen laughed and then grew more serious. "You sound better today. I'm glad."

"Better? What do you mean?"

"Ever since you didn't get that detective job, you've seemed kinda off. And then the Cheeseburger gets his wings, extra sauce, whatever that lieutenant stuff is, while you got kicked in the teeth. Anybody would be bent out of shape after that. The timing sucked."

Sometimes Darleen's insights surprised Bernie. "He deserved that promotion. I'm happy for him." It was true.

"Tell him hey for me. He's my favorite brother-in-law. And before you ask, Mama seems good today. Wanna talk to her?"

"Yes. Nice chatting with you."

"You too. Here's Mama."

It took a moment, and then she heard her mother's voice.

"Yá'át'ééh."

"Yá'át'ééh. Good morning, Mama. I hope your day is off to a good start."

"My daughter, we have coffee here. I will pour a cup for you."

She loved her mother's coffee, strong and black with just the right bitterness. "Thank you, but I can't come this morning. I have to meet with someone, another law enforcement person."

"Did you get arrested?"

"No. It's business. I'm fine."

"I think something troubles you. I think you are not fine. I think you are mad at me."

The statement caught her off guard.

"Oh no. Not one bit mad." As she said it, she realized that wasn't totally true. She felt angry at how Mama had become weaker and more forget-ful. She wasn't mad at her mother but at a decline both of them seemed powerless to prevent.

"OK, then." Mama paused. "You hear that barking?"

"Yes."

"It's Bidziil. Your sister is helping with him."

"That's nice of her." Bernie didn't like dogs, but she'd made peace with the dog that belonged to Mrs. Darkwater, her mother's longtime neighbor and friend. After Bidziil had saved the woman's life, Bernie asked its name. How appropriate, she thought, for a dog with such a brave heart to be called Bidziil, "He Is Strong."

"Daughter, if you don't need to say something else, I have to go. Mrs. Darkwater just got home, and she brought us some cookies."

"Goodbye, Mama. I hope you have a lovely day."

Bernie slipped the phone into her backpack and grabbed her coat and keys. "I'll drive," she told Chee. "Easier than telling you how to get there. Let's go."

He reached for his jacket. "I've been thinking about that trench you fell into. How odd to do that around a site."

"That's how it seemed to me."

"I'm glad you didn't get hurt."

"Only further damage to my already bruised self-esteem." She said it lightly, as a joke, but Chee heard the truth in it.

She turned on the truck's ignition and then climbed out to join him in scraping the frost from the windshield while they let the defroster blow full blast. She was eager to see the site in the daylight, hoping the visit would put her apprehension to rest. Perhaps the BLM person would know the reason for the odd trench and the tools that had been left there. But she couldn't think of an explanation for the nearly deadly encounter with the truck, the rifle blasts, or the defaced petroglyphs.

Mid-December's early-morning sun filtered through the low clouds. The red rocks and cliffs around Bluff sat in soft light that belied the no-nononsense reality of the landscape. The little settlement of Bluff, named by the hardworking families who settled in the area and fought with the Indigenous people who already called it home, sits in the midst of some of the West's most iconic and challenging geography. The natural beauty of Bears Ears draws curious vacationers, hard-core hikers and mountain bikers, rafters and kayakers. Other visitors come expressly for the area's rich archaeology and geology, including layers of stone saturated with fossils.

This landscape spoke to her. She wondered if the old white politicians in Washington, DC—a place so far removed from here—had seen it. If they had, would they have realized sooner that it was sacred space that deserved protection?

The truck with the Bureau of Land Management logo waited at the place where she had parked last night. A plume of exhaust steamed from the tailpipe into the frigid morning air.

"Your directions must have worked, honey. She's here already."

"What's her name? Cassidy . . . ahhh . . . something."

Chee had a great memory. "It's Kingsley. Ranger Cassidy Kingsley."

Bernie flashed the headlights at the BLM truck as they pulled in next to it.

The darkened window in the BLM truck low-ered, and she saw a young, blue-eyed woman in a BLM uniform.

"You Manuelito?"

"That's me."

"You gave great directions. Got here quicker than I expected. Then I wondered if I was in the wrong place. I'm still learning the area."

"Happy to help."

Bernie noticed Kingsley looking at Chee. She introduced him as her husband and fellow officer and added, "He's a good investigator. I'm glad he could come with me."

"Pleased to meet you, Lieutenant. We try to keep an eye on the rock art, on all the archaeolog-ical resources, but it's tough. We rely on folks like Manuelito to let us know when there's trouble."

"Becenti mentioned you," Chee said. "He said he was glad to have some help."

"Ajax is a good man. He hadn't come in to work yet when you phoned, so I got the duty. Just had time to get my snow boots. I was expecting more of the white stuff out here."

Bernie nodded. "They say the brunt of the storm is due later."

Kingsley said, "I'm not used to this weather. It was clear last night, beautiful full moon. And then after midnight, a touch of snow and more in the forecast." She shook her head, then switched to business. "So, where was this trouble?"

"I'll show you." Bernie locked the truck and slipped the keys into her backpack. "Let's take a walk."

The San Juan River, the same waterway that

flowed past their Shiprock home, had carved some of this timeworn landscape. The place reminded Bernie of how ancient the earth was, and of how blessed she and Chee were to live in the place where its rocky bones were so readily apparent. The landscape looked friendlier in the morning light.

Kingsley zipped her coat. "I'm surprised that you stumbled onto vandalism and some digging out here. As I understand it, most of the places where Indians lived are closer to the river."

"Do you come across many disturbed sites?"

"I haven't, but I've only been here a few months. Before that, I was in the California State office."

"California?"

"Sacramento. I have to admit that I miss it. This is totally different." She frowned. "You should talk to Becenti about petroglyphs, he's the old pro. Never lets me forget it. I think he sees me as a city girl who'd rather talk to visitors about fire restrictions and scold people for illegal camping or whatever than learn about fossils or the archaeological resources here."

Chee said, "With the tightening of the market for grave goods and more buyers' insistence on a provenance, I thought the people behind the illegal trade in artifacts would have figured out another way to make money."

The ranger looked puzzled.

Chee was tactful. "Grave goods. That's what we call items stolen from burials at the early Pueblo sites. Buyers are after provenance because it gives them a history of where the pot or whatever came from. Stuff found on private land is OK to sell, but not things from public land like this. But it's hard to prove that something was stolen from a national park or a national monument or elsewhere. Some crime still pays. And some crime pays better than others."

Kingsley stood a bit straighter. "The same restrictions you mentioned about archaeological resources apply to mammal and dinosaur bones, fossils, stuff like that out here. Once I get a look at what Officer Manuelito found, I'll figure it out. We take vandalism and looting very seriously. I'm glad you called me about this."

They walked for a while, and then Kingsley spoke again. "So, what are you two doing in this part of Bears Ears anyway? Just hiking and watching the sunset?"

Chee gave her a condensed, generic version of his assignments, leaving out the meeting with Hosteen Grayhair. "Bernie had some time off coming, so I persuaded her to leave Shiprock and tag along."

"I have a close friend who has a home in Santa Fe. Is that close to Shiprock?"

"No. Shiprock is in northwestern New Mexico, about an hour's drive from here when the weather is good. It's four hours from Shiprock to Santa Fe. New Mexico is a big state."

"I see. Are you enjoying your trip?"

Considering why Kingsley was with them, Bernie found the question odd. "It was fine until I went for a hike out here to see the sunset, and those two yahoos in a truck tried to kill me."

Kingsley nodded, realizing her mistake. "That's

terrible. I'm not aware of any other incidents like that, thank goodness. We want to make sure our visitors stay safe."

They reached the place where Bernie had first realized that the truck driver meant to harm her. In the distance, she saw the area where she had discovered the tools, the trench, and the damaged images. But it looked different.

Someone had removed the equipment and filled the trench.

The unexpected change stunned Bernie. "Wow. Stop a minute. I need to take a look at all this." She shrugged off her backpack and set it on the ground next to her as she scoured the place that she had found so disturbing. "Someone's been here since last night."

"You think so?" Kingsley sounded skeptical. "Are you sure this is the same location?"

"Yes. Of course. Maybe the people in the truck were concerned after they saw me out here, and came back to clean up."

"Officer Manuelito, that seems strange to me. Are you certain this is the right spot? I don't see a sign of anything odd down there. Sorry." Kingsley smiled at her. "It was dark. You were tired."

Bernie took a breath. She scanned the landscape, judging her position against that of the most notable sandstone formations she'd seen in the fading light. They had seemed larger last night in the moon glow, and the dusting of snow gave the landscape some softness. But she knew this place. Her sense of direction was accurate.

"Right down there. That's where I saw the trench and the tools. We can't see the petroglyphs from here, but I noticed them on that sandstone cliff face, sheltered by the overhang."

Chee studied the scene. "I wonder if, after what they did to you, they figured they could be in trouble. Tell Ranger Kingsley about the truck and rifle."

"I already did."

"I know what Officer Manuelito says happened. The BLM takes incidents that impact the well-being of our visitors very seriously. I'd appreciate it if you would review the encounter again for me, now that you're in the landscape where it occurred. Perhaps you'll think of a new detail." Kingsley rubbed her gloved hands together and put them back in her coat pockets. "Could you identify the driver or the guy with the rifle?"

"No. It was too dark." Bernie paused. "I heard a male voice, so I'm assuming at least one of the two was a man."

"OK, I understand. Let's head on down there."

They descended the ridge in silence until Bernie found the place where she had squeezed into the crack in the cliffside to escape the truck's lights. She studied the landscape, then headed toward the road. "I walked down this way before the truck came after me. Then I tossed away my coat and changed course, headed into rougher country, but they followed me."

"What was wrong with the coat?" Kingsley looked puzzled.

"Nothing. I loved it. But it was white. It made me an easy target."

"Look here." Chee pointed to tracks where the

truck had left the road. The snow partly covered them. "This must be where they began to chase you."

Kingsley looked at the dirt. "They could be old tracks."

"They could be, but they aren't. Squat down here, and I'll show you."

She complied while Bernie watched.

"See how these edges are sharp? We're lucky the snow hasn't completely covered them."

Kingsley stood. "I get it. I didn't get much experience tracking in Sacramento."

"Come this way." Bernie looked beyond the tracks. "I want to find my jacket."

They walked through the sand and rocks and low shrubs for a few moments.

"I think that's the place."

She leaned forward and studied one sandstone boulder and then another. "OK. See this rock?" She ran her hand along the place where the bullet had chipped the stone. "That's where I tossed it. The truck slowed down here, and the passenger held the rifle barrel out the window and shot it off that bush. Then the truck drove closer, and someone got out and picked up my coat and shook it."

Kingsley frowned. "Why were you out here by yourself in the dark?"

"What?" Bernie resented the implication. "I came to see the sunset, like I told you before. I have every right to enjoy the scenery without being terrorized."

"Of course you do. That's what public lands are for. I was just wondering, that's all."

Chee smiled at Bernie. "A friend of mine suggested that she hike here. He told her the monuments were especially beautiful at sunset." His voice carried its trademark calmness.

"Is that right? I haven't had a chance to get out here that time of day. I'm too busy working." Kingsley looked at the place where the bullet had ricocheted off the rock. "That's weird about the jacket getting shot, and it's odd that it isn't here. Maybe in the dark whoever fired that rifle thought it was you."

"Or maybe they picked it up when they came back to fill in the trench." Bernie studied the spot again.

"You really believe they'd be that smart, huh?"

Bernie didn't respond.

Chee pointed with the toe of his boot to a place where the earth had been disturbed. "Right here's where the truck stopped. Notice these tracks?"

"Yes. What a bizarre event. I've never heard of such a thing happening." Kingsley shook her head. "I'm sorry about that. Let's move on. Where are the petroglyphs?"

"We'll be there in a minute. They are a bit above where I found the tools last night. We need to look at that place first."

They continued down the slope toward where she'd tripped into the trench and seen the excavation tools. The exertion, less challenging in the daylight, helped Bernie shake off her surprise and disappointment that things weren't exactly as she remembered them from the night before. She had expected irrefutable evidence of the disturbance. Without the tools and with the trench filled in, she knew Kingsley found her story less believable.

They reached level ground and moved quickly toward the site. Bernie recognized the litter of potsherds she recalled from her earlier visit. She noticed even more broken pottery than she'd seen in the glow of sunset.

Kingsley bent forward to study the array of broken ceramics. "When you see these, an archaeologist told me, it's an indication that you're close to or standing on top of a place where the Pueblo ancestors left their garbage. Did you know that?" She sounded like an overeager teacher addressing her third-grade class. Bernie felt a prickle of resentment. How dumb did this woman think they were?

"It's called a midden." Chee's voice lacked even a hint of irritation. "Archaeologists love them because they mean that the people who generated the garbage lived nearby."

Bernie said, "It's clear that someone refilled the trench I stumbled into last night."

"Really?" Kingsley's tone was somewhere between puzzlement and disbelief.

"Yes. They did it before the snow came, and they didn't bother to smooth the surface. Look at this." Bernie tapped the ground with the toe of her boot. "A fresh footprint."

Chee studied the earth more closely. He pointed with his chin to another spot along the newly added dirt. "And see here? A different boot sole. Two people. Maybe the driver and the shooter."

He rose and motioned to the women. "And

look at these tire tracks. Another match. The same truck."

Kingsley frowned. "I believe your story about the attack, OK? But don't jump to conclusions. There are hundreds of trucks out here. Just to play devil's advocate, what if some tire place in Monticello had a sale? Half a dozen trucks could have the same tires, right?"

The ranger gave them a conciliatory smile. "Maybe these workers were sloppy, forgot to finish, and then had an attack of conscience and came back so they wouldn't get in trouble. Maybe the archaeologist in charge didn't know when the job would resume and figured they needed to rebury this ASAP."

Bernie looked at the place where the trench had been. "You're saying that it seems like a lot of trouble for someone to go to on the off chance that a person they terrorized might be a cop, right?"

"Right." Kingsley continued to press her point. "I've already seen that it's common out here for crews to rebury the structures and do some site restoration. The archaeologist might give instructions to cover up a site as a way to protect it, you know, to store it for the future when we might have better tools to decipher the past."

Bernie studied the area again. "Sure, with the advances in technology and all, reburying a site makes sense. But why do that in the middle of the night? You wouldn't unless something odd was going on here, something underhanded. I get what you're saying, but this still makes me suspicious."

Kingsley pushed a strand of hair away from her face. "What if they missed a deadline or something and had to rush to finish the cleanup? But don't worry. I'll do a report about the truck and the guy shooting at you. We work closely with the San Juan County Sheriff's Office, and they will probably call you to follow up after they get my information."

Bernie said, "I spoke to a deputy last night."

"Who was it?"

"Douglas Dayton. He said he'd tell the sheriff."

"I know him. He's a good man, so you've got nothing to worry about. Weird stuff happens everywhere, unfortunately. Even here in this so-called paradise. Why don't you show me those petroglyphs? That's clearly the BLM's problem. I'm sure Dayton can handle the truck incident."

Chee shifted his weight from heel to toe. "Ranger, wait. Focus on this." Gone was the prior calm. Now Chee's voice took on a commanding tone. "Bernie could be dead. The average person probably would be. Those guys need to be caught, and we haven't heard anything from the sheriff."

As he talked, he had been walking slowly, methodically examining the ground. He stopped. "Look."

Bernie moved toward him. "More footprints."

"Right. See here? The same two sets of shoe soles among the potsherds. My bet is that they stood here before they began to refill the trench."

Bernie saw a scrap of burlap and something that looked like chalk next to it. "Hey. Come see this."

"What?" Kingsley squatted to look closely. "Some modern trash?"

"Modern trash buried at what we assume is an archaeological site. That could be evidence."

"Evidence of what? Illegal dumping?" Kingsley laughed. "You guys act like the freakin' FBI or something. But hold on. Don't touch that stuff." She took out her phone. "Let me get a picture of it in place. It could just be trash, but you're right. It could be evidence of something amiss out here. You never know."

Bernie decided to take the FBI jab as a compliment. Even if the Navajo Police didn't think she had what it took to be a detective, following up on something out of place came naturally to Officer Manuelito. The burlap and chalk might mean nothing other than someone's sloppiness, something that bounced out of a loaded pickup on the way to a landfill—or an illegal dump site. But they might mean more. Perhaps Kingsley's inexperience kept her from understanding the gravity of the situation, Bernie thought. She knew she had not imagined the danger that stared her in the face last night.

When Kingsley was done with the photos, she turned to Bernie. "I have to get back to Monticello. I really need to see those petroglyphs."

Bernie nodded. "I want to find out what's in this trench—if there was something worth coming back to hide in here, and if it had anything to do with why they tried to kill me." Bernie glanced at the ridge ahead of them. "The rock art is up there."

Kingsley shook her head. "That stuff in there must be garbage. Someone certainly has a permit for this site. I'll follow up on that and make sure it's legal."

Chee frowned. "I'm not telling you how to do your job, but if this excavation is not permitted, when Bernie stumbled across it, whoever was working here would have cause to conceal the evidence. You ought to check on that."

"Of course." Kingsley's voice had a touch of arrogance now. "I know there's lots of archaeology going on out here. And a man from the Natural History Museum of Utah has a paleontology permit to look for some kind of rare bones and fossilized teeth. And another guy hired a crew chief from around here to run the show for him. Dueling bone hunters of Bears Ears. Maybe the folks in that truck figured your wife here was a spy, checking up on the competition."

Kingsley saw Bernie's dark look. "But hey, Manuelito, I understand your concern and your curiosity. So between us, I'll look the other way on any unauthorized digging you want to do here after I leave. You're both law enforcement, and I trust you to behave yourselves. Keep me in the loop in case you discover something important, like a fresh dead body. If you come across any artifacts, you know enough to rebury them and leave them be. There's a shovel in my truck. You can use it."

"Thanks."

They headed toward the area where Bernie had seen the disturbing petroglyphs. The exertion warmed her, and she slipped her red cap into her coat pocket. Kingsley kept quiet until Chee asked a question.

"Ranger, do you know if they have discovered any old burials around here?"

Bernie thought of the time he'd spent in the sweat lodge. Was this what that cleansing was preparing him for—an unexpected encounter with the restless spirits of the ancient dead?

Kingsley shook her head. "Not many, and none in the area of that trench. Becenti told me some archaeologists unexpectedly discovered human remains in caves in the cliffsides around here. From what I've heard, that was a common practice of the people who lived here when it came to death."

The hike was longer and steeper than Bernie remembered, and she began to think she'd made a wrong turn when she came to the rock face. In the daylight, she realized the sandstone had more carvings than she'd noticed the night before, and not all of them had been vandalized.

The damage to the ancient figures chipped out of the red rock was intentional and selective. Someone had obliterated the face of the long-legged person with the square head, and that of the shaman-like character with the large, roughly triangular body. Other images had their eyes scratched away. Bernie and Chee quickly moved to a place on the trail where they couldn't see the vandalism.

Kingsley used her cell phone camera to record the destruction. "This is heartbreaking. Criminal. Of course it's nearly impossible to catch these fools in action unless they really screw up. Usually they chip off the panel and try to sell it. But this is different. Whoever did this wasn't even after money." She shook her head and put the phone in her coat pocket. "I hate to see stuff like what happened to those rock people. Some of the folks who come to Bears Ears, to any park for that matter, just don't appreciate what we have."

"Do you?" Bernie smiled to soften the question.

"Probably not as much as I should. I'm still learning about the area, and it doesn't feel like home yet."

Based on her upbringing as a traditional Navajo, Bernie viewed the defacement as the intentional work of Diné witches. Or of someone pretending to be evil for unknown reasons. She knew that Chee would agree.

They walked with Kingsley to their trucks in silence. The ranger handed Bernie her shovel.

"Bring it back to the BLM office when you're finished screwing around." Kingsley laughed when she said it, but that didn't disguise her disdain.

Kingsley started her truck and then rolled down the window. "I'll do a report on the petroglyphs and check with Ranger Becenti on the trench permit when I get back to the office."

"OK." Bernie took the statement as a gesture of goodwill. "Thanks."

"Follow me, and I'll show you how to drive closer to the place where you want to dig."

Chee drove, following the BLM truck and turning where Kingsley indicated.

"What about that?" Bernie pointed to a pair of wooden sawhorses with No Trespassing signs nailed to them.

"Go ahead and move them," Kingsley said. "They shouldn't be there in the first place."

Bernie hopped out and carried the sawhorses to the side of the road. The ranger left, and they returned to the site. Bernie put the tool Kingsley had loaned her to work, and Chee shoveled with the old favorite he kept in the truck. They dug together silently, not sure of what they were looking for except something out of place, out of the ordinary. The softer earth in what had been the trench made the job easier, but not easy.

After a while Bernie unzipped her coat, the old jacket she'd found in their truck last night. When she put the shovel down, the abundance of broken pottery caught her eye again.

"These sherds are everywhere. I don't think I've ever seen so many. And some of them are so different it seems like they came from separate villages, or even different periods."

Chee nodded. "Either something strange is going on here, or these ancient ones must have been awesome traders. And time travelers."

Bernie frowned. "But it's odd that we haven't discovered a corn cob, part of a sandal, discarded stone tools—you know, the stuff that normally comes up in middens like this. All I've found is more of the fabric and that chalky powder."

"I think this is, or was, a different sort of excavation—that the people behind this didn't care about Native stuff. That's just a smokescreen. I think whoever did this was a fossil hunter. Maybe they got an archaeology permit but really wanted fossils."

Bernie stopped shoveling. "Why would someone do that? How curious."

"It's puzzling. Maybe for scientific research that couldn't get funded. Maybe whoever worked here did it just for his or her own entertainment, a sort of hobby."

Bernie nodded. "Maybe for some other reasons we haven't thought of yet."

"Questionable, that's right, but none of our business. And maybe this shoveling you wanted to do is useless busywork."

She didn't like his tone. "Hey, don't get snippy. I wanted your opinion, not a lecture."

He turned his palms toward the sky. "Sorry, but I'm starting to wonder what we're doing here, Bernie. Two guys tried to run you over and then shot at you, or your coat anyway. I get it. But we can come up with a better way to figure that out than digging for another hour. Especially when we aren't sure what we're looking for, and we aren't finding anything except odd sherds and more of the trash Kingsley took pictures of." He straightened up to stretch his back. "Another blister, sweetheart, and I'm quitting."

Criticism always made Bernie defensive, but she tried to put her feelings aside and think logically. "You are one who always keeps looking, even though you don't know exactly what you're looking for. I'm not ready to quit."

Chee said nothing and kept digging.

"You can stop right now if you want," Bernie said. "But remember, nothing much good happens in the dead of night."

"Unless it's a baby coming into the world." As soon as he said it, he regretted it. They'd discussed the possibility of parenthood, but Bernie had seemed less enthusiastic about the idea than he was. They hadn't talked about what had happened, and he hadn't meant to raise the unspoken sadness.

Instead of arguing or, worse, giving him a cold stare, she put her shovel down and walked toward him. He dropped his too, took her in his arms, and whispered, "Oh, honey. I didn't mean to bring up such a sad thing."

She moved gently from his embrace. "You might be right about this digging, but I want to give it a little longer, OK? Five minutes?"

"That's fine."

They shoveled, and then she called out. "Hey, here's something weird. A dental pick."

"What?"

"No kidding. Come look."

After that, they found more coarse brown fabric scraps and rocks, small and large. She took pictures of it all, and then, based on Chee's protest and Bernie's agreement, they stopped digging.

She reached for the water bottle in her backpack, took a sip, and offered it to Chee.

"What do you think?"

He took a sip before he spoke. "I think someone was working here, probably without a permit or with the wrong permit. But I don't understand why all these different sherds are in here, or what whoever was here wanted to find, or why they had to clear out in the middle of the night, unless seeing you spooked them."

THE WAY OF THE BEAR          67

Bernie thought about it. "The young man, the father of the baby, acted nervous when I told him I'd been out here. He mentioned defaced petroglyphs, and he told me to be careful."

Chee laughed. "So this is the guy with the wife having her baby in the car, right? Are you sure the damaged rock art was what made him nervous?"

She grinned. "Well, OK. More nervous. And this was after the baby got here. I didn't mention the trench or the men in the truck. When he asked why I was here at night, I said someone suggested I come to look at the geology and the view at Valley of the Gods, and time got away from me. Anyway, I asked him why he was concerned, and he just said this place wasn't safe."

"And you asked why, of course."

"And he said something like, 'Some places out here are dangerous in the dark,' but he didn't get into the details. If he knew about the specific drawings I saw, I could tell he didn't want to discuss that, especially with the baby arriving just then."

"You know, honey, bad stuff happens everywhere. All the time."

"I know. But there is an odd vibe to this area. It makes me uneasy."

"I think some of that comes from dealing with Miss California there. She has a lot to learn." Chee grabbed his shovel. "It's time to go. Let's make sure Becenti and the BLM archaeology department know about this. And we will follow up with the sheriff on your assault."

Bernie bent down to tie her boot lace, and that's when she spotted something blue on the ground.

As she extracted it from the dirt, she realized it was a small turquoise bear on a pink ribbon.

"See this? Kingsley would call it trash because of the ribbon, but I'm taking a photo or two of it in place."

Chee looked at the little necklace. "After that, slip it in your pocket. A bear at Bears Ears? You should keep it safe."

# 4

Her partner had already arrived when Jessica pulled up in the blue van.

They often met there to steal a kiss and strategize, a quiet spot outside Bluff on a county road that never had any other traffic and offered a heart-stopping view of Comb Ridge.

"Hey, sweetheart, I'm glad you wore that outfit. Makes it easy to recognize you."

They laughed.

"Those Navajo cops booked at the same motel where Kyle and I are staying," Jessica said. "I'm glad I asked Walter for the room next to theirs. I'll keep an eye on them."

"Great." Her partner smiled. "You know, I can't wait to be done with our project. I'm looking forward to saying goodbye to this ugly place and seeing something green again, to getting away from all this stupid rock."

"That's where we're different. I love this landscape, the way it shows us the bones of the earth. It holds so many secrets about the people who lived here and the ancient animals, even before that. Even the Bears Ears name makes me smile."

"What's hidden appeals to you, doesn't it? You're good at secrets."

Jessica laughed. "They helped me survive back in the day when I had nothing. When I had to struggle to get by on wit and charm. When every penny mattered. You've been poor. You understand."

"You bet I do." Her partner smiled. "I'm so glad you are in my life, sweet one. I'm ready not to worry about money, or about secrets, anymore."

"Hang in there with me, then the Caymans with money to spare. And no one except the two of us to share it with."

"Too bad about Kyle."

Jessica said, "He wrote that script himself, you know?"

"I know. Let's get down to business. We have a lot to talk about."

5

Chee reached for Bernie's shovel, the loaner from the BLM ranger.

She handed it to him. "I think it's interesting that Kingsley seemed more concerned over the damage to the petroglyphs than about my story."

"I agree. It sounded like she's expecting the sheriff's office to stay on top of that."

They heard a vehicle and then saw a pickup with a custom paint job approaching them.

"Is that the truck from last night?"

"No. Not even close." Bernie studied it. "This one is a lot newer, and the grille looks normal."

The driver slowed as her vehicle passed the spot where Bernie had removed the improvised road-block. She seemed to study their parked pickup. Then the truck stopped within shouting distance of them, and the driver, a Navajo woman, lowered the window.

"Yá'át'ééh." She stayed behind the steering wheel, drumming her fingers—uncertain, Bernie speculated, about this unexpected encounter with two strangers.

Bernie walked to the truck and returned the greeting, introducing herself the traditional way with her clans on the maternal and paternal sides. The woman followed. As they recited their clans, Bernie observed that they had none of the 140 or so extended family groups in common. The driver's name was Lilakai Zonnie, and she said she lived a mile down the road. She may have been in her sixties, with a cheerful face and a few gray highlights in her long black hair.

Chee watched and listened from a distance for a few moments as the women spoke, then went back to digging.

"Who's that?" Lilakai pointed with her lips toward Chee.

"My husband, Sergeant—I mean, Lieutenant—Jim Chee."

"Lieutenant? That's good. He's a Marine?"

"No. With the Navajo Police."

Lilakai smiled. "I bet he looks good in his uniform. And he's got two shovels. That's in case one breaks on him, right? Or maybe he figured out how to use both at once."

"Oh, he's a clever one."

"Handsome and hardworkin', too. You're a lucky woman. Any kids?"

"No." Bernie surprised herself with how easily she said it. "How about you?"

"Me neither, but some nieces and nephews. I got a husband back home and a boyfriend in Kayenta. Them, the rest of the family, and my job, that keeps me busy." Lilakai ended with a wink. "So far as I know, there's no buried treasure out here. What's he hopin' to find?"

Bernie thought about her answer. Instinct told her this woman could be an ally; experience said a good extra set of eyes could come in handy if the area needed more watching. "We don't know exactly what we might find. I can't get into a lot of detail, but I'm a police officer too, like my husband."

The woman nodded. "I know something isn't right out here."

"What do you mean?"

"That crew has no right to block off our road. I tried to talk to them about it, and they just ignored me. My husband sits and honks until one of the men moves the barriers when we're going out or coming in. They oughta know us by now."

"Does anyone else live up your way?" Bernie knew the traditional Navajo system was for families to live close together.

"Sure. My sister Pam and her kids and her son and his boyfriend. Pam's eldest daughter comes to visit once a week. And my nephew works in Blanding, and he comes too with his little one and the wife. And lots of other relatives."

Bernie watched Lilakai fiddle with a knob on the dashboard, and felt a soft flow of heat waft out the open window.

"So now, your turn. Tell me why you and your handsome husband are here."

"I came for the sunset view at Valley of the Gods yesterday, and I saw something that made me curious." She gave Lilakai a condensed version of the events of the night before.

The woman listened with rapt attention. "Did you call the sheriff or the BLM?"

Bernie nodded. "I spoke to a deputy sheriff last night, and I called the BLM this morning. A ranger met us here, but she didn't think there was anything funny going on."

"She? That fat blond one?" She used the Navajo word. "Why not the Diné officer?"

"We asked for Ranger Becenti because my husband knows him, but Ranger Kingsley said Becenti hadn't arrived at work yet, so she got the assignment."

"That's not right. He's never late." Lilakai made a clicking sound. "Too bad it wasn't him. He's smarter, and cuter too."

Before Bernie could think of the proper response, Lilakai laughed. "That man is my clan brother. You know his first name?"

She almost remembered. Something unusual. "Atlas?"

"Close. It's Ajax." She laughed. "We call him 'the Cleaner.' He's one of the good guys."

Bernie remembered that Ajax, besides being a brand of cleaning supplies, was a famous leader in Greek mythology, a warrior known for his huge, strong physique as well as his bravery in the Trojan War.

Lilakai grew serious. "You know, there's evil out here. I don't like to speak of it. I don't want it to come around me. But you should know about it because you're with the police."

"Go ahead. Tell me."

"Well, the children went out here on their horses. The girl's horse acted crazy, and she and her brother got separated on the way home. When she got back, she told me some men had talked to her and taken her picture. We drove out here, but the workers didn't know about it, and the girl couldn't say who it was. That wasn't right."

"Did the men hurt her?"

"Not exactly, but they scared her. My sister told her to stay away from there. Then Sister got that photograph in the mail. It showed her girl, all pretty with her new necklace, standing next to a man. The picture didn't show his face, just from the chest down. But that wasn't the bad part. Next to them was . . ." Lilakai exhaled. "OK, next to them were figures in the rock that the old ones made, petroglyphs. But somebody had carved away the faces, destroyed the eyes. You know who does that, don't you?"

Bernie nodded. Receiving such a photograph was an omen of impending evil, witchcraft that could make a person sick or crazy or dead.

"Was there a note with it?"

"Sort of. On the back of the photo of our sweet little Crystal someone had written, 'Stay away. Stay alive.'"

"What did Crystal say about what happened?"

"When we talked to her again, she said the men had a big truck. She said one of them had a tattoo on his arm. A skull. And that the man who took the picture was missing two fingers."

"Did she describe the truck?"

"A big, black, shiny pick-me-up truck."

Black trucks were common in the Four Corners country; skull tattoos and missing fingers less so.

"What did the Cleaner say when you told him?"

Lilakai's eyes opened wider. "That man was furious. He said he would find those people and take care of it. But he hasn't done it yet. He thinks they might be connected to the workers over there."

"Ranger Kingsley mentioned that she'd check on the permit, but other than that, she didn't seem to think anything underhanded was happening out here."

"Well, except for the Cleaner, the BLM don't seem concerned about much. He says they all are overworked and underpaid. My brother pays attention because his family lives around here." She adjusted the truck's heater. "Whatever these guys are doin' isn't my business. But to tell it to you straight, I think they're up to something. Why else would they try to block my road? But messing with the road wouldn't especially bother me if someone hadn't taken a picture of Crystal, Pam's daughter, in the place of witches." Lilakai shook her head. "Lucky for us, she's too young to understand about that deep evil. But now she and the boy can't ride out there. It limits their freedom."

The story made Bernie angry. "My husband and I will stop by the BLM office and say hello to the Cleaner. I'll tell him about last night."

Lilakai picked up a rock sitting on her dashboard and absent-mindedly stroked it. "Tell the Cleaner his sisters Chatterbox and Pam need to talk to him."

"Chatterbox?"

"That's me."

"I'll tell him." Bernie noticed that Lilakai's stone had an unusual ridged surface. It reminded

THE WAY OF THE BEAR                    77

her of a tooth. "That's an interesting fossil. Where did you get it?"

"I found it over there." She pointed toward the cliff face. "If you're curious about what they're doing, with chain saws and sledgehammers, you should check it out. They even had a dump truck out here. Sometimes they put something white on the cliffside and then chip off big chunks of it. And they like to explain things. I think they get bored just working on the rock, you know, separating stone from shells or old plants or bones."

The people she'd encountered didn't fit that description, Bernie thought. "If they are so friendly, why block the road?"

"I don't know why. It's not like any dig I've seen for pots or Indian stuff. They have a different approach."

"Have you watched a lot of those?"

Lilakai shrugged. "Around here, it's full of ruins, and they attract attention like bees to flowers. Those people who look for pots and stuff in ruins, they might go inside a cave or something, but these folks are different. They're interested in the rocks. Pot hunters don't use chain saws unless they're stealing petroglyphs, you know, cutting them off the cliff face." Lilakai glanced at the excavation plaza, the filled-in trench, the hillside, and back at Bernie. "Have you and Mr. Muscle over there found anything interesting?"

"We are puzzled by all these potsherds."

"I noticed those too. It makes me uncomfortable, you know, thinking of all the aunties and grandmothers who shaped those jars and bowls with their own hands, brought water here, cooked in the pots. They probably cried when they broke."

Chee, who had been digging while they spoke, walked over to the women and introduced himself.

"Sorry to interrupt, but I need to go. I've got that meeting back in Bluff, remember?"

Lilakai shifted in the driver's seat of her pickup. "I gotta get goin' too. Nice talking to you."

"Hold on a minute." Bernie took her little notebook from her backpack, wrote her name and number, and gave it to the woman, regretting that she hadn't brought business cards. "Would you call if you hear anything else about the men in the truck who took the photo of the girl?"

"You bet. If I don't shoot them like vermin first." Lilakai offered a set of numbers. "That's my phone. Of course, it only works when there's service."

Bernie started to open her notebook, but Chee said, "I've got it." He repeated ten digits back to her.

"That's right." The woman started the engine. "You guys look tired. Try to have some fun while you're here, OK? And when you tell the Cleaner hello for me, remind him not to forget the birthday party."

"Oh, a party?"

"Right. Our boy is turning six."

After the woman left, Bernie motioned to Chee. "There's something white on the hillside. Odd. I think it might be connected to the white stuff we found in the trench."

Chee smiled. "We have to leave. I know you're curious, but this isn't our case. You can ask Ranger Becenti about that white stuff. Or come back here after you drop me off. But I have to go now."

"OK." As was their habit, because Bernie had driven to the site, Chee drove back to Bluff. They sat without talking for most of the trip, and then Chee's phone vibrated. He glanced at the screen. "It might be the donor I'm supposed to meet with." He took the call. His part of the conversation consisted mostly of "Sure, that sounds good" and a few thank-yous.

"So, are you all set?"

"I think so. That was Dr. Dulles's security guy. He wants to talk to me, so he's taking me up to Chapman's place."

Chee's phone rang again.

"You're popular."

"It's Triple X. I'll put him on speaker."

Captain Texas Adakai was new to the force, having been hired from Farmington, New Mexico. The other cops referred to him as Triple X because of his heft. The captain took the nickname as a compliment.

"Hey, Lieutenant, how's it going?"

"Fine, sir, but they postponed the award ceremony I came for because a big storm is supposedly on the way."

"I saw that. What about the meeting with Dr. Dulles?"

"His security guy just called. He said the house is hard to find, and that he'd meet me at a restaurant in Bluff and drive me to Chapman's house

from there. I'm on my way to the restaurant now."
Chee laughed. "I think this security guy is looking for a job with us and wants to sound me out
about that."

"Chat him up, tell him how working with the
Navajo Police is heaven on earth. Because he's already doing security, he could be a good hire. Let
me know what you think of him, OK? We could
use more help."

"Will do, sir."

"What's happening with the storm?"

"I can't tell. The weather forecast called for
heavy snow, but so far nothing. It's just cold."

"Same here." Adakai paused. "Shiprock is supposed to get some of the weather that's predicted
for Utah. The whole Four Corners and then some
could receive a ton of snow—an early Keshmish
gift. The first blizzard of the season always catches
people off guard, and we know what big storms do
to the roads. This one is predicted to be a beast.
I'll need you and Bernie back here ASAP if this
forecast is right."

"Yes, sir. I'll be in touch after I've met with Dr.
Dulles."

The call ended as they reached Bluff. Chee
stopped at a cozy-looking restaurant with a few
cars in front. "Wanna come in and get a quick
lunch?"

"Thanks, but I'm not hungry."

Chee looked into Bernie's wonderful dark eyes.
"How are you doing today?"

"Better. I've got more energy, and talking to
Chatterbox stirred me up."

"I noticed."

"Call me when you're done. I'll pick you up." She could have offered to leave the truck with him, but she wanted to start packing in case the storm arrived as predicted. And she wanted them to have plenty of time to visit with Mama and Darleen if she felt like stopping.

"No need for that. I can walk back to the motel. It's only a mile or so." Chee gave her a kiss and climbed out.

Bernie slipped into the driver's seat and made the adjustments for her height. Or what Chee called lack of height. She noticed the low clouds, gray and heavy with snow. A few lonely snowflakes drifted against the windshield and melted. When she arrived at the motel, she saw a San Juan County sheriff's unit parked outside their door and a banged-up SUV with a BLM logo on the door next to it. She parked. The sheriff's unit sat empty, but an officer climbed out of the SUV and sauntered toward their truck. He looked like a Navajo, so she offered the traditional greeting.

"Yá'át'ééh."

He returned the welcome, and then Officer Ajax Becenti formally introduced himself with his clans.

Bernie did the same. "Glad to meet you."

"You too. I understand you and my buddy Chee were looking for me."

She nodded. "We were. I just dropped him off at the Bluff Diner. He had to meet someone there. How did you know we were staying here?"

He grinned. "I'd say it's because I'm psychic or something, but I'm here on business with Sheriff Gillman. I didn't expect to run into you."

"What's happening?"

Bernie knew that the Navajo way of telling a story was to start at the beginning. She wondered how far back the Cleaner would go.

"You know how it is with missing person cases that involve healthy adult men? Usually they work themselves out with the guy being OK."

She knew the normal scenario. Sometimes the "missing" person just wanted a break from ordinary life. Sometimes the men were involved with romantic interests and didn't want to tell their partners the truth. Sometimes they really were lost: they suffered a medical incident, succumbed to addiction, or became crime victims. At other times, as in the case of some Native women who had disappeared, they were exploited in the sex trade.

"So this woman from out of town calls the sheriff and says her husband is late from returning from the grocery store and she's worried."

Bernie thought this was the woman she'd met last night.

"Just by luck, one of Gillman's deputies discovered the man. The officer was heading back from Monticello when he spotted an old Land Cruiser off the road on US 191 north of Blanding. The cabin light was on and the vehicle was empty, so he pulled behind it. He called for the driver, heard nothing, then saw something bulky and green on the shoulder. He found the body of a man in a big green coat, a guy from Santa Fe, according to the driver's license. He called it in and learned that a woman from Santa Fe staying at the Bluff Inn had been in touch with the sheriff's office when her husband didn't come back from getting groceries. The dispatcher had her name. Same last name as the dead man."

"What happened next?"

"The sheriff put it all together. It was a good thing the wife called from the Bluff Inn to report him as missing. Otherwise, it would have been a lot harder to figure out how to notify next of kin. Which was her. That's how I got involved. Gillman recognized their names and called me. He's a smart man."

"So did you know the dead guy?"

"Actually, no. But I met the wife. She came into the BLM office to ask if and how they could get a permit extension for her archaeology work out by Comb Ridge. She's a nice gal. I never would have suspected she was married, because she did all the work and never mentioned him. Not that she had to, I guess.

"Anyway, when Sheriff Gillman figured out who the deceased person was, he called me. He thought it would be easier on the wife to get the bad news from someone she knew. And he had questions about some items his deputy found in the vehicle. He thought they might be related to her archaeology work, and wanted me to ask her about that. You know how it is with any unattended death. Always a suspicion of foul play."

"Chee and I met her last night. She came over to talk about her missing husband, ask us what she should do. Chee told her to sit tight and check back in the morning if he was still missing. We didn't hear from her before we left. Was the car found on the route back to Bluff?"

"Sort of. That's funny, now that you mention it. It was on the other side of town, as though the driver had missed Blanding, driven out toward Monticello, then turned around to come back. And boom."

"Did it break down?"

Becenti shrugged. "I assume so, or it ran out of gas. I figure the man wandered away from it. Collapsed in an old snowdrift. Or maybe the car was OK and he parked, climbed out to pee or look at the stars, and tripped and hit his head or had a heart attack or a stroke or something. Other than the coat, the deputy said he wasn't dressed for a night outside below zero."

Bernie agreed. "Did you tell the lady her husband was dead?"

He sighed. "I hardly had to. I think she knew it was bad news as soon as she saw the two of us pull up to her room. Most people do. Gillman asked me to wait out here while he got some information from her, you know, and told her what to expect. I said I would wait, and I'm glad I did so I got to meet you."

"I ran into a clan sister of yours today out at Valley of the Gods. She said to tell you hello, and don't forget the party tonight."

"If she's talking to you about me and the party, that must be Chatterbox, Lilakai Zonnie, right?"

"Right."

"Were you out there enjoying the scenery?"

"It started that way. It's kind of a long story—it

begins with a suggestion that I take a hike and ends with my coat getting shot."

"I've got time." He pointed to a sheltering wall that was absorbing the morning's weak sunlight. "Let's stand over there. It's chilly out here."

Bernie shared the story, adding in all the details she remembered. "I persuaded Chee to return with me this morning. Before we left, I called your office to report that vandalism. I asked for you, but instead that other ranger joined us."

Becenti had been listening intently. "What did you find?"

"Well, for starters, the trench had been filled in. Chee and I thought that was odd. Ranger Kingsley said we could do some digging to figure out what had been dumped and buried there. Mostly we found potsherds, rocks, and some burlap and coarse white powder that looked like chalk."

The Cleaner chuckled. "Rocks in a trench, huh? That seems normal to me."

"A few, sure, but this was more than that. And why cover rocks with dirt? That made me curious."

Becenti nodded. "What did the people in the truck look like?"

"It was night, so it's hard for me to give you a good description. It was too dark to see much."

"How about the truck?"

"It was old. Maybe black or dark blue." She thought about how to describe it. "It didn't make a lot of noise, so I guess the muffler was good. There was something odd on the front of the grille. Like a roll of paper towels. Some kind of cylinder."

"That's not much to go on. Considering how big the area is that Kingsley and I keep an eye on,

I don't expect the sheriff to have much luck finding the guys who tried to run over you without a better description. Sorry."

Bernie nodded. "I get it. A load of rocks isn't really worth the bother, and I couldn't ID them. But it's not just that." She described the defaced petroglyphs. "Chatterbox told me that you know about the incident with Crystal and the photograph that shows those."

"If I ever—" He stopped talking when they saw an older man in uniform close the door to a motel unit and walk toward the parking lot. The sheriff tipped his hat toward Bernie.

"Ma'am."

Then he looked at Becenti. "Your turn to talk to the lady."

"Sheriff, this is Officer Bernadette Manuelito. She's with the Navajo Police. She's the one who had that disturbing incident last night in Valley of the Gods."

"First I've heard of it." Gillman wrinkled his brow. "What happened?"

She gave him the short version. "I told Deputy Dayton all this when he stopped me to give me a message from my husband. He said he'd pass the information along to you."

"Dayton? That guy is on probation. He shouldn't have left the station. Never said a word about this."

"Then why—" Bernie read Gillman's expression and stopped talking.

He frowned. "Long story, but the plot line is lack of follow-up on incidents like this where BLM jurisdiction overlaps ours. And then there's a stench of profiting from illegal excavations out here."

Gillman asked her the right questions and didn't make her feel guilty for not being able to identify the driver or the shooter and having only a dim description of the truck. "I regret that happened, Officer Manuelito, and I'm glad you weren't injured. I'll keep it on our radar."

Bernie and Becenti watched the sheriff drive away.

Becenti stood. "I need to check on Jessica and ask her some questions. Since she's met you, do you wanna come with me?"

"No, but I will. I know how tough these situations can be."

The woman was sitting on the bed in a room like the one she and Chee shared, except that Jessica's space was crowded with cases of bottled water and flats of unopened cans of iced tea and soda pop. The only chair was piled high with packages of hot dog and hamburger buns and bags of potato and corn chips.

"I'm so sorry about your husband," Becenti said.

Jessica patted the bed next to her, the only available seat, but Becenti continued to stand.

Bernie said, "I'm sorry too. Can I do anything to help?"

Jessica gave her a blank look. "Do you work with Ranger Becenti?"

"No. I'm Bernie, from the room next door. We met last night when you came by to ask for advice about your husband."

"Oh, that's right." But Jessica showed no sign of recognizing her.

Becenti softened his voice. "I'm going to ask Bernie to sit in with me for this interview. She's an experienced officer with the Navajo Police in New Mexico."

"That's fine."

"The sheriff asked me to talk to you about some things they found in your late husband's car." Becenti pulled out his phone and held it toward her. "Please take a look at these photos."

"Is Kyle in them?"

"No, ma'am."

Jessica leaned in to see the pictures, and Bernie did too. The images included a knife and two large machetes, a pickax, sharp-looking chisels, several shovels, buckets, nylon rope, a collection of sealable plastic bags, gloves, and a camera.

Jessica looked at the photos awhile. "So what's the problem? What does this have to do with my husband freezing to death?"

"Sheriff Gillman found this puzzling and asked me to check with you."

She frowned. "That's it? Those are just tools of the trade, you know, equipment Kyle and I use for excavating sites."

Bernie said, "What about the pickax?"

"Oh, that's for his geology side of things." Jessica paused. "None of this is for murdering anybody if that's what you're wondering, OK, officers? Anything else?"

Becenti turned the phone's screen black. "I'm sorry for your loss."

"Thanks."

"Me too. Much sympathy." Bernie thought the woman seemed remarkably composed for someone who had been told her spouse had been discovered dead by the side of the road.

Jessica sighed. "I always told him that this is high country. Weather changes. Dress for it. Don't be dumb. But he didn't listen. He wore that big coat, but no hat, no gloves, the wrong pants, the wrong shoes." She stood. "Maybe you two can help me with a problem. I was planning a celebration tomorrow for the end of my archaeology project. Of course, now I have to tell everyone that's canceled because of Kyle's death, but what will I do with all this stuff?"

It wasn't the question Bernie had been expecting. "What do you mean?"

Jessica waved an arm at the clutter in the room. "All the food, drinks, the meat in the ice chest, plates, napkins. Things I bought for our party. I don't need them. I don't want them now. Nothing to celebrate."

Bernie waited a moment for Becenti to jump in, but, like other men she'd met, he didn't seem to be a natural when it came to celebrations. "I know a family having a birthday party tonight for a little boy."

"Right." Becenti came to life. "My clan sisters and our extended relations. It's a big deal. I bet they could use some of this. Want me to ask?"

"Please do."

Becenti started typing into his phone.

"If they say yes, can you take this stuff to them?" Jessica didn't wait for Becenti, who was still typing, to respond. "I have to get home to Santa Fe. I need to get to work on the funeral arrangements, notify our colleagues, wrap my head around this. Poor Kyle." She looked at Becenti. "I still can't believe this. Do you know when his body will be released to me?"

Becenti looked up from his texting and raised a finger to say *Wait until I'm done here*, and Bernie answered instead. "The release depends on the autopsy in a case like this. Becenti can give you the medical examiner's information, and you can try calling there."

"Why do they need to do an autopsy? My husband froze in the desert. Poor bastard. I should have told him to take a hat and his gloves, but he never listens to me when it . . ." Her voice cracked. "I need to take Kyle home."

"An autopsy is legally required for unattended deaths like this." Becenti stopped at that.

Bernie assumed Sheriff Gillman had photos and possible evidence from the site where the body was found. The autopsy would help determine if Kyle Johnson's demise warranted further investigation. If it turned out that his death was more than a matter of terrible judgment, then the new widow's life would become more complicated.

Becenti's phone chimed. "My sister says she would love the food for her party."

"That's great."

"I'll tell her. I've got to get going. My sympathy, again. Call me or Sheriff Gillman if you need anything."

She sighed. "Do you have a reason to think Kyle's death was not an accident?"

The Cleaner hesitated. "It's not my jurisdiction, ma'am. That's up to the sheriff. I'm working on other cases."

"Like what?" She gave him a questioning stare. "What's more important than a dead man?"

He ignored the question and changed the subject. "I'm glad my sister can take that food. I get off work at six today, and I could come by for it then."

Jessica said, "That's too late. What about the big snowstorm that's supposed to hit us? Can she come and get it? I'd like this all to go to a good cause, and I can't haul it back with me."

Bernie had an idea. "What about this? I can take a drive out to the Zonnies' place and use my truck to deliver this stuff."

Jessica nodded. "What if I go with you? Taking a drive seems better than sitting here feeling sad."

The Cleaner swung his attention back to Bernie. "Do you know how to find the place?"

"No, I don't."

He rattled off the directions.

"Got it." Bernie smiled. "You mind if we remove the roadblock?"

"Do it. That shouldn't be there in the first place. Want some help loading up all this food?"

Jessica looked at the pile. "No thanks. Bernie and I will get it. I'm sure you need to get back to work."

The BLM officer left, and Bernie and Jessica began to move the food outside. Together, they lifted and stowed the big cooler last.

"So what's this about a roadblock?" Jessica put

her hands on her hips. "I've worked out there plenty, and I never saw it."

"Oh, someone improvised it trying to restrict access. But the route they have blocked off is also the road to Ranger Becenti's sisters' home. They can't do that to a public road."

"Where is this?"

"We'll drive right by it. I'll show you what the dig looks like, and maybe, with your experience out here, you can help me understand what they're looking for." Bernie paused. "Actually, I thought it might be the place where you or your husband had applied for a permit."

"No. I've been working in the Comb Ridge area, and he's moved into research for a commercial fossil business." Jessica's tone changed. "You know Bears Ears is rich in archaeological sites. That helped make it a national monument. There's a lot I'd like to do here if and when I have the money."

Bernie started the engine while Jessica grabbed her coat. The cab had cooled, and Bernie pulled her red knit cap down over her ears and slipped on her gloves.

Jessica climbed in. "I like that hat. It will make it easier for me to remember you."

"Really! What do you mean?"

"I have some issues recognizing people, that's all."

Bernie drove out of the parking lot and turned toward Valley of the Gods.

"Hey, before we drop things off, could we see the place where the deputy found Kyle's car?"

"Sorry, but that's not on the way." The request surprised Bernie. "You know this area, don't you?"

"I do. I'd appreciate it if you could head up toward Blanding. I'd like to see where he died. Please."

Bernie hesitated at the note of desperation in the woman's voice. "I can't. I have to get back to New Mexico before the storm. I'm already delaying to help with this food."

"OK." Jessica sighed. "I can't get the image out of my mind. Kyle leaving the car like that, freezing. It just isn't right. It doesn't seem real. I can't wrap my head around it."

"Death is shocking. Especially something like this."

Bernie considered how much time she had spent with people confronting the unexpected death of a friend, colleague, or loved one. She had heard some of them argue with fate. "Accidents are always unexpected. That's why they're called accidents. Cars have unanticipated problems. Our bodies have reactions to things we eat or germs we catch. A curb pops up to trip us and we break a leg. We get trapped in a blizzard or stranded by a flash flood. A spider bite makes it hard to breathe. Other things can happen."

"Of course. I know all that." Jessica's voice had a sharp edge of frustration. "But this kind of death, or whatever you'd call it, is totally out of the blue. Kyle was on his way to the grocery, that's all."

A heavy silence hung in the truck's cab, a mood that matched the cold gray day.

"Bernie, what about his car and our tools?"

"Talk to the sheriff about that. He'll tell you what to do."

They drove in silence for a while, and then Bernie remembered something. "When Ranger

Becenti asked you about the things in the back of your husband's car, you hesitated. I had the feeling that you were trying to figure out the best answer to that question."

"I didn't know for sure what Kyle might have in there, that's all." Her voice dropped lower, and Bernie had the sense Jessica wanted to confide in her.

"But . . . ?" Bernie prompted.

"But I think Kyle might have been into something he shouldn't have been messing with."

"Something like . . . ?"

She shook her head. "Illegal or borderline legal. Questionable. Dangerous. He denied it, but I know he was lying."

"You need to tell Sheriff Gillman about that." Because, she thought, Kyle Johnson's death seemed increasingly suspicious.

Bernie's phone buzzed with a text. Their truck was linked via Bluetooth with Chee's phone, but she had installed hers as well. And with Mama's fluctuating health, she liked to stay on top of things. She handed the phone to Jessica. "Could you read that text to me, please?"

"It's from someone named Lilakai. 'Men there now.' That's it."

Bernie remembered Lilakai's positive impression of the workers. She hated unanswered questions, and the trench was a mystery solved best by asking the people who were behind it.

"Could you text her 'Thanks' for me?"

Bernie continued on to where Comb Ridge rose before them, steep and forebodingly beautiful with Monument Valley in the distant background. The ridge stretched eighty miles south to north, from Kayenta, Arizona, into what was now the Shash Jáá Unit of Bears Ears National Monument, ending in the foothills of the Abajo Mountains near Blanding. Or starting there, Bernie thought, depending on one's perspective.

From the air, the layers of rock that tilted toward the sun resembled a snake. In the Diné stories, this was the place where Big Snake, one of the monsters killed by the Hero Twins, turned to stone. More than a mile wide in places, the monocline had arisen some sixty-five million years before, geologists found, when tectonic plates deep beneath the earth's surface slipped. A massive ancient earthquake had created this beautiful scar.

Jessica sighed. "I'm going to miss this landscape when I get back to Santa Fe. If only there were real money in my kind of fieldwork."

"This part of Utah is amazing. The Bears Ears area has special relevance for us Diné, you know. We regard it as a place of healing. Maybe it will help with your loss." As she said it, Bernie realized she had been less obsessed with her own recent losses.

"Working out here really did give me joy, but now it also will remind me of my dear Kyle and how much I miss him."

They turned off State Route 163 at the sign, onto the dirt road that wound for seventeen miles through the startling, large-scale landscape someone had named Valley of the Gods. Jessica stared out the window as they bounced along, cruising their way among the formations. Millennia of exposure to wind and water had carved the towering red sandstone into buttes and spires, unusual shapes that stirred the imagination. The landscape was a gift from the Holy People, the Diyin Diné, a marker that reminded their five-fingered children to think big thoughts. To be brave and bold, Bernie thought.

What should she do next? Could she return to contentedly working for the Navajo Police as a beat cop? Or was it time for a big change?

They passed flat, deserted spots that looked promising for camping—in the summer. The temperature on this December night would certainly plunge below freezing, even to single digits. The predicted snow had yet to arrive, and she and Jessica needed to drop off the groceries and get back to the motel so Chee and Bernie could return to Shiprock. Triple X wanted them there in time to help with traffic duty if the storm made a mess of the maze of dirt roads that linked the Navajo Nation.

Jessica readjusted her seat belt. "Valley of the Gods makes me think of Monument Valley. It's something special, isn't it? It lifts my spirits."

"Mine too." In fact, keeping her eyes on the road was a challenge because of the seduction of the huge open spaces furnished with massive Halgaito shale and sandstone cliffs, and red buttes with slim, rocky tops stretching toward the sky. She noticed a formation that resembled a saddle.

"Do you know any stories about these formations?" Jessica asked.

Bernie thought of an appropriate answer. "Some people say Diné warriors are frozen in the rock here and respond to prayers asking for their protection. Because they are warriors, young people joining the service might ask for their help. Some visitors place special stones at the base of the pinnacles as an offering."

The truck followed the ribbon of road through the startling landscape, one that dwarfed humans and their problems. Even though Bernie had been there earlier in the day, the monuments looked different now as the changing light accented different features.

They turned onto a rougher dirt track. They stopped to move the sawhorses and the Road Closed sign that formed the roadblock, and then she drove on slowly to the place where she'd seen the trench. She stopped so Jessica could take a look from the truck window. "This is where we found the fabric and the rocks and the white powdery stuff."

"And you and Chee were concerned about that?"

"Ahhh. Yes."

"Well, it doesn't look like a traditional archaeology site, that's for sure. Maybe these guys are high-tech."

"High-tech? The trench looked traditional to me. What is high-tech archaeology anyway?"

"I should have called it noninvasive. Haven't you heard of it?"

Bernie shook her head. "Tell me."

"The idea is that old pueblos, settlements, habitations, whatever, can be explored with radar and other kinds of ground-penetrating equipment. That means we don't take a chance on destroying something accidentally with physical digging.

The theory is that scientists in the future will have more tools at their disposal to learn about these ancient people, so we need to save some undisturbed habitations for them to look at years from now."

"Makes sense. So what do you think was going on here?"

Jessica studied the scene out the side window. "As I remember, this specific area has no major ancestral sites. I looked at it when I was working on my grant, because I figured the quicker the drive from Bluff the better."

"Did you see that white against the red stone on that cliffside?" Bernie asked. "Why would someone paint something white there?"

"It might not be paint. Do you want to take a look?"

"I'd like to." Bernie had been disappointed when she and Chee weren't able to investigate the white scars before he had to head back for his interviews. And unlike Jessica's earlier request, this detour was only slightly out of the way.

She pulled the truck off the road and locked it after Jessica climbed out. The Zonnie birthday delivery could wait.

Jessica tied her boots. "I remember some interesting petroglyphs up that way too. Let's walk up there, OK?"

Bernie didn't exactly believe in witchcraft, but if the images Jessica remembered were the ones she saw, they gave her the creeps.

# 6

Jim Chee was a patient man. His training as a hatáálii had helped contain his natural tendency toward restlessness. He had learned to study a situation, see what developed. He had found that observation, in the proper circumstances, offered as much knowledge and information as asking questions.

Arriving at the restaurant a few minutes early allowed him to settle his mind and focus on the job ahead. He tried to sweep his worry about Bernie aside and replace it with the happier outlook the sisters at St. Michael's Indian School had taught him as a boy. "Do the best you can, but remember that God is the architect who drew up this beautiful master plan. You and I, all of us, we're just his tools."

As a cop, he'd seen too much that wasn't beautiful. Bernie's rejection for the criminal investigator job, a position for which she had natural talent, experience, and passion and more than met the qualifications, had left him saddened, confused, and annoyed. She had raged about the unfairness of the decision and then stopped complaining, internalizing the disappointment. After that she had pulled away from him and gone silent.

Chee had selected a table in the rear of the restaurant with a view of the entrance. About five minutes before the security officer for Dr. Dulles was due, he saw an old Chevy sedan pull into the building's parking lot. The young man in the driver's seat lowered the visor, used the mirror to check his hair, climbed out, and began walking toward the front door. He radiated confidence.

Chee wasn't in uniform, but he was the only man sitting by himself. The security guard headed right toward him. "Lieutenant Chee?"

"Mr. Black?"

"That's me. I wasn't sure you were here. I didn't see your unit outside. Thanks for meeting me here."

"My wife dropped me off." Chee noted Black's good observation.

"Of course. I appreciate the opportunity to talk to you for a few minutes before heading up to my boss's place. And, hey, I'm happy to give you a ride back to where you're staying when we're done so you don't have to bother your wife." And then Black switched to Navajo and introduced himself with his maternal and paternal clans.

Chee noted that Black shared some clan connections with the acting captain. That would come in handy at the Shiprock substation. He gave his own formal Navajo introduction to the young man and then asked the obvious question.

"Do you know our new boss, Captain Adakai?"

"No, sir. My contacts have only been with Navajo law enforcement up here in Utah." Black stuttered a bit and backtracked. "By contacts, I don't mean that I've been arrested or anything like that. I just meant, well, you know, connections through my family or my wife's family or friends we've made down there. Beautiful country."

Chee motioned to the empty chair across from him, hoping to put Black at ease. "Please sit down. I just ordered coffee. Want something?"

"You bet." Black took his phone out of his pocket, switched it to mute, and set it on the table where he could see it.

Chee wrinkled his brow.

"Sorry, but I need to leave it on because my wife is home with our little one and I have our only car. You know, in case she has a problem."

Black looked toward the server, a young woman with the tattoo of a tree on one arm and what might have been a raven on the other, and she came to their table.

She smiled at Black. "Hot chocolate as usual?"

"That sounds good."

"I heard that there was some excitement for you last night."

He smiled. "Hannah's relieved that everything turned out well. So am I."

"Congratulations to both of you."

"So how are things with you and Ned?"

"We're fine, thanks. It's been tough, but we made it through." The waitress took a breath.

Black spoke before she could continue. "Glad to

hear everything is moving forward. We'll catch up later. The lieutenant and I have to get to business here."

As the woman walked away, Chee silently gave him a gold star for the gentle way he'd ended the conversation.

"So you and our server know each other?"

"That's how it is in a small town. Everyone knows everyone and half their business."

"It's like that in Shiprock, too. Impossible for a cop to be an anonymous crime solver. Not that I'd want to be." Chee took a sip of his coffee. "Thanks for being my escort up to Dr. Dulles's place. So you currently work as his head of security, is that right?"

"Yes, sir. I'm head of security, the security force, and his handyman when necessary."

"Sounds like an interesting job."

"It was, but I'm ready for a change. I'm thinking the Navajo Police might be a good fit for me. I was hoping you could answer a few questions I have about that. We've got some time. I just tried calling Dr. Dulles, and he's not home yet."

"What kind of doctor is he?"

"The PhD kind. He wants people to call him Chap."

"I'm happy to talk to you about our police force, but I'd like you to tell me about Dulles in exchange. I'm here to discuss the Fallen Officers Memorial Fund. I was curious about why he's interested in helping the Navajo Police. But before we get into that, give me an idea of why you think you'd like to come and work with us."

"Well, I'm ready for a change." Black smiled.

"So how can I get a job in the Shiprock district as soon as possible? I've been working security for a year now, so I think I might have an edge over some candidates. What do I need to do to make this happen?"

The question, Chee thought, underlined Black's youth and lack of sophistication. He answered it with one of his own. "Why do you want to be a cop?"

Black didn't hesitate. "I'd like to make the world safer. It bothers me to hear about people exploited, hurt, taken advantage of, especially vulnerable elders, women, children, and people with disabilities. It's not right, and I don't want to just stand by and see it happen. I was in the army, so the idea of service, of rules and order, makes sense to me."

Chee nodded. "Law enforcement everywhere seems to be hiring. Why the NPD?"

"That's easy. Besides being Navajo, I also believe in the Navajo Way, in trying to work things out between family members or even strangers with disagreements, between the victim and the one who caused the damage. I am all for restitution and restorative justice both for the offender and the offended. I like the fact that we Diné can handle these problems without always sending people to jail or prison." He grinned. "And it's personal, too. My wife has family in Shiprock. We'd like to live there."

As they spoke, Black's confidence continued to emerge. Chee realized the man had brains. He looked physically fit. He wanted to move to a small town on the Navajo Nation, which was not true of everyone.

Eagerness to start something new was welcome in a recruit, but Chee remembered Wilson Sam, a young officer who'd looked promising on paper but turned out to be nothing but a headache. Sam had finally left for a job in Flagstaff.

Black asked more questions about the job—not the ones Chee anticipated about salary or shift hours or what kind of additional training he might need. Instead, they dealt with corporate culture and the personalities he might be working with. Then the young man came up with a scenario.

"Suppose I drive out on a call, and it turns out that what's going on there is not really a crime?" Black looked toward the ceiling. "Or if it's more of a safety issue?"

Chee wrinkled his forehead. "Can you give me an example?"

Black thought for a moment. "What if a family calls because their fifteen-year-old son has run away? That's not a crime, but we respond in case the boy is in danger or was abused or used for sex trafficking or whatever, right?"

"Probably right. After a dispatcher talked to the mother or whoever made the call and if it seemed that the kid might be in danger, we would respond. We'd hope the situation turned out to be nothing more than an adolescent temper tantrum. But just to be sure, as long as we had someone available, we'd send an officer out there."

Black's phone lit up with a call. He glanced at it on the table for a moment and ignored it.

"OK," Chee continued. "So you're the responding officer. You get there just as an uncle is driving up with the boy, and the kid's got a couple of black eyes and he's scared and the uncle is angry and maybe drunk or high. Neither he nor the boy want to talk about the obvious problem. And let's assume there are more children in the family and some other adults. How do you deal with this situation?"

Black spread his hands on the table and gave it a moment. "If it was me, I'd hang around awhile. Try to figure things out. I would work on building some trust with the adults and the other kids, and try to see what the backstory was. Get the boy who's hurt to talk to me if I could, assess what happened to cause the child to leave home and how he got injured. Try to talk to the uncle about why the kid had the black eyes and was scared. Basically, I would do what I could to make sure that he and any other kids were safe there. I'd try to go back and follow up. See if there was any point in getting social services involved."

Chee sipped his coffee. He was beginning to like this guy.

"And I'd probably worry about that young man." Black sighed. "I'd rather handle a traffic accident than a case like that one, just because it's easier to resolve."

Chee smiled. He appreciated the answer. "So would I. Tell me about the job you have now."

Before Black could answer, the server came with his hot chocolate. He thanked her, took a sip, and put the cup down.

"Dr. Dulles hired me as his security consultant after someone slashed his tires and he started getting a bunch of anonymous phone calls. I set up a security system for him with cameras and replaced the front door with something that couldn't be kicked in. I do several patrols of the property, you know, his house and the outbuildings, and make sure the locks all work and the windows close. I tried to talk him into replacing all his outside doors with something sturdier, but he said he didn't want the disturbance of having workers at his house. He told me I worried about him more than he worried about himself."

Chee nodded. "That's the job of a security guy, right?"

"Yes." Black smiled. "My wife and I keep him company sometimes now that his . . ." He searched for the word. "His female companion is gone."

"Did she leave or die or . . . ?"

"He told me he asked her to move out."

Chee nodded. "Does this guy work for a living?"

"He works hard. He's outside finding fossils and then inside doing brain work and writing. He's one of those scientists who study the hills for bones in the rocks, petrified wood, dinosaur tracks, fish skeletons, stuff like that. He told me he grew up in the East but got himself to Utah as soon as he could. He loves Bears Ears because he says there's more than three hundred million years of early life here, everything from little sea creatures to dinosaur claws. Cool, huh?"

"That's interesting." Chee put his cup down. "When I think of this area, I think of Cedar Mesa ruins, burials, and sacred places for the Diné and the other Natives who live around here. I thought that was what Bears Ears was known for."

"It is. But the boss says the wealth of fossils here is just as spectacular. Bears Ears is one of the richest places in the Southwest for finding that stuff. He's been studying fossilized teeth and jaws as clues to puzzle out how some animals survived the extinction that killed off dinosaurs. More than you needed to know, right?"

"No. It's fascinating."

"Before I went to work for Chap, I never realized how important fossils were. They can tell scientists how ecosystems respond to sudden temperature increases or decreases, what they call the icehouse-greenhouse transition. You know, from glaciers to steamy tropics."

Black's phone flashed on the table. He glanced at it for a moment and again ignored the call.

"As I understand it from Chap, one of those climate changes hundreds of millions of years ago marked the beginning of the age of dinosaurs because they could adapt better to the new environment. According to the boss, we're in an icehouse stage now, with glacial ice on the earth's north and south poles. When it's all melted, we'll be in the greenhouse stage."

Chee glanced at the time. "My appointment was five minutes ago. Nothing from Dr. Dulles yet?"

"No. I'll call him again. You'll get a charge out of his house, Lieutenant. It has the best views in the county."

Chee listened as Black left a message.

"Do you know why your boss is interested in making a donation to the Navajo Police?"

"Sort of." Black leaned in toward Chee. "A cop saved his sister's life. It's a long story. So how come you got picked to be a fundraiser?"

"I asked myself that. I just made lieutenant,

and I think it's either a little test, or everyone else talked his way out of the trip up here. I don't mind, actually. I've never done anything like ask for money. I might learn something." Chee spread his hands on the table. "So how about you? It sounds like you've learned a lot from Dr. Dulles and enjoy the job. Why leave?"

Chee could almost hear Black thinking.

"Like I said, I'm ready to get back to my roots, back to Dinétah, and start something new."

"What else?"

Black waited a few beats. "Dr. Dulles seemed to resent my advice about changes to his house and life that could keep him safer, even though he ultimately agreed to the cameras and updated security system. Lately he's tense, cranky, anxious all the time. He's become an iceman himself. It's not as pleasant to work for him as it was when I started."

"What happened to make your boss grumpy?"

"Oh, it began when his girlfriend left, and then a business deal went south—a consulting job with a group of other paleontologists. And then he got his tires slashed, and some abusive phone calls started."

Chee finished his coffee and thought of another question. "Do you know anything about some excavations out by Valley of the Gods? My wife was hiking out there and had a strange experience."

"No, I don't. Chap's been renegotiating with the BLM for an extension on his paleontology permit out that way, though. The boss asked me not to talk about that." Black hesitated. "Wait. Is your wife a cop named Bernie? Short, kinda bossy, and full of energy? Drives a truck?"

Chee was surprised. "That sounds about right. It sounds like you met her. Maybe last night?"

Black gave him a huge smile. "She's the one who delivered our baby."

The phone flashed again. Black glanced at the screen and then at Chee. "This is the sheriff. Third call. I've got to take it."

He picked up the phone.

# 7

Dr. Chapman Dulles had always been a morning person, and today he awoke with a smile. He was looking forward to meeting the Navajo lieutenant that afternoon to talk about the memorial fund. Before then, he could go to his workshop and put the finishing touches on the amazing replica he had created of an even more amazing fossil.

Dulles agreed with those who considered him obsessed and took no offense at the description. In fact, if it was meant as criticism, he pitied their small-mindedness. He relished his obsession with petrified jawbones and stone teeth as strongly as some humans loved power or jogging or drugs or new sexual encounters. His all-consuming passion for dinosaurs and their relatives had enabled him to make a living, enjoy the beautiful out-of-doors, and share ideas and insights with like-minded scientists and amateur enthusiasts.

Chap dressed quickly, had some breakfast, and then savored the view from his living room window as the sun began to rise. The panorama of buttes, cliffs, and rust-red sandstone spoke to him. He found it endlessly fascinating. The sky, usually pale blue this time of day, was filled with gray clouds, typical of an early-winter morning in the Bears Ears country with snow in the forecast. The predicted storm had left a light cover of snow the night before, most of which quickly melted. The main event, forecast to arrive later that day, seemed to have changed direction.

Yesterday, he'd watched a pair of ravens glide against the deep, brilliant sky, southern Utah's morning sun reflecting from their wings as if they were black patent leather. The ravens' shadows had played against cliffsides rich in fossils. Today the early-morning view was somber, moisture-rich clouds filtering the light. A good day for staying in the office, putting finishing touches on a replica he'd made of an important find, and working on his paper about that discovery and why it would turn paleontology on its head.

Chap, like many children, had loved dinosaur books, dinosaur models, dinosaur toys, dinosaur movies—everything dino. Unlike most youngsters, he never fell out of love with them, and his insatiable curiosity led him to degrees in geology, paleontology, and a residency through New York's Museum of Natural History. The job in New York eventually brought him to Utah for fieldwork. As a young man he had been fortunate to help excavate the site where the best-preserved and most complete sauropod skeleton ever found was discovered. Sauropods, those giant vegetarians of the dinosaur family, had held his attention for years.

Happily, he'd discovered a way to share his love for dinosaurs and at the same time make a living. He consulted with companies that sold fossils—only those common ones of no scientific value—and his fees paid for life's necessities not covered by his trust fund. Why not give a child the chance to hold a real *T. rex* tooth, when there are literally millions of them preserved as fossils?

His place on its ten acres outside of Bluff offered everything he needed for work and life, everything except the partner of his dreams. He had designed the house with a lovely large bedroom and ample space for his lab and office, along with a two-bedroom guest house. The second building came in handy to accommodate apprentices or consultants he invited to help him, or who invited themselves to see what he was working on. His guests didn't have to drive to motels in Bluff or Blanding, and they could go to sleep early or work late without bothering their host.

And best of all, his home was relatively convenient to Valley of the Gods, where he had done his most important research. He saw the area as an archive of the final stages of the late Paleozoic ice age, a treasure house of information about animals that had either become extinct or led to life as we know it today.

Everything had gone well until the breakup with his girlfriend, the slashed tires, and the threatening phone calls. He tried to forget her betrayal, bought new tires, and changed his phone number. He hired a good man to help him with security.

Chap pulled himself away from the view and went to his bone shop. He had intentionally designed it without windows, letting big skylights provide the natural light while avoiding the lovely distractions to be found by a glance out the window.

He powered up his laptop and focused on the fossil on his lab table, which could, to an untrained eye, be mistaken for a rock with bumps. In fact he was looking at a remnant of a dinosaur ancestor, a close-up of a fossilized jawbone connected to something even more intriguing, a once-in-a-millennium find—the skull of the animal itself. He called the skull Mary.

The skull was a rare and valuable find, as he had recorded in his research notes yesterday, even without its surprise—a nearly complete set of differentiated teeth. Using his high-powered magnifier on the surface of the rock, he found what appeared to be the start of a new tooth arriving to replace one that had been lost.

He made a note, then stashed the fossil away and focused on the replica. He reached for a dental pick to remove a bit of residue from the replica's jaw. He wanted Mary's clone to be as perfect as possible.

It was easy to lose track of time when absorbed in his work, and so the sound surprised him.

Then his doorbell buzzed again.

Odd, he thought. It was too early in the morning for most people to even be awake. Deliveries came to his office in Blanding. Maybe whoever was there would leave if he ignored them.

He glanced up at the security camera screen.

A nervous man wearing a sweatshirt printed with the sketch of a *Utahraptor* that Chap had designed stood at the entry door.

Chap sprang out of his desk chair and put his hand on the gun safe.

# 8

"I'm worried about your sister. I don't know why she's mad at me." Mama frowned at the passing landscape, a platform of brown earth with a few parched plants against the cloudless blue sky. "Sometimes my remembering isn't good."

"No, that's not it. You didn't do anything you need to remember, Mama." The hay bales on the bed of the truck in front of Darleen wobbled whenever the vehicle hit a rut, but the road was too curvy to risk passing. She slowed down and listened for what else Mama had to say about Bernie.

"My daughter is too quiet. Not even arguing with me or with you. What did we do to make her angry?"

Darleen sighed. They'd had a version of this conversation last night when she had reminded Mama of the doctor's appointment and of the fact that Bernie was in Utah, which meant Darleen got the job of taking their mother to the clinic.

"I don't think she's mad at you or at me. She's

disappointed that she didn't get that job. And before that, Mrs. Darkwater's injury and especially the fire at your house really bothered her."

"What fire?"

The truck slowed some more, and Darleen tapped her foot on the brake. She tried to think of a concise, polite response to Mama's question. "That fire that burned our old corral." She had learned not to say, "Don't you remember?" because obviously Mama didn't remember, even though the blaze had almost spread to the house.

"Did my neighbor catch on fire?"

"No, Mama." Sometimes Darleen amazed herself with her patience. "The fire at your house startled her, and she tripped over something in the dark and hit her head. Bidziil let me know she needed help."

"Bidziil is a good dog. He's a strong one, just like his name."

The truck driver stuck his arm out the window to signal a turn. Darleen could see no other traffic, but the man came to a full stop in the middle of the highway before creeping left across the pavement onto a dirt road. The hay shifted but stayed in the truck.

Darleen breathed a sigh of relief and enjoyed the open road ahead of her.

"I know that lady neighbor is all right. We talked this morning. She's worried about your sister, too. Why do you think she's mad at me?"

"I don't think she's mad at you, Mama. She loves you as much as I do. Getting rejected for that detective job really shook her. My sister cried when she told me."

"Oh. Your sister doesn't cry much. You should talk and find out why she's so angry with me."

"She never said she was mad at you, Mama."

"Then what is it?"

Darleen squeezed the steering wheel a little harder. "I don't know, Mama."

"Well, why don't you ask her?"

"I have. She said she didn't want to talk about it." Darleen remembered how awkward she felt raising an uncomfortable subject. "I told her that we both saw her unhappiness. I asked her what was up."

"And why she's so mad?"

Her sister had seemed more disappointed than angry, but she let Mama's opinion stand. "She said not to worry about her, and that speaking of it made her feel worse." Darleen shrugged. "She's sad, Mama, maybe upset about not getting a job she deserved. I don't know what else to say."

They rode in silence for a while, heading toward the town of Shiprock for Mama's appointment at the clinic, lunch at Thatsaburger, and groceries at Basha's.

Mama reached over unexpectedly and patted Darleen's hand. "So there's nothing to do. We have to wait until she wants to talk or until her pain goes away. She's strong, that one. She'll be OK. I think it's time for her to have a baby. That would be a good thing."

The car filled with quiet again except for the sound of the engine and the tires on the old pavement, and for a moment, Darleen imagined that Mama was OK too.

They turned onto NM 491 toward Shiprock,

passing the convenience store where Darleen
sometimes pulled over for fuel and a snack.

"You stopping here?"

"I can if you need the restroom."

"I mean for gas. You don't want to run out."
Mama reached for her purse. "I have some money."

"It's OK, Mama. We're good." Thanks to her
steady boyfriend, Slim, who had borrowed the car
a few days ago, the gas tank was nearly full.

Traffic into town was light, and Darleen snagged
a parking spot close to the entrance of the clinic.
The nearly empty parking lot made her nervous.
As was their habit, Mama waited in the car while
her daughter went inside to check her in and see
how long the wait would be.

Darleen was back in less than five minutes, a
scowl on her face.

"The doctor is sick today, so they had to cancel
all the appointments. They said they called and
left a message, but I didn't get it." She shook her
head in disgust. "We'll have to come back."

Mama frowned. "Are you sick, my daughter?"

"No, Mama. This was for you. A checkup." The
purpose of the visit was to discuss Mama's memory
problems. Bernie had done some research, which
she passed on to her sister, about new drugs that in
some cases delay the progress of certain dementias.
Bernie had planned to come with them, but then
she had the chance to go to Bears Ears.

"I don't need a doctor. Let's get the groceries."

"What about lunch?"

"We had lunch."

Darleen knew better than to argue, and in fact
they were closer to Basha's than to the restaurant.

They grabbed a grocery cart for Mama to push and to help with her balance and were headed toward the veggies, Darleen's favorite department, when her phone signaled a text. She pulled it from her back pocket and saw that the message came from Chee.

"Hold on, Mama. It's the Cheeseburger."

Mama kept walking. "Tell that man we are busy. You can't talk now."

"It's a text message."

"A test?" Mama pushed her carriage toward the potatoes.

"No, a text, a little note someone can send you over the phone."

"That's wrong. Phones are for talking."

Darleen took a moment to read it:

What if we stop by on our way home from Utah? B could use some cheering up.

She texted back a thumbs-up emoji and Dinner? Then, How's Utah? and, out of politeness, How's U? But he didn't respond immediately, so she caught up with Mama, and they did their shopping.

Of the three Manuelito women, Darleen realized she was the best cook. Mama was barely cooking anything these days, and when she did, her daughters helped. Bernie left the kitchen to Chee except for homemade fruit pies.

Cooking for her brother-in-law made Darleen happy. Chee ate with gusto and gratitude. He loved spaghetti, and Bernie and Mama tolerated it. She got a package of ground beef, a box of pasta, a jar of sauce, onions, fresh garlic, and, as a splurge, a plastic box with fresh oregano inside. She added veggies for a salad to the cart—part of her ongoing but failing campaign to help Mama and her sister improve their diets. On the way to the cashier, she tossed in some cookies for dessert.

Mama complained that everything was too expensive but remained on her good behavior in the store and at the little restaurant for lunch and most of the way home. Then she asked the question that led to what Darleen and Bernie privately referred to as the Big Problem.

"Are you looking for a job?"

"Not right now, Mama."

"You know I can't make those rugs anymore. My hands fail me." Mama had been an expert weaver in a section of the Navajo Nation where competition for that title was fierce. But arthritis had ended her career. "It's hard to find a job, my daughter, but don't give up."

"I'm not looking for a job right now because I'm heading back to school. I'm going to get some training so I can be a nurse's aide. Then it will be easy for me to get a job." She and everyone else in the family liked the plan and supported her idea. Everyone except Mama. That was the Big Problem.

"You graduated already." Mama shook her head. Darleen remembered how she'd squeaked by with barely enough passing credits to leave Shiprock High with a diploma. "And then you went to that place in Santa Fe, the eye school or something, for your drawings."

"That's right. The IAIA." She'd taken a summer program at Santa Fe's well-regarded Institute of American Indian Arts. She'd fallen in love with the classes and with a fellow student who turned out to be the wrong man. She had returned to live with Mama again, bringing a sketchbook filled with images and a heart full of heartbreak.

"You draw real good now. You should do that."

"I'll always love to draw, Mama, but I need a better way to make a living. I registered for classes, and I start in January. That's about a month from now." She paused to give Mama time to process the information. She had applied for grants and a scholarship. Bernie and Chee had agreed to help financially if necessary. And when he wasn't teaching his elementary school students, Slim volunteered to stay with her mother so Darleen could study.

"You already got that job making pictures of those women for Leapfrog." Mama always called Lieutenant Joe Leaphorn, Bernie's and Chee's former boss and mentor, by the wrong name. "You didn't have to take any classes to learn how to do that. Why are you always such a problem for me, my daughter?" Mama made a clicking noise with her tongue.

Thanks to the retired lieutenant, Darleen worked when needed designing posters for the Navajo Department of Public Safety to help publicize missing and exploited Navajo women, men, and children and try to bring them home. But even though Leaphorn and his committee found a bit of grant money to pay her, and she loved the work, Darleen needed a steady paycheck.

"Mama, try to think of it this way. I went to Chinle to be with our old neighbor when he returned from the hospital. I enjoyed that. I felt like a valuable person because I could make that man's life easier and help him get well. And when Mrs. Darkwater got hurt, I wish I had known more so I could have been a better helper to her."

Mama frowned.

Darleen felt her patience start to fray. "In these classes, I'll learn new things, kind of like a nurse."

"No. After Dikos Ntsaaígíí, that work is dangerous." Dikos Ntsaaígíí—coronavirus, the Big Cough—had changed life on the Navajo Nation. It had killed almost two thousand people and sickened more than seventy-five thousand. And the illness continued.

"There will always be something contagious out there," Darleen said. "We have the vaccine now for that, and the classes will teach me to keep myself as safe as possible, and how to help you more, too."

Mama shook her head. "No. You are a good artist, my daughter. That is how you should live. Let someone in their families take care of those old ones. No. That's all I have to say."

Mama fell quiet, and Darleen drove home in silence.

The trip from Shiprock to their house in Toadlena took them past a familiar landscape of gentle hills, sage, and piñon trees. December clouds had begun to build, and the air smelled of winter. The moisture of snow would be welcome.

Darleen had grown up here and knew this slice of Dinétah like an old friend. With deep roots as her anchor, she looked forward to a positive change. She tried to push her concern about her sister and her irritation at Mama aside and think about Slim.

For the first time, she believed that she'd found a man she could love forever, and who would love her back just as fiercely. It wasn't what he said; it was what he did. He'd noticed that the driver's door on her car didn't open and figured out how to fix it. He had researched grant and scholarship opportunities for her. Best of all, when she talked, he listened.

Slim was in his first year of teaching third grade at Shiprock Elementary, a promotion from his work as teacher's aide. He enjoyed it, but the job came with tremendous responsibility and lots of stress. When he got grumpy and she pushed him to tell her what was bothering him, he reassured her that it wasn't her fault and said he'd talk about it when he figured it out. And true to his word, he did.

Mama had drifted off to sleep—although she would argue that she never slept while Darleen was driving—and so the old woman didn't see the coyote that emerged from the roadside and dashed to the other side of the pavement. Darleen had been told that if a coyote crossed her path, she should turn around, find a different route. Mama always said it meant bad luck was in the air. But Darleen had never had a reason to believe that, and anyway, there was no other way to get home. She said a prayer for protection and continued on the route.

Mama awoke when Darleen stopped the car in front of their house. She helped her mother inside and to the bathroom, then went out for the groceries, and came back to settle Mama on the couch. Darleen had put the refrigerated food away and was about to start on the rest when her phone buzzed with a text. She hoped it was from Slim, but Chee had sent it. On assignment that's taking longer than it should have. Bernie off with the truck. Dinner? He added a few snowflake symbols.

She responded, No worries. Hope to see you.

Then she texted Slim. Maybe her boyfriend could come, even if Bernie and Chee couldn't make it. Mama tended to be less openly critical of her daughters' choices in men if the men she would have criticized sat at the table. Darleen could tell that, after several years of having the Cheeseburger as a son-in-law, Mama liked him, even if she wouldn't say so.

She thought about Chee's text. Where was Bernie anyway? Probably getting gas or something.

# 9

"Damaged petroglyphs aren't really that unusual." Jessica sounded like an expert. "If you consider that some of these are a thousand years old or more, it's no wonder the elements have done some harm to them."

"Right. I know that." Bernie kept walking. "But this was clearly vandalism. Whoever made them purposely found a sheltered place. Out of the way, too. This wasn't an act of nature. I'm surprised someone went to the trouble to harm them."

As the two women hiked to the cliffside, Bernie realized that the potsherds were less noticeable here. She wondered if someone had dumped them at the trench on purpose, to make an illegal search for fossils look like an archaeology site. The pieces of her theory didn't quite come together, but it was the only logical explanation she had at the moment.

The massive sandstone walls and the intense, primitive beauty of the area made her feel like a human standing in a space intended for the gods.

Some of the sandstone formations resembled enlarged versions of the walls you might find at a ruined pueblo. If she used her imagination, she could see one formation as a giant chicken sitting on her nest and another as a rooster. One reminded her of twin owl chicks perched side by side. Light beige sand lay in the shade of the cliffs, a striking contrast to the red rock. Bands of dark brown and cream-colored stone encircled the buttes.

Bernie searched the cliffside for the rock art. Nothing yet.

"Jessica, did you and your husband work together very much?"

"I guess you could say that, even though our fields were different. He helped me organize some of my excavations. Kyle loves . . . I mean, loved it out here." Jessica stopped and sucked in a breath.

Bernie paused too. The day seemed to be getting colder.

Jessica pointed to a place in the cliffside. "Wow. Look at this."

Bernie stared at the odd dark rock, shaped like a section of broomstick.

"You mean the stone?"

"It looks like rock, but it's a fossil. Bone turned to stone."

"Very cool. How can you tell?"

"Because Kyle was a paleontologist, he had a second sense about this. After so much time in the field with him, I learned how to spot fossilized bones, teeth, claws, tracks. Even dinosaur poop."

"You're teasing me."

"No. We call it coprolite."

Bernie laughed.

Jessica ran her fingers along the protruding stone bone. "Kyle's field of interest was climate change and what adaptations helped mammals become the world's dominant animals."

Bernie said, "My theory about that trench back there was that it had to do with grave robbing. But that doesn't seem right. Do you think someone was stealing fossils?"

"I don't know what to think." Jessica looked at the cliffside. "Some dinosaur skeletons sell for huge amounts, in the millions. Someone paid nearly thirty-two million dollars in New York for a skeleton of *Tyrannosaurus rex*—the most expensive fossil ever sold at an auction. Of course, it was a complete skeleton."

"Wow. That's huge money. Do all fossils go for that much?"

"Not at all. It's almost unheard of for a complete or almost complete skeleton like that to come up for sale. And everyone loves a *T. rex*."

Bernie thought about it. "If the fossil market is anything like what happens sometimes in archaeology, I bet there's also a pretty active black market for fossils."

"Well, most commercial fossils don't sell for anything even close to that because they're smaller, more common, and therefore less desirable. And legally, all the commercial stuff has to come from private land, places like the Hell Creek Formation north of here. A person can't legally remove anything from public land, like Bears Ears, without a

permit, and those are only issued for research. If
someone is into looting, it certainly would be easier
to be a pot hunter. Pots are a lot lighter than dinosaur bones."

Bernie laughed. "I think the petroglyphs are
just a bit farther."

They climbed the ridge. Bernie showed her
where to look beneath the overhang for the art;
she didn't need to see the disturbing images again.
Jessica spent a few minutes examining the pictures, and then they headed for the truck.

Bernie walked a bit faster than usual. She
wanted to drop off the gifts, get back to the motel,
pack up, and head for home.

Jessica fastened her seat belt. "How long to get
to the house where we leave the food?"

"I've never been there, but they say it's only a
few miles or so from here. We'll see what state the
road is in." When Lilakai had texted directions to
the house from the turnoff, she mentioned that
the last few miles were a little rough.

"Whatever." Jessica adjusted the heater vent.
"I'm glad to be out of that motel room, not taking calls or visits from the BLM or the sheriff.
After seeing the damage, I agree with you about
that rock art being vandalized. That's a shame.
I've rarely found that kind of purposeful destruction. You probably know that there's always talk of
witchcraft when that kind of defacement happens.
I mean, the figures have spiritual power according
to some cultures, so destroying them, wounding
them, might transfer the power from good to evil.
I don't buy the witchcraft stuff." Jessica laughed.
"Do you, Bernie? I think sometimes people just

get bored. Or they feel a need to destroy something beautiful."

The topic made Bernie uncomfortable, and she saw no need to answer the question. She started the engine and then noticed a dark truck heading toward them. It reminded her of the one that had tried to kill her last night. She didn't drive off.

"What's wrong?"

"I'm curious about that vehicle coming our way."

"Why?"

Bernie didn't feel like explaining. "It's a long story."

She noticed that the truck didn't hesitate to pull up to her vehicle.

The driver lowered the window, and the stench of old cigarette smoke wafted out.

"Hey there, honey. You lost?"

"No."

"Did you and your girlfriend there take down that roadblock?"

"Absolutely. Ranger Becenti of the BLM says it's illegal to block a public road."

Jessica shifted in her seat. "Let's go."

Bernie ignored her. "Now I've got a question for you, something I think you can help me with. I was hiking out here last night, and a truck that looked just like this one tried to run over me. Then somebody used a rifle to shoot my jacket. I was wondering if you could tell me anything about that."

The driver winked at her. "So what were you doin' here in the dark, sweetheart?"

"That doesn't matter."

Bernie saw the rifle in the gun rack behind the

man's head and put her hand on her own gun. She had no jurisdiction here to arrest him, but she had every right to protect herself if it came to that.

The driver laughed, and Bernie heard the meanness. "Honey, what happened to you is a darn shame. You know, there's a lot of trucks out this way and a bunch of coyotes, too, just lookin' for trouble. Maybe that's what you heard, you know, someone trying to bag one of those varmints. One big problem with coyotes is that they don't mind their own business."

"I think this truck tried to run over me, and the buddy who was with you last night took the shot."

The driver gave her a wicked smile, revealing a gold eye tooth. "You have to be careful out here, especially at night. I hear that your Navajo witches fly around in the dark. And like I said, there are packs of coyotes. Ranchers sure don't appreciate the way they harass the livestock."

Jessica stared at the driver. "I remember you and that gold tooth. You're Donray, right?" Jessica didn't wait for the man to answer. "You and a friend of yours, a guy missing some fingers, both of you worked for my husband, Kyle, and me up by Grand Gulch last year, didn't you?"

"Yeah, we did." Donray's voice was cold and flat. "Until you fired me. And then Dev quit."

"You kept forgetting to come to work, remember? What are you doing here at Bears Ears?"

"An old fossil guy from outside Bluff hired me to work for a company he was with, and it paid better than you ever would. Dev works for him too. Chap is good to us. And he's gonna be famous someday."

"Chap?" Jessica spoke a little more quickly. "You work for Chap? Dr. Dulles? What do you do?"

Bernie remembered Chee mentioning the name Chapman Dulles. The connection to the "fossil guy" made sense.

Donray laughed. "I didn't think you pot diggers paid much attention to the old-bone dudes. But Kyle knows Chap, right? Those guys are in the same crazy cage, sweating their butts off for a dinosaur turd."

Bernie waited for Jessica to correct the verb tense and explain about Kyle's death, but her passenger let it slide. Bernie motioned to where she had tripped and fallen. "What's up with the trench that was here, and why did it get filled in with rocks and that burlap stuff?"

"We do whatever the company asks, and that is none of your business. And while we're talking about that, there's no trespassing on the site. Someone could get hurt out here." He glanced toward the sawhorses. "Put those back when you leave."

Donray made a U-turn. The truck drove off the way it came.

Jessica turned her head to watch. "Donray always bothered me. An arrogant jerk with a love of violence. And his friend Dev? That guy is strange, too."

"Did they work for you very long?"

Jessica nodded. "Too long. Donray is smarter than he seems, and we shared a love for nice vehicles. He actually worked more for my husband than for me, but Kyle gave me the job of firing him."

She lightly squeezed Bernie's arm. "Let's drop off the food and get back to the motel. I have a friend coming to help me deal with the details of Kyle's death. And I want to be sure I don't miss the call from the medical examiner. You know cell coverage can be spotty here in the valley."

# 10

Chee sat across from Roper Black as he answered the call from the San Juan County Sheriff's Office. He couldn't deduce much from Black's end of the conversation, except big trouble somewhere. Black rattled off a set of numbers. His frown deepened as the conversation went on, ending with, "I'll tell him to get over there."

He looked at Chee. "The alarm I put in at my boss's house is going off. Chap isn't answering the sheriff's call. Hold on a minute while I give my boss another try."

Chee listened as Black placed an unanswered call and left an urgent message with both his phone number and the sheriff's.

"They think it might be a burglary, but it's probably nothing. The sheriff is on the way, and he wants me there too. I'd appreciate it if you would come with me to the house." Black launched into a quick description of the views and the home's construction, all of which sounded like an extravagant real estate ad. "When Chap shows up, I'll

disappear so you can talk to him about the donation. Then I'll give you that lift back to the motel
I promised."

"Let's do it." Chee rose and put some bills on
the table for their drinks and a tip. "That's one
advantage of the Navajo Nation. A lot of people
have dogs as their alarm systems. They might go
off by accident, but they don't dial the cops."

Black stood and looked at the car keys in his
hand. "I don't mean to give you a false impression
here. I tried to install a system that would resist
false alarms but also dial 911 automatically. Something could be going on up there at the house."

Chee nodded. "I understand."

It was about a half-hour drive from the restaurant to Chapman Dulles's place. The site was
as grand as Black had described, perhaps even
grander. A heart-stopping panorama of mountains
with snow-topped peaks stretched along the horizon to the north. Then came open chaparral country and Bluff's famous cliffs. A few stray snowflakes
tumbled from the leaden sky onto the windshield.

Chee put in a call to Bernie and explained to her
voice mail that he was on the way to Dr. Dulles's
house and would see her at the motel. Black drove
with silent focus, a bit over the speed limit.

They pulled into the broad circular driveway,
noting that neither the sheriff nor a deputy had
arrived yet. They saw no other cars. Good, Chee
thought. The odds were slim that, if it was more
than a false alarm, the bad guys were still there.

They parked and walked toward the house.
Black hadn't exaggerated; the place was a knockout.
It had exterior walls of natural stone that helped

it blend into the environment. Chee admired the thoughtfulness reflected in building the structure with minimal disruption of the landscape. But then he saw the shattered front door hanging from a single hinge at an odd angle. Followed by blood on the driveway and the person it had once belonged to, obviously dead.

Black gasped. They backed away in unison. Both men had their weapons drawn, pointing at the house. Chee felt his heartbeat accelerate.

"Is it your boss?"

"No. Chap is older and bigger."

"Did you see the door?"

"Yeah. It looks like someone blew it nearly off the hinges."

Black pulled out his phone for a quick call. Chee heard the sheriff yell, "On the way. Don't touch a thing." Immediately after that, Black tried to reach Chap again. "You need to get here. There's a dead man in the driveway." Then he slipped the phone into his pocket.

Both men studied the house.

"Chee, I've never been in a situation like this. Where's the killer?" Black's voice carried his tension.

"I don't know. Maybe inside. Maybe gone." Chee found the weight of his Glock in his hand reassuring. "Probably gone. There are no vehicles in sight, and whoever did this must have had some kind of getaway transportation."

Chee looked toward the house; he pictured Black's boss dead inside. "Have you spoken to Chap at all today?"

Black shook his head. "But that's not unusual.

He likes to traipse off into the backcountry. Leave his phone in the car. Except he knew you were coming up here with me and even said he looked forward to meeting you. He's very reliable about keeping appointments. What do we do now?"

"We wait."

The men retreated to Black's vehicle and stood behind it, eyeing the house, waiting for the sheriff to arrive and take charge.

Black sighed. "This is going to be a long day. If you need to go, you can take my car and just leave it at the motel. I'll get a ride from someone when this is done. My boss ought to be here any time, but he'll probably not be in the mood to talk about the donation."

"Thanks for the offer of the car, but I'll wait awhile to see if Chap shows up. If we don't hear from him in ten minutes, I'll go in to look for him."

"You?" Black's anger was palpable. "Why not me?"

"I'm a cop. I know how to handle situations like this." Chee looked at the scene again. "Let's hope the sheriff gets here soon."

Black nodded.

"Tell me more about the man who lives in this house."

Black studied the heavy sky a moment. "He's complicated. If I had to sum him up in a few words, I'd say he expects too much of himself and projects that same expectation on everyone around him. On the one hand, that inspires me to do my best. On the other hand, my best is never good enough."

The description reminded Chee of his old boss, the legendary Lieutenant Joe Leaphorn.

Black spoke quickly. "Dr. Dulles is really smart, and he works hard. He went to school somewhere in the East and got a couple degrees, then became interested in dinosaurs and their ancestors. He told me he was lucky to find a job at a museum where they had a treasure trove of fossils from Utah, and that figured into his decision to move near Bears Ears. He's, well, I guess I'd say quirky. Not your average boss."

"Are you worried that he's not returning your calls?"

"Not yet. He turns his phone off when he goes to the places he loves out here. He enjoys revisiting the spot where he found the allosaurus bone or the cliff where he saw the claw of a raptor or the expanse of sandstone that held the theropod tracks. His favorite at the moment is where he found that old skull with teeth still in the jaw." Black smiled. "He's kind of like me. He loves hanging out in the Bears Ears boonies."

"Does he keep a lot of cash at the house, maybe to pay his workers?"

Black shook his head.

"Does your boss have anything especially expensive in the house?"

"Not that I know of. He has what you'd expect: TVs, computers, a gun or two. But nothing exceptional."

It was hard for Chee to imagine any possession worth enough to warrant murder. "I'm going to take a walk, check outside the house, while you wait for the sheriff."

Chee checked the exterior of the building, looking and listening for sounds and sights of disturbance, or for someone in need of help. He noticed the open double-car garage with no vehicles parked inside, no signs of forced entry other than the front-door damage. Besides that—and the body—nothing seemed unusual. The fact that the house was quiet reassured him. Time to go in and look for Chap, or his body.

As he walked back to where Black stood, a San Juan County sheriff's unit pulled up. They met Sheriff Gillman at the top of the driveway.

"Sheriff, this is Lieutenant Jim Chee with the Navajo Police. He was with me when I got your call."

Chee acknowledged the sheriff with a nod, grateful that Gillman knew enough about Navajo tradition—and the changes brought by COVID—not to offer a handshake.

"I thought I might be helpful," Chee said.

"I'd like that." Gillman gave him a cursory look and then spoke to Black. "Anyone else here?"

"I don't think so. Us three and the dead man."

Chee said, "I walked around the exterior perimeter. Nothing unusual except the garage is open and it's empty. I mean, no cars there. I didn't go in the house."

Gillman looked out toward the mountains for a quick moment. "Even though it's obvious, I need to make sure the victim is deceased. Protocol. Then I'm going inside to look for Chap."

Gillman knelt by the body, and checked for a pulse while Chee and Black waited. He got up, shaking his head. "Roper, have you heard from Chapman yet?"

"No, sir. I'm starting to worry. What if he's inside, hurt or something?" Black looked at the mess in the driveway. "Hurt or worse."

The sheriff quickly put on a pair of latex gloves. "You two walk to the front door with me and wait there. Come if I holler for you, or if you hear a shot or a scuffle. Be careful."

Chee nodded. "I've been in situations like this. We've got your back."

They stepped around the blood freezing on the driveway and trotted to the open doorway, guns drawn, Gillman leading the way. Gillman disappeared inside the house, and they heard him calling Chap's name.

Black stepped closer to Chee. "Lieutenant, I've never been involved with a murder before. Should I have gone inside the house when we first got here? What if Chap was near death, and I could have—"

"Don't go there." Chee answered the question with the by-the-book response. "You did just right. The sheriff is in charge. He's the pro. He's old enough to have seen this rodeo a few times."

They continued to hear Gillman calling without a response. No shots, no sounds of violence, no criminal running toward an exit.

Chee read the sheriff's relief, and perhaps disappointment, as he walked out of the house toward them. Gillman resembled the human equivalent of a sputtering engine, but the man gathered his thoughts as he drew closer and assumed a more assertive posture.

"Chap's not in there, as far as I can tell. The detective and the medical examiner are on the way." Gillman took a breath. "I didn't see signs of a struggle in the house or any more blood."

"Good." Black's voice rang with relief.

"What type of vehicle does Dulles drive?" Gillman asked.

Black thought for a moment. "He has a Lexus SUV, but it's at the dealership in Salt Lake City for repairs. The dealer gave him a loaner of some kind."

"So where is he? Where's Chap?"

"I don't know. Hopefully on the way home."

"Maybe. Maybe he's on the run because he killed that man." Gillman shook his head. "It's odd. It looks like someone disabled the security equipment. There probably won't be a record of who was here or what they did."

Black began to pace. "I should have been here. At least the 911 call worked. Could you tell what got stolen?"

Gillman paused. "That's another thing odd about this. There's lots of nice stuff inside, stealable things like TVs, video game players, electronic tablets, some attractive gold coins on display, a fancy leather jacket on a chair in the living room. All that is in there, in plain sight and untouched."

Chee sighed. "Maybe whoever broke in abducted him. Maybe they were after the man himself, not his TV."

Gillman looked back at the house for a moment. "The only room where there might have been an intrusion resembles a workshop or a laboratory or something. I noticed a bunch of stuff on the floor, as though someone had rifled through there, looking for something. A closet and a file cabinet were standing open, but maybe Chap left them that way."

"I doubt it." Black readjusted his hat against the cold. "Chap likes order. Sir, I just installed that security system, and it has a solid backup. When I have access, I can check the automatic camera tape. It might show us something."

Chee said, "The fact that the system was disabled tells me that whatever happened here wasn't spontaneous. Did Chap know how to turn off the cameras and the rest?"

"Yes. Chap asked me how to turn it off. He joked that he didn't want any recordings of him and his girlfriend if he got a new one." Black stopped his explanation and blew on his hands. Chee realized he felt colder, too. "The system isn't very complicated. Anyone comfortable with electronics could figure it out quickly."

Gillman said, "Who's the dead guy?"

"I don't recognize him." Black paused. "I know most of the people Chap hires, but not all of them."

Chee had been listening quietly, gathering his thoughts. "Let's look at this scene again. If this was a break-in, did Chap kill the invader? Is that why there's a dead man in the driveway? Who blew the door off its hinges? I didn't see a weapon by the dead man. Did he have one? And why isn't Chap here? Why hasn't he responded to your calls?"

Gillman bristled. "I was just going to ask Roper about that. Since you brought it up, Lieutenant, what do you think?"

"Well, either Chap is on the run for killing this guy, or Chap got kidnapped by the killer. Or, like Black told me, he's just out enjoying the sights." Chee shook his head and changed the subject slightly. "I suspect the dead man had at least one accomplice. If one of his partners shot him, that brings me to why. Maybe an argument over the crime? Maybe the dead guy got cold feet?"

Gillman looked toward the body. "The crime scene investigator can clear up some of these questions. He's good at his job. Black, do you know if Chap has enemies?"

"He's never talked about any. He's focused on his work."

"Well, he must have annoyed someone seriously enough to get his tires slashed." Gillman exhaled. "Deputy Dayton handled the case. He said that Chap seemed embarrassed to file a report on that incident, as though it were a waste of time."

Chee turned to Black. "Maybe embarrassed because he knew who did it."

Black shrugged. "He never let on, if that was the case."

Gillman nodded. "Dayton asked him about it, and Chap said he had no clue."

"Did you track it down?" Chee knew the answer before Gillman shook his head.

"No. Dayton let it fall through the cracks."

Black jumped in. "I told Chap he should have reported that and those threatening calls a lot sooner."

"Does Chap have a gun?" Chee said.

"Of course. Several. It's practically a requirement for residency out here." Black paused to think. "He kept one in his car."

Chee glanced toward the dead man. "We ought to cover his body out of respect."

"Of course," said Gillman. "I've got a tarp in my car. Parker and Carson should be here soon. A deputy is down there, securing the scene at the entrance to the house."

Gillman left for the tarpaulin, and Chee turned to Black.

"Who are Parker and Carson?"

"Nathan Parker is the department detective. He's a Ute. A good man. I don't know Carson." Black looked at the ground. "I can't believe Chap would shoot someone. He's not a killer, but maybe the dead man scared him enough that he had to defend himself."

"Some people go ballistic when they feel threatened. What's the real story with Chap not being here and ignoring your calls?"

"I don't know, honestly."

Gillman returned and covered the body himself, a gesture Chee and Black appreciated, both as a way to limit their exposure to his chindi, the malevolent spirit that lingered after death, and as thoughtful recognition of the victim's humanity.

The sheriff left the corpse and walked to where they stood. "Parker texted that he's on his way. I left another message for Mela."

"Who?" Black asked.

"Mela Carson. She's the one who comes to examine the body."

"Oh."

"After she's done with the prelim exam, her crew takes it to the morgue for a full autopsy." Gillman changed the subject. "Do you know what your boss was working on in there?"

"Not exactly. Something about ancient teeth. Fossilized. Turned to stone."

"Like shark teeth or something?" Gillman shook his head. "My boy got some of those from a catalog that had dinosaur stuff. He thinks they're pretty cool."

While they spoke, Chee fiddled with his phone, searching for something. "Hey, I just found this. Chapman Dulles is famous in the world of pale-ontology. The website at the university where he worked says he's an expert in the ancient ancestors of the animals that ultimately became mammals. And he discovered evidence that the early Pueblo people who lived here in Bears Ears intentionally built with stones that contained fossils when they could. This article says his specialty is researching the evolutionary changes reflected in the fossils in Valley of the Gods and Cedar Mesa." He put the phone back in his pocket.

Black looked puzzled. "Chap never told me he was famous. Lately he'd been spending a lot of time talking about teeth that turned to stone. He found a skull that came from some ancient creature. He said its teeth show the kind of de-velopment he's interested in—how early animals became mammals—and that fossils like this are extremely rare."

"That's interesting." Chee thought about it. "Where did he find it?"

"In Valley of the Gods. He named the skull

Mary. He told me it was a priceless discovery, the thrill of his lifetime."

"Mary?" Gillman chuckled. "He gave the skull a name? You're kidding. Where did he keep Mary—the skull, teeth, the jawbone, whatever? Where is she, or it?"

Black seemed surprised by the question. "I don't know. He never offered to show it to me, and I never asked to see it."

Chee waited for Gillman to pose the most important question, but he didn't. So he asked it himself. "Where do you think Chap is now?"

"I don't know that either. I wish I'd . . ." Black trailed off and shook his head.

"What?" Gillman pressed. "You wish you'd what? Found a ransom note?"

"No, no, no. I wish . . . I should have taken better care of him. I was still on the payroll, but he gave me time off for the baby. None of this would have happened if I'd done my job."

"Baby?" Gillman raised his eyebrows.

"My wife had our little girl last night. She wasn't due for two weeks. I had to be with her, but this wouldn't have happened if I'd done my job."

"You don't know that," Chee said. He'd been in that dark place of self-doubt too. "You could be as dead as the guy under the tarp. And the security system you built got the sheriff here. What about your wife and daughter? What would they do without you?"

Gillman turned to Black. "We need to figure out where Chap is, if he knows about this, if he had any involvement in what happened here, and if anything was stolen. And we need to ID the dead man and find out who killed him."

"The fact that the security system was disabled says smart criminals came here for a planned home invasion," said Chee. "This wasn't kids acting spontaneously."

Gillman nodded. While they watched, Black dialed Dulles's number again and left a "call me now" message.

"Give me his number." Then Gillman called as well as sending a text, ordering Dr. Dulles to respond as soon as possible. He looked at Chee. "You had an appointment here, right?"

Chee nodded. "He'd asked to talk to someone from the Navajo Police about making a donation to our Fallen Officers fund. I got the assignment."

Gillman smiled. "So maybe one reason he's not here is that he changed his mind, didn't want to talk about giving money to the police."

"Wrong." Black's tone offered no room for argument. "He's a people person, and politeness is another of his strong points. It's totally unlike him to dodge an appointment. Especially with a cop."

"Why is that? Law enforcement in his family?"

"Sort of." Black shifted his weight. "His family was living in Albuquerque, and Chap's sister Emily went skateboarding with a couple of friends. They were doing tricks in a drainage canal, something the city created for flood control. He described it as basically a cement tube that becomes a rushing blast of water after a thunderstorm. Well, the friends had started skating before it rained uphill from the canal. And even though it was just sprinkling in Albuquerque, the water surged in fast and strong. Her friends climbed out, but the power of the current swept Emily away. The friends ran for help, and amazingly, the first person they found was an off-duty Navajo cop in town, visiting his cousin. The officer saved Emily from drowning and risked his own life in the process.

"Because of that, Chap has always honored people in law enforcement and had a special affection for the Diné. He likes to quote something from President Jonathan Nez about the need Navajos have for helping others."

Chee was familiar with the line and pulled it from his memory. "I know that one. 'Our people have the power within us to do anything and overcome anything. True sovereignty is the ability to take care of our own people and then to help others.'"

Gillman said, "OK, then. Anything else?"

"Not from me."

Black shook his head.

They watched a car head up the pavement toward the steep driveway that led to the residence, pausing at the request of the officer stationed at the driveway entrance as crime scene security.

Gillman said, "Let's hope it's Chapman Dulles. He has some questions to answer."

# 11

Bernie and Jessica followed the directions to the Zonnie house. The condition of the road as they neared the place made driving a challenge. The turquoise pickup was not there, Bernie noticed. Neither was Lilakai Zonnie, but an attractive younger woman walked out to meet them.

"I'm Lilakai's sister Pam." The tall, slim Navajo woman introduced herself to Bernie with a grin. "Same clans as Chatterbox. She told me you were coming. She had to do something, but she said she'd be back in a few minutes." She smiled at Jessica. "Hello there."

"This is Jessica Johnson," Bernie said. "She's the woman who wants you to have all these things for the party."

Jessica extended a hand. "Pleased to meet you."

Bernie cringed, surprised that Jessica didn't understand the traditional resistance to touching a stranger as well as the extra caution the devastation of the coronavirus had created about contact with outsiders.

Pam declined the handshake, looking puzzled. "Thank you for the food and drinks. Nice of you, Jessica." But from Pam's action and the tone of her voice, Bernie sensed something was amiss.

"Where would you like all this?" Jessica motioned to the supplies that filled Bernie's truck. "I have to get back to Bluff soon, so we better unload it."

Pam slipped on some warm-looking gloves to help, and the three of them worked hard moving the boxes from the truck into the house. It was colder than when they left Bluff, and Bernie tugged her hat over her ears. She noticed that from time to time, Pam gave Jessica an odd look.

When they had finally finished, Pam motioned them to a large kitchen table. "Sit a minute, you two. That was a lot of work. I'll make some coffee."

Bernie knew it would be rude to refuse. "Thank you, but we can't stay long. I have to get back to Bluff to pack and drive home to Shiprock before the storm causes problems."

"I understand." Pam reached for the Folgers can. "I can make it real quick."

"No. We have to go now. Thanks for the offer, but we can't do it." Jessica underlined the *can't* with her tone of voice, confirming her lack of Diné politeness.

Bernie spoke to offset the growing tension in the room. "Jessica's husband died unexpectedly just yesterday. We don't mean to be rude."

"That's right. His death means I have a lot of things to attend to."

"Oh, I'm so sorry about that man. I didn't

know. I used to work for you and your husband, and I liked him very much." Pam pressed her lips together. "You don't remember me, do you?"

Jessica gave her a blank stare.

Pam motioned with her chin to the chips and drinks they had just carried inside. "Take some back with you. You might need this food. Keep it for your family. I didn't understand what was going on."

"No, no. All this is yours. I'm glad you can use it for a happy occasion. My husband would be delighted for you to have it. I heard it was someone's birthday, is that right?"

"Yes." Pam grinned. "It's our first big family celebration in a long time."

COVID-19 had hit the Navajo Nation hard, and as a result, tribal government stressed the need for masks, vaccines, handwashing, and social isolation. Gatherings of all sorts had been discouraged and even forbidden to keep the virus from spreading. Now that the Nation had a high percentage of completed vaccinations and boosters, extended family, clan, and community gatherings were safely returning. It was a time for celebration.

"A birthday party for our little Matthew. We appreciate all these gifts. Ahéhee. And if the storm gets bad, it's nice to have extra in the house, you know. It will come in handy. This road gets awfully slick, first with the snow and ice, and then comes the mud. That's even worse." Pam shook her head. "And those guys digging out there, with trucks and their equipment. That doesn't help."

Bernie frowned. "We ran into a man in a black

truck as we were headed up here. He wasn't very friendly."

"Was it Donray?"

"Yes."

"I know his friend Dev better. He's usually with Donray. Dev's the quiet one who was born around here. He told me his relatives were part of the first LDS group that homesteaded out this way, the one they talk about at Bluff Fort. He's quiet, but I've heard he has a wild side. I don't know the one who drives, but he seems kinda mean and grumpy."

Jessica nodded in agreement. "Donray, that's the other guy. He was a punk when he worked for me. I kept him on at first because he was strong, but I was glad to have a reason to fire him."

Pam glanced out the window. "I can tell you don't remember, but you fired me, too. Not when I worked with you and Kyle, but when you lived in that big house with the views."

"You're right. I don't remember ever seeing you." Jessica didn't apologize.

Bernie stood to signal that she and the rude white woman were leaving. "I hope the weather doesn't interfere with your party."

"Oh, you know us Utah Diné. We're tough, and we are used to winter. The parents with little ones and elderlies will leave early when it's snowing, and they'll probably be in bed when the worst of the storm comes in. If it gets bad, we have plenty of floor space and extra blankets. But our relatives are used to driving on these roads. We try not to do it, but we know how if we have to."

Pam went on, giving a description of who would be at the party, where they were coming from, the connections between them, and more. As she listened, Bernie thought of how much she missed Mama. She usually called every day, but lately staying cheerful with her mother was difficult, and the idea of politely hearing another of Mama's lectures seemed impossible. And Darleen, as usual, was facing a life transition. Her sister liked to use her as a sounding board, but Bernie had been a poor listener over the past few weeks. Another failure.

By the time they finished their goodbyes and were back on the dirt road, the snow was drifting down lightly, melting on the windshield and dusting rocks and brown earth as it fell. Bernie turned on the wipers periodically to clear the moisture.

Jessica, so talkative on the way out, fell silent. Bernie appreciated the quiet. She realized she owed her husband an apology for dragging him out on a cold morning to dig in a trench when he should have been focusing on the gentleman he planned to talk to about the police fund donation. Oh, well. Time to return to Bluff, deposit Jessica, and meet Chee. If she planned it right, she'd have time to get the truck packed for their return trip before he arrived.

They reached the junction with the main road. The Valley of the Gods road was a long loop, and Bernie decided to go out the other way so she could see more of the pinnacles and stone figures.

A few miles along, she noticed a car parked on the shoulder, a new-looking smallish white sedan with Utah plates. A Lexus. She slowed down. "On a quiet winter day like this, I could enjoy being alone out here in Valley of the Gods. I hope the person who came in that car is savoring the peace here."

Jessica glanced at the vehicle. "I envy that driver."

"Do you want to stop for a moment?"

"No. I'm not talking about the peace you mentioned, I'm talking about the car. I used to be crazy jealous of people who own cars like that."

"Really? Why?"

"I'd see cars parked like that all the time when I was working out here as a student in the summers. I never got to take a vacation. Too many debts. I was barely squeaking by, always tired and sunburned. When Kyle and I married, I thought things would improve, but he never thought twice about how to pay the bills or improve our finances. He lived in the world of old bones and new ideas. It was all up to me to figure out how to earn enough not to worry. How to make what I needed to buy a car like that if I wanted. I guess growing up poor left a big hole."

Bernie listened. Making money had never been on her to-do list. She was glad her husband felt the same.

Jessica looked out the window. "Now, today would be a good day for a hike. It's cold, but the air smells good—rich, you know, with the promise of moisture in the snow. I could park here and enjoy nature's beauty if I didn't have to get back to the motel to meet Chris."

"Chris?"

"Oh, he's the business associate I mentioned.

He's doing me a favor by coming to help with Kyle, and I don't want to inconvenience him."

Jessica was right about the tantalizing smell of moisture in the dry desert air, but Bernie didn't see it as a good day for a hike. The people who'd left that car might need help if the storm arrived as predicted and caught them unaware.

They jolted over the ruts and skirted rocks and potholes until they reconnected to the pavement. The snow seemed to have lightened. Jessica was chattering about the time she and her husband had found a macaw skeleton near Comb Ridge, and how the paper she had written about the poor dead bird resulted in a bevy of speaking invitations. Bernie made the I'm-listening sounds she knew non-Natives appreciated.

Jessica finished her story, and Bernie spoke.

"Donray mentioned that your husband knew Chapman Dulles. My husband had an appointment with him today. That's one reason we came out here."

"Was it about a donation?"

"That's right."

Jessica shook her head. "That man works hard for his money and then gives it away."

"It sounds like you know him too."

"Yes. He and I got along better than he and Kyle did."

"I heard that they were both paleontologists?"

"That was part of the problem. They had worked together successfully on some projects to link Indigenous stories of monsters with the dinosaur tracks and bones discovered at Bears Ears.

Then Chap wanted to spend more time researching the development of teeth and jaws in mammal
ancestors. Kyle tried to persuade him that he was
wasting his time. Chap told Kyle that his work was
too commercial." Jessica said *commercial* as if it had
been a swear word. "As if there was something
wrong with selling fossils science doesn't need."

"Did they stay friends after that?"

Jessica shrugged off the question. "I couldn't
tell and I never asked."

When Bernie reached a place with better cell
service, she called Sheriff Gillman and left a
message with a brief description of the vehicle
she'd seen, including the license plate number
and its location.

"You're worried about that car, aren't you? I
think it's great that you're such a good citizen,
but I've seen lots of vehicles left out there." Jessica sighed. "I wish someone had paid that much
attention to poor Kyle last night. If only somebody had spotted him and stopped. If someone
had found him outside, freezing because of his
stroke or heart attack or whatever happened, today would be a lot different."

Bernie didn't respond.

Jessica sighed. "Can you go any faster? I need
to get back. Chris is driving to Santa Fe with me.
We have to load up the equipment and see if we
can retrieve anything that was left in the Land
Cruiser Kyle was driving. I'd like to have those
tools he had with him."

If Chee died unexpectedly, Bernie thought,
she probably wouldn't be thinking about tools, or
about anything except the shock and heartbreak.

When she looked at her phone again, she saw a text from Chee: Call me. He answered on the first ring.

"Hey, Lieutenant. Are you about ready to head back to Shiprock?"

"Uh . . . Not quite."

"Oh. What's going on?"

He answered her question with a question. "Where are you?"

"Driving back to the motel in Bluff with Jessica. She's meeting someone in a few minutes. You sound worried."

"Call me back after you drop her off, OK?"

"Sure thing."

She saw the question in her passenger's eyes and let it stay there.

By the time they arrived at the Bluff Inn, the asphalt was moist with melted snow, and some of the snowflakes had begun to stick to the trees and to frost the rocks. A red Jeep Grand Wagoneer with a New Mexico license plate and a University of New Mexico "Go Lobos" logo on the rear window was parked in front of Jessica's room. Emissions from the tailpipe made a white cloud that drifted over the mostly empty lot. The driver wore a cowboy hat that brushed the ceiling of the vehicle.

"Looks like Chris is here." Jessica sounded pleased. "He will be a big help." She pulled out her phone, tapped a short text, and put it back in her pocket. "Will you thank your husband again for his help last night? And thank you for finding a home for that food and for giving me a shoulder to cry on."

"You haven't done much crying."

Jessica looked surprised. "I guess I can't believe he's gone."

For easier loading, Bernie backed the truck into the parking spot in front of the room she and Chee shared. They climbed out, and Jessica waved to acknowledge the man in the cowboy hat waiting in the Jeep. She hurried down the sidewalk to unlock the door to her room and disappeared inside.

Bernie went inside, too, and turned up the heater. Before she began packing, she called Chee.

He answered after a few rings. "You alone?"

"Yes. I've been thinking about you ever since you called. What's going on?"

"A murder, to start with. I didn't want to talk about it where Jessica could have overheard. You know how quickly bad news spreads."

Especially in small towns where such news is rare, Bernie thought. "What happened?"

"There was a break-in at the home of Dr. Dulles, the donor I was supposed to meet with. His security guy and I found a dead man in the driveway but couldn't confirm that anything was missing. The medical examiner just got here, and we're waiting for the detective. And hoping Dr. Dulles shows up, but he hasn't returned phone calls or messages."

"The security guy is named what?"

"Black. Roper Black. Smart, confident, not too much ego. He says he wants to join us at the Shiprock station."

Bernie sucked in a breath. "Tall, thin Navajo guy in his thirties?"

"Yeah. He told me you delivered his daughter."

She collected her thoughts, remembering his

concern for his wife and his appreciation for her help. "Odd, isn't it?"

"It is. I'm staying until the detective arrives. I'm hoping Dr. Dulles will come home too, and I can at least set up a new appointment with him."

"That makes sense, I guess, but why not just drop him an email or a text to reschedule and get on back to the motel so we can beat the storm?"

"Well, sweetheart, the whole scene looked strange to me, as though it was an inside job orchestrated by someone who knew the layout and knew exactly what they wanted. I don't like it. It's not right."

"But think of this: it's not your case." She took a breath, remembering something from the night before. "Black was talking about his boss, and he made a joke that he'd have to kill him or find a new job, or both."

"Today he's regretting that he wasn't here to prevent this. At least, that's what he's saying. Did he mention what the problem was?"

"I don't remember. We were busy with the baby."

"Oh, of course."

"So you want to stay here until you figure this out? Even though there's a big storm on the way." She knew she sounded grumpy. She was.

"Honey, I know you dread disappointing your mother and your sister. If you need to leave, go. Take the truck. I'll figure it out."

"I'll think about that." Bernie really didn't want to leave Utah without Chee. She had been on this road before, down to the junction where Chee's sense of duty overrode any other commitments, including a promise that they'd join Mama and Darleen for dinner. The desire for justice pulsed deep in his heart. Not only justice, but hózhó, the sense that all was in balance. It was a quality she deeply admired and also something that irritated her when it meant a change in plans. When it meant she and her wishes came in second place.

Although she hated to admit it, she knew that they were alike in this way. She had tested his patience with cases she couldn't let go. She tried to take off her injured-wife hat and think like an investigator. "While we're talking about the dead, anything else on Jessica's husband?"

"It's not official, but he died from a bullet wound. The deputy didn't notice it because Kyle's layers of heavy clothes contained the blood. From the initial investigation, it looks like the gunshot killed him, not the cold."

"Jessica told me she was waiting for a call from the medical examiner's office. She mentioned that she'd warned her husband not to go outside in the winter without the right clothes. She assumed that he'd frozen to death because of how the body was found."

"Well, she was wrong about that."

"Interesting."

"That's what I think. Gillman and his team haven't found the weapon yet. It wasn't at the scene."

"Poor Jessica. I don't think she suspected murder." Bernie knew the medical examiner or someone on that staff would give Jessica the news as objectively as possible and then, if they operated with the same compassion as the office in her home state of New Mexico, refer her to a support group for families dealing with violent death.

"Where were you when I called?"

"Jessica went with me to Valley of the Gods." Bernie mentioned the Zonnie party. "On the way, a man showed up in a truck that looked a lot like the one that tried to kill me. Jessica knew him and said she'd fired him. He'd worked for her and her husband before taking a job with Dr. Dulles, your missing paleontologist."

"Interesting connection. Anything else?"

"Nothing important. I saw a car parked along the road. I left a message about it at the sheriff's office. Jessica said that happens all the time, but it bothered me because of the weather. Not the best day for a hike."

Chee laughed. "No kidding."

"How's Roper Black doing?"

"He's never been at a murder scene, so he's shaken up. But he'll be OK. Hey, another car just drove up. It might be the detective. Gotta go."

"Are you working the case?"

"Maybe. Gillman invited me to consult, and I've been asking some questions. Call you in a few?"

"If you want. Better yet, finish up and head back here so we can leave for Mama's house."

After Chee hung up, Bernie thought of the mother and the new baby. She wondered how enmeshed Black would be in the case with those two on his mind. If he was a normal person, he'd get home to them as soon as he could. But her own husband had nothing that compelling to distract him, and he loved making things right, solving mysteries such as the identity of a dead man and the reason for his murder.

Her phone buzzed. It was Darleen, as if her sister had been reading her mind.

"Hey, Sister. Hi there. Where are you?"

"Shash Jáá."

"Are you and Cheeseburger leaving soon?"

"I hope so."

"Me too. I could really use you. Mama's having a bad day. She's restless and whining at me."

"Why?" Bernie was used to Mama's swings in mood, but they always worried her.

"I don't know."

"I'm sorry you have to deal with that. What if I talked to her?"

"You used to always call her, remember?"

She heard the criticism and switched from asking to being in charge. "Tell Mama I'm on the phone and that I need to talk to her."

"Sure thing."

While she waited, she braced herself for a rocky conversation. It took Mama a few moments to come on the line.

"Daughter, why aren't you here?" She spoke in Navajo, the language of their hearts.

"Hello, Mama. I'm up at Shash Jáá."

"Shash Jáá? That's a long way from home. I remember that place. I've been there, but it was many years ago."

Bernie waited for the story to unfold.

"I remember seeing those rocks that look like a big hat. Have you seen that?"

"You mean Mexican Hat?"

"No, it's called Ch`ah Lizhin."

Bernie knew they were talking about the same dramatic rock formation.

Mama kept talking now. "I remember that ridge of stones. Tséyík'áán. It was beautiful."

Bernie silently translated it to Big Snake, the Comb Ridge monocline.

"Daughter, that is a place of power. Have you seen it?"

"Yes. Tséyík'áán is near where I was today. That and another beautiful spot, Valley of the Gods in Shash Jáá."

"That's good." Mama sighed. "I worry about you, my daughter."

They had been down this road before, more often lately. Bernie wrinkled her nose but stayed quiet.

"I don't know why you are mad at me."

"I'm not mad at you, Mama. I'm not mad at my sister either."

"Then stop your police work and come to help me for once."

Bernie drew in a breath. "Help you how, Mama?"

"You should know."

Bernie let the silence rest between them. If anything, she could use her mother's help. The reassurance Mama used to often give her when she'd complain about her job, about Darleen, about the boyfriends she had before she met Chee—all of that had raised her spirits. Now she wondered how she could help her mother return to hózhó and again walk in beauty.

She heard Darleen in the background, asking for the phone. Then her sister was on the line.

"Cheeseburger said you'd be coming for dinner tonight, so I got the groceries. Will you let me know when you guys are ready to leave so I can start cooking?"

"I don't know for sure that we can make it to-day." She wondered why her husband hadn't mentioned the conversation. Or, if he had, why she didn't recall it. "I'd like to get out of here soon. But Chee's involved with some police work."

"I thought you two went up there to get away from that."

"Well, I did. He was supposed to represent the department at an event, and he agreed to talk to some rich Utah guy about a contribution to the Fallen Officers Memorial Fund. Then things got complicated."

"Complicated? That's your middle name. Both of you, actually." Darleen laughed. "Things are complicated here too. Slim is taking his kids to the Natural History Museum in Albuquerque over winter break next week. He wants me to go along to help him. I told him I'd have to see if you could stay overnight with Mama."

"Your boyfriend has kids?"

"No. Well, yeah. I mean his students." Darleen gave her more details.

"I'll see what I can do." If she resigned from the Navajo Police, she'd have plenty of time to figure out what came next. Plenty of time to offer Mama a hand with whatever it was her mother thought she'd been neglecting. Plenty of time to let Darleen take a break from caregiving.

But police work had been central to her life and, next to Chee and her family, her main love.

What would come next? Could she leave her pride behind and go back to her old job? What effect would Chee's promotion have on all this?

Bernie was ready to hang up, but Darleen changed the subject. "I need to talk to you about something else. Something that bothers me. I'm not handling it well at all."

Why was it, Bernie wondered, that her sister always wanted to have deep conversations when she itched to get off the phone? "What is it?"

"It's about Mama."

Of course it was. Bernie tensed.

"Now she's having trouble sleeping. She wakes up around two a.m., and she thinks it's morning. She wakes me up and wants me to fix breakfast. I show her on the clock that it's too early, but, well, you know how she can be."

"So you've been getting up at two a.m. too?"

"Yeah. Believe me, this is getting old quick."

"I bet it is. What have you tried to get her to sleep longer?"

"First, I tried ignoring her, but that doesn't work. And anyway, I'm afraid she might hurt herself or wander off."

Bernie listened.

"I've tried giving her some relaxing herbal tea before bed, but then she has to go to the bathroom. I've been taking her out during the day for more walking, thinking that might make her tired, but she gets mad and won't go. Slim said I should try to keep her from taking that afternoon nap she loves. When I do, she gets *really* grumpy, and then she falls asleep in front of the television.

No matter what, at two a.m. she pops up like a prairie dog."

"Did you ask her why she wakes up?"

"No." A few beats went by. "I'll try that. Maybe she's hungry. Maybe if I give her a snack before bed she'll sleep longer. Do you have any other ideas? I'm getting desperate."

And exhausted, too, Bernie thought. "Sorry, I'm not thinking of anything else right now. We can brainstorm when we're together."

"Tonight. Your husband can help too. He's a good problem solver." Bernie heard relief in her sister's voice. "I hope we'll come up with something. See you then."

Darleen hung up, and Bernie stared at the phone. She knew that she hadn't been much help and, worse, that dinner together might not be on that night's menu.

In good weather, it took less than an hour to drive from Shiprock to Mama's house in Toadlena, but it seemed as though these women she dearly loved were a lifetime away. Now she was a little more than a hundred miles, or about two hours, from Mama and Darleen, assuming the predicted storm held off or amounted to nothing.

Chee could deal with whatever he had to, she decided. She'd go to have dinner, chat with Darleen about Mama's insomnia and her new boyfriend and the Albuquerque trip. Chee could stay in Bluff if he had to, and she'd collect him in the morning. When she and Chee had checked in at the Bluff Inn, the kind man who ran the motel had offered them another night in the room at half price if the weather got too sketchy. This time of year, Bernie knew, the motel didn't have many customers. Her husband could manage without her.

She stepped outside the motel room to check the sky and clear her head. The snow had stopped. She filled her lungs with the crisp air, thinking about when to tell Chee her plan, hearing his plea to wait until he could come with her—even though he himself had suggested she go alone. Was her own restless need to be in the company of family she loved a valid counter argument? Bernie pulled her red hat down over her ears, snuggled into the old coat of Chee's she had found in their truck, and tried to think of something more cheerful.

She saw Becenti's truck heading toward the motel again. Based on what Chee had said, she assumed that Sheriff Gillman had persuaded the ranger to tell Jessica about her husband's bullet wound, to explain that a death not from "natural causes" had a more complicated legal trajectory. In other words, a murder investigation.

The ranger greeted her. "I'm surprised you guys are still here."

"Just me again. My husband's out. The home of a man he needed to talk to is now a crime scene, and he offered to help."

"Oh, you mean the shooting at Chap's house. You and Chee show up, and the place goes crazy. A veritable crime wave." He grinned.

"Tell me what happened."

"All I know is what I heard through the blue grapevine. The victim might have worked for Chap. No weapon on-site. And Chap is missing."

Becenti looked at the door to Jessica's room.

"I have to talk to the lady again. Do you know if she's here?"

"Yes. We got back a few minutes ago from taking the food to your relatives."

"Thanks."

"Are you here with more bad news for her?"

Becenti nodded. "Her husband didn't pass away from exposure or natural causes."

"Chee told me about the way the man died. Come back, and let me know how it went, OK?"

"I will. I hate giving people that kind of news. It's hard enough to have to announce a death and then to go back and say it was murder . . ."

"I agree." Bernie frowned. "That's a tough job."

"I better get going. It never gets easier. I'll knock on your door when I'm finished, OK?"

"Sure."

Bernie had just gotten into the book she was reading when she heard Becenti's knock and rose to let him in.

"How did she take the news?"

"It was weird at first." Becenti shook his head. "She looked at me as though we'd never met. Like I was a total stranger, even though I'd talked to her earlier. So I introduced myself again, told her my name, and she said, 'Oh right. You had on a different jacket.'"

"Have a seat." Bernie motioned to the chair at the desk. "And then?"

"She handled it well. You know, I think she felt relieved that her late husband wasn't such an idiot that he'd get stranded outside his car and die from hypothermia. She asked the right questions."

Becenti took a breath. "I've seen people fall apart at the news of a murder. Her friend Chris helped too. I reassured her that we'd get to the bottom of this."

"I think a situation like that is easier if the person you have to give that news to already knows that the loved one is dead. That way it's just one shock, not two."

"Right. I still hate doing it."

"Me too." If she changed careers, she'd be spared that job.

"Chatterbox said to tell you she was sorry to miss you when you dropped off the food, but that it will be perfect for the birthday party, and enough to give the guests some to take home."

"I'm glad it's going to a good cause. I'll let Jessica know about that if I see her." Bernie wasn't planning on running into her motel neighbor again.

"Speaking of Jessica, she had photos on the table in there of a handsome Navajo. Since it wasn't me, I figured it was your husband."

Bernie's eyes opened wide. "Photos? What photos? Are you serious?"

"I thought it was odd, too." Becenti rubbed his chin. "Did Chee mention anything about Jessica wanting a picture of him?"

"Not a word." She felt a cold wave of worry roll up her spine. "This is seriously creepy."

"I asked Jessica what was up with the photographs, and she made a joke about how it was someone she met last night, and she didn't want to forget him, so she had those printed up from her phone."

Bernie shuddered. "I don't know what's going on here. That's weird, and it makes me angry."

"Weird and disturbing. That's what I thought. I told Jessica no one in law enforcement appreciated someone taking their picture without permission. She laughed it off."

"She laughed at you? I'm going next door to ask her about it."

"I'll go with you. Let's talk to Jessica together."

"No, I'll handle it. You need to get to work so you can help with that party later."

# 12

Jessica took a step away from Bernie and stood at the motel doorway.

"Pictures of your husband?" She rubbed her temples. Bernie knew a lie was coming. "I don't have a clue as to what you're talking about."

"I'm talking about photos of Lieutenant Jim Chee. Ranger Ajax Becenti saw them on the table in this room a few minutes ago."

"Photos?"

Bernie spoke more loudly. "Photographs. Pictures. What's going on?"

"Oh, that. There's no reason for you to be so upset. Let's talk." Jessica turned and patted a clear spot on the bed behind her. "Sit a minute, and I'll explain. It's kind of embarrassing."

Bernie didn't move. "Go ahead. Start talking."

"At least come inside. You're letting winter in."

Bernie moved into the room, stood three steps away from the door, and closed it. "Jessica, show me the photos. Now."

"Sure. It's really not a big deal. I don't know

why you're so upset. Your husband was the perfect gentleman. He even stayed outside the room rather than coming in here with me."

The idea that Chee would have done something inappropriate with Jessica had not occurred to Bernie. She knew her husband, and the idea that he'd been anything less than the perfect gentleman further stoked her anger.

"Ma'am, I guess you haven't followed the news. Don't you realize that those of us in law enforcement, a dangerous job to begin with, are even more at risk if some kook has a grudge against us and our pictures at his fingertips? What were you thinking, or were you thinking at all?"

"Calm down."

Being told to calm down made Bernie angrier. "I need those pictures. Now."

"I'll get them." Jessica raised her voice. "Hey, Chris?"

"Yeah, babe? What do you need?" The male voice came from the other room.

"Come in here. And bring the photos."

"Sure. Give me a second."

Jessica sat on the bed. "I need to explain something. I've got a condition known as prosopagnosia. It means I can't remember faces. I see a person I've known for years, and unless he says something, or has an unusual walk or always wears the same cologne or gives me other nonvisual clues, I won't recognize him."

"I've never heard of it."

"Few people have. Prosopagnosia is also called face blindness. Most people who have it are born with it, like I was. The even more unlucky ones get this way from a brain injury or maybe encephalitis. It's harder on them, you know?"

"No, I don't know. I think you're making all this up because I caught you doing something you know you shouldn't have done."

"Just listen. I've had this condition my whole life. Until I went to school, I thought I was normal. Then I realized I had to struggle to act normal, to try to work around the disability. People who acquire it later in life have issues with depression because they remember how they used to recognize people, how they could watch a drama on TV without getting confused like I always do. Before face blindness, they could tell the actors apart, and now they can't."

Bernie glared. "You waved at your friend Chris. Do you have pictures of us hidden away?"

"I know Chris's car."

"I want to see those pictures of Chee."

"Of course. Chris is bringing them. I use photos as a tool to help remember a person I think I might be encountering again. I try to memorize some aspect of the face that goes with the name. When I met Lieutenant Chee last night, you know, before I found out about Kyle, I figured I'd be seeing him again. I didn't want to embarrass myself with a policeman. That's why I took the pictures. It's just a little something I do to seem normal. I guess you could consider it my medicine, a partial antidote to the ailment."

"You photographed him without explaining any of this or asking permission, right?"

Jessica shrugged. "Yeah. It's easier, and permission doesn't really matter because I'm not making the pictures public."

"It matters to me, and I know it would upset my husband." As she said it, Bernie realized that this condition could explain why Jessica hadn't recognized Ranger Becenti or Pam Zonnie.

The man in the cowboy hat emerged from the bathroom. He was in his forties, solidly built, and handsome for a white man, although Bernie noticed that his belly extended over the belt buckle and around the waist of his jeans.

"Hey there. I want to introduce you to someone. This is Officer Bernie Manuelito, Navajo Police."

"Christopher McDouglas. Pleased to meet you. Call me Chris."

Jessica cleared her throat. "The officer is wondering about those pictures of that Navajo man you printed for me. He's her husband. The officer with the BLM noticed them earlier when they were on the table."

"I want to see them now." Bernie unzipped the coat she'd borrowed from the truck. The heat in the room was catching up with her. "And I'm wondering what you have to do with any of this, Chris."

He looked puzzled for a split second, then opened a computer bag that sat on the floor and pulled out three sheets of printer paper. He handed them to her.

The pictures were candid shots of Chee in the civilian clothes he'd been wearing the night before, standing in the doorway to Jessica's room.

She could see the woman's blue van behind him in the dim light of the motel parking lot.

Chris spoke while she studied the images. "Jessica doesn't have a printer here, so she sent the photos to me so I could print them for her in Santa Fe before I drove out this morning. Taking pictures helps her with her work for Dinostar, you know, an aid to identifying her coworkers and staff and keeping everyone involved in the business— or not involved in the business—straight."

Bernie took a moment to absorb it. Then she tore the pages into shreds and dumped them in a nearby wastebasket.

"Jessica, call up every picture you have on that phone of my husband and show me."

"What? What's on my phone is none of your business. Why don't you settle down?"

Chris put a hand on her shoulder. "Let her see the pictures of her husband. That's all she's asking."

Bernie watched as Jessica scrolled and then called up a screen with about a dozen pictures of Chee.

"Is that all?"

"Absolutely."

"Now delete each one while I watch. I'll tell Chee if he ever runs into you again to introduce himself."

Jessica seemed to think about it for a split second and then made the pictures disappear. "No hard feelings, OK? I didn't mean any harm."

"OK." Bernie gave her a subtle nod. "What is Dinostar?"

Chris answered the question. "Dinostar is our company. We have a permit from the BLM to search for particular fossils here, and a contract with the University of Utah for the research."

"Dinostar?" Bernie said the name again. "So you're looking for dinosaurs?"

"No. Not at all, but that's a common misperception. I bet you don't know much about the paleontology here in the Bears Ears, do you?"

Bernie bristled at the white male's assumption that a Navajo woman would be uninformed. "You'd lose that bet. This area is extremely rich in fossils, and that's partly why Bears Ears became a national monument. Some of the material here dates back to around three hundred million years ago, when this part of southeastern Utah was a coastal desert. Scientists have found animal fossils here that can be tied to the opening chapters of the age of dinosaurs, as well as to the period just before the mass extinction. I could go on about *Dineobellator* or *Dilophosaurus* . . ." She paused, and gave Chris the stern look a teacher might flash at a misbehaving junior high student. "I know something about the paleontology here, but I never heard of Dinostar. So tell me, why might the company think that Jim Chee posed such a threat that Jessica should take his photo without permission?"

"Happy to." He smiled, as if her depth of knowledge was no surprise. "Let me back up a little. Few people have heard of Dinostar because we keep a low profile. But we are one of the largest operations of our kind anywhere in the United States. We find and sell things like this."

Chris reached into the pocket of his plaid shirt and pulled out what looked like a small stone.

"Here." He extended the object to her.

He'd given her a rock. No, she realized on second glance. It was a fossilized shell.

"I call her Amanda, my favorite ammonite from Nevada. Dinostar doesn't deal with bones, just the stuff like this that's pretty and easy to ship. There are trillions of commercial fossils like Amanda out here in the West."

"Commercial fossils? What does that mean?"

"Things we can sell to collectors, interior designers, classroom teachers, whoever. Things that scientists like Kyle, bless his soul, and me are tired of looking at already. Dinostar has contracts with ranchers and other private landowners in places where a variety of prehistoric animals have been discovered. We find fossils like Amanda, beautiful common fossils sold with no loss to the scientific record. If we come across an unusual specimen, something Kyle and I think may offer science a new look at the past, or a fossil we have questions about, we bring in our consulting paleontologist, Dr. Chapman Dulles, and follow his advice to determine if what we've uncovered is important or not. We always come down on the side of caution. Everything strictly aboveboard."

Jessica interrupted. "Chris forgot to mention that this is our first venture in Bears Ears."

"I didn't forget, babe. What Kyle and I were doing here isn't part of the normal Dinostar operations. This is pure science." He said it again for emphasis. "The research Dinostar is doing out here is important and potentially controversial. We need to keep it secret. We're not keen on trespassers."

Bernie handed the fossil back to him. "Trespassers? Bears Ears is a national monument. Public land."

Chris seemed flustered, but Jessica intervened. "We just don't want anyone to get hurt, that's all. And sometimes people aren't who they say they are. Keeping track of everyone, not just by name but by sight, is a huge challenge for me."

Chris nodded, encouraging her to continue.

"You know, Bernie, you and Chee aren't in uniform, but I never asked either of you for ID because I sensed that you were who you said you were. But just as my partner here explained, we have to be wary of intruders until we have made enough progress that we can announce our scientific findings."

"That's right." Chris's face relaxed. "Because Bears Ears is a national monument, we're not allowed to do any kind of commercial work. So Kyle and I returned to our first love, pure science. We were looking for tooth structures that help explain how some animals became omnivores, you know, developed so they could eat a variety of food, and—"

"I know what an omnivore is." Bernie interrupted, even though she knew it was rude. She resented this man's attitude. "Where are you doing the excavation?"

"We're not at liberty to disclose that." Chris smiled again.

"But it's the site I saw in Valley of the Gods, right?"

He ignored her question. "The research Kyle and I were doing was on the cusp of paleontological investigation. Dinosaur teeth are a big commercial seller. Some folks might irrationally fear that what we are finding would jeopardize their livelihoods."

After a moment of silence, Bernie dug deeper.

"Jessica, you acted like you had barely heard of Chapman Dulles, but now I learn that he's on your team. Why the lie?"

"He's not on the team anymore." She looked at the floor when she spoke. "We never used him much, even though he was a professional associate of Kyle. He's an odd duck. And he resigned as a consultant to Dinostar. Left us in the lurch."

"Why are you even involved in this? You told me you were an archaeologist."

"I am an archaeologist." Jessica's voice had an edge to it. "I'm on the team because, unlike the other team members, I'm good at numbers and enjoy the financial side of things."

Chris resumed his role as spokesman. "Dr. Dulles is a bit unusual, but a lot of paleontologists are. He seemed solid enough until a year or so ago. Then he started canceling his work for us because of his own related project in or near the same area where we were working. He officially left Dinostar a month or so ago."

Bernie took a moment to consider what she'd learned. "So why were there potsherds at that site Chee and I saw? And why didn't you tell me what was happening out there?"

Jessica said, "Indigenous folks who live out here don't like to be in close contact with ruins because there could be graves there, out of respect for these ancestors. I had access to a trove of potsherds that had been illegally collected in this area by visitors and even sometimes by scientists. A lot of people believe that bad karma goes with removing them from their burial sites, so the finders returned them to a museum I'm associated with, and I received the go-ahead from the Bears Ears Inter-Tribal Coalition to bring them home to Bears Ears. As for the rest of your question, it really was none of your business."

Bernie turned to Chris. "Were you and Jessica's husband working in competition with Chap's research?"

"No. Chap's project has morphed into something different. He moved on. And speaking of moving on, Jessica and I need to get going."

"Oh, back to Santa Fe?"

"Yes, of course." Jessica sighed. "We need to make arrangements for when Kyle's body will be released."

"Before you go, did you take pictures of Becenti and of me? We're law enforcement too."

Jessica sighed. "Becenti is easy for me to remember because of the BLM uniform. And you are wearing that red hat you wore in the truck and a leather cord, a necklace or something. Those make it easier for me to place you both."

She knew Jessica was referring to her jish, the medicine pouch she wore for protection. She accepted the explanation, at least for the time being.

"Tell me about the guy in the truck who works for you. When we ran into him he said that he and his friend used to work for Chap, and now they work for a company."

"She means Donray and Dev." Jessica looked at Chris and then continued. "When Chap quit, Dinostar kept them on for security at the site and to haul away the debris, other odd jobs. They don't work for me." Jessica underlined the statement with her tone of voice. "I'm at my own site at Comb Ridge."

"Why didn't you tell me this earlier? Donray is a thug. I nearly got shot and run over when I was hiking out there."

"Are you sure it was on purpose?"

"Yes. Your research put me in danger."

Chris frowned. "What happened to you?"

Bernie gave him a shortened version of the incident. Just thinking about it made her furious.

She noticed Chris's growing restlessness as she spoke. Finally, he interrupted her.

"Chap hired those idiot losers, and when he left, Kyle and I kept them on." He sounded flustered and less arrogant now. "I'm so sorry. I—I don't know what else to say except I'm going to fire them. I apologize for what happened out there. Inexcusable."

Bernie's phone buzzed, and she saw that the number was the San Juan County Sheriff's Office. "I've got to take this. We're done here."

Bernie answered the call as she walked back to her motel room.

"Manuelito, this is Sheriff Gillman. Got a minute?"

"Sure."

"Tell me about that vehicle you saw on the Valley of the Gods road."

"It was a Lexus sedan. It looked new, in great shape but maybe a bit short of clearance for that dirt road. It was white, coated with red road dust."

"You checked in the glove box, right?"

"No, sir. I drove past it. I had Jessica Johnson with me—the woman you spoke to at the motel about her husband, whose body was found last night. She knows the area. She told me hikers frequently leave their vehicles out there. It didn't look especially suspicious, but I figured I would alert you."

Bernie heard a gentle rumble that she assumed was Chris's red Jeep leaving the parking lot.

Gillman spoke quickly. "Could you swing out there now and take another look?"

She hesitated.

He read the pause correctly. "The situation here is that I'm shorthanded, and if the storm comes, I might need the deputies to work a bunch of overtime hours. I can't reach the BLM, Becenti, or Kingsley. And since you already know where the car is, well, what do you say?"

"I was planning on heading back to New Mexico."

"I guess you heard that a man, a well-known resident, is missing."

"Chee told me about Chap."

"Well, his security guy mentioned that Chap's fancy SUV was out of commission, so he was driving a loaner. It makes me wonder if that expensive vehicle is just a random tourist's, or if Chap drove it out there. We need to talk to him about the shooting and the home invasion and, well, make sure he's safe."

"I've been wondering about that car you mentioned out there, too. Something's off. Let's make a deal."

"What?"

"If I do this, will you ask my husband to explain whatever he can about that crime quickly and then get back to the motel? Chee has a hard time leaving a case before he knows all the details, but I'd like to get home tonight."

"You've got it, Officer. I'll let him know he can keep giving us his bright ideas over the phone. I appreciate your help. Let me know what turns up. Cell service can be spotty, but you might be able to text. Or call when you get some bars. If my number doesn't work, use this." He gave her another phone number. "When can you go?"

"I'm leaving now."

"Thanks." She heard the relief in Gillman's voice. "And be careful out there."

# 13

The car that was headed up the steep driveway to Chap's house came to a stop. The driver, a gray-haired woman in black pants and a puffy blue coat, climbed out and headed toward them.

"Hey, Gill. How's it going?"

"I've had better days. How are you?"

"OK. Waiting for the big snow."

The woman gave Chee and Black a quick, hard look, then turned back to the sheriff. "Who are these guys?"

Chee introduced himself. "I had an appointment with Dr. Dulles. I'm here at the request of his security director, Roper Black." He motioned toward Black with a jut of his chin.

"Mela Carson, Utah Office of the Medical Examiner. Lieutenant, I'm sure you know about crime scene protocol." She said it as a statement and looked at Black. "Just do what he does, and follow the sheriff's direction, and you'll be hunky-dory. All right, then." She began striding up to the body, and the sheriff followed. Chee and Black stayed behind, close enough to be of help if needed but keeping their distance from the dead man.

Carson stopped a few feet away from the victim's shoes and stared at the way the blast had blown the heavy front door off its hinges and turned what probably had been handcrafted vertical stained-glass windows into sparkling rubble. She squatted to look at the victim, belly-down on the concrete driveway. "It's not Chap, is it?"

"No." Gillman looked away. "I'm glad I met him so I can say that for certain."

"Thank goodness." She cleared her throat. "I mean . . ."

"I know." Gillman put his hand gently on her arm. "It's OK. People out here speak well of Chap."

She studied the dead man a moment longer, then rose to standing. "Do we know who the victim is?"

Chee would have expected the same question. It was a small town with a lot of longtime families. People knew people. People had friends, and people held grudges.

"No. I can't recall having seen him. Black didn't recognize him either."

She stared at Black, and he nodded in agreement. "I don't think I've ever met him."

She turned again to Gillman. "Have you told Chap about what happened here?"

"Black and I both have calls in to him. No response yet."

"Where is he?"

Gillman shrugged. "Good question."

"Before I do the prelim, what do you know that I should be aware of?"

The sheriff shifted his weight from foot to foot. "He was shot from behind. I felt for a pulse, checked for breathing when I got here. He was seriously dead. I searched his pockets. No ID. No pills or needles. I found a pack of cigarettes. No smell of beer."

"OK. After my field exam I'll arrange for transport for the autopsy."

"The detective in charge says he's on the way."

As if on cue, they heard a vehicle approaching. Black stopped pacing. "Maybe that's Chap," he said. "I hope it's him."

"That's got to be Parker." Gillman grinned. "He only rides his motorcycle when his wife is out of town."

Detective Nathan Parker roared up the long, steep driveway on his BMW RT and parked behind the sheriff's unit. He removed his helmet, and Chee noticed his gray crew cut. Parker, a big, muscular man, moved like a guy who stayed in shape.

"Well, hello there, Detective. Glad you could finally join us." Gillman spoke louder than necessary. "You know Medical Examiner Carson?"

Parker ignored the jibe. "Mela and I have met."

"And this is Roper Black, Chap's head of security, and his buddy and adviser, Chee."

Chee jumped in. "Lieutenant Jim Chee with the Navajo Police, Shiprock. I've worked some murders, so Gillman asked me to be a consultant."

"No kidding?" Parker chuckled. "I guess a dead guy on the property means there might be a little problem with security." He turned to Black. "I heard you quit."

"I did. But I'm on the payroll until the end of

the month. So yeah, this was on my watch. Let's figure it out."

Parker looked toward the body. "Who is the dead guy? Chap, right?"

Gillman handled the question. "Not Chap. I don't recognize him, and he's not carrying ID."

"Maybe he was one of those temp workers," Black said, "or an intern Chap decided to mentor. He's wearing our sweatshirt."

"Where is Chap?"

"I haven't been able to reach him."

"He's in the wind, I figure, if he shot this dude." The sheriff exhaled. "I looked around inside. No more bodies."

Carson straightened up, stretching her back. "Gentlemen, so you know, the crew to remove the body is on the way. They don't like waiting any more than I do. I realize you need to get everything photographed and all the evidence collected. So, Detective, stop gabbing and get cookin'."

"Of course." Parker gave her half a smile. "Sorry to have inconvenienced you."

"I'll be in my car doing some paperwork, finishing my coffee." She walked away, stiff with irritation. "Come get me soon."

Gillman reached in his pocket for his car keys. "Detective, don't let these two screw things up. And, by the way, they were together at the Bluff Diner when the alarm went off. They were here when I got here, but they aren't suspects. Make sure the technicians get fingerprints, blood splatters, all that."

"Sure thing, boss," Parker said. "At your service."

Chee heard the sarcasm and noticed that Gillman didn't react.

"Let Chee help, and put Black to work," the sheriff said, and turned to Black. "When and if Chap calls you, I need to talk to him pronto. Understand?"

"Yes, sir."

"Do you know the interior of the house?"

"I do." Black thought for a moment. "I was inside day before yesterday helping Chap figure out how to hook up some speakers to his TV."

"OK, then. If Parker asks, go in and do what he says. He's in charge. Remember that."

They watched Gillman walk to his car. Parker gave his back a salute. "Gill does a good imitation of a jerk, doesn't he?"

"I've seen worse," Chee said.

"Jim Chee, huh? I've heard of you. My wife's brother-in-law works for the Navajo PD in Tuba City." Parker mentioned the name.

"I know him. A good man."

"They say the same about you."

Parker walked toward the house, studying the environment as closely as if he were an alien freshly plopped down on Planet Earth. He took photos of the deceased from many angles, then the porch and the damaged door and the stained-glass inserts. He made notes.

"Hey, you two. Help me look for the shell casings."

They searched without finding anything, then Parker walked to Carson's car. He knocked on the window and gave her a thumbs-up. The body was all hers.

Parker turned back. "So, Chee, why are you here? Not that I can't use your assistance, but I wasn't expecting company."

"I had a meeting with Chap scheduled for this afternoon to talk about a donation to the Navajo PD. Black came to drive up here with me, and he got the call about the incident. I've covered too many homicides. I'm glad to help if I can."

Parker nodded. "Roper, who would want to break in here and why?"

Black repeated what he'd told the sheriff.

"Anything else I should know about the situation?"

"Someone busted the security camera, but the backup in Chap's office could have something."

"I'll be sure they dust it for fingerprints."

Chee said, "I checked the exterior. No signs of other intrusions. No tire tracks or footprints, but the garage doors are open. There's an old sedan parked on the other side of the house along an access road."

"Thanks. We'll deal with the car after we check the house." Parker pulled out three pairs of gloves. "I want you both to come inside with me."

He gave them gloves and put on his own. "Roper, don't touch anything. Don't move anything. Don't lean on anything. Don't straighten anything that's crooked. And don't be shy in there. Tell me if you see something that doesn't seem right. It's better to be wrong about it than to overlook something important."

"What do you mean, doesn't seem right?"

"Furniture that someone moved. Something that used to be there that's missing. Got it, buddy?"

"Yeah."

Parker looked at the damaged front door. "Do you both have a weapon?"

Black opened his jacket to show Parker his holstered gun.

"I do," Chee said. "But whoever was here is long gone."

Parker nodded. "That's my guess too, but I have guessed wrong once or twice."

They followed Parker through the wide entrance hall, which opened into a great room with a million-dollar view of the mountains and the heavy clouds of the approaching storm. The house, Chee noticed, had been built with care inside as well as out. The abundant windows captured the Utah light and the panorama of snow-dusted peaks. Other than the damage to the entry and some unusual yellow dirt on the hallway floor, both of which Parker paused to photograph, the home's interior seemed undisturbed. Odd, Chee thought, after the violence done to the front door. Were the intruders sloppy breaking in, or did they make a statement with the destruction?

They continued down a hallway illuminated by skylights, past a bathroom and bedroom.

Black said, "All this looks normal."

"I wonder if the man at the door terrified Chap, so he killed him."

"No." Black's tone was adamant.

"Listen to the theory," Chee said. "After that,

Chap disabled the camera to hide the evidence and then left because he was scared of getting caught or getting shot by the man's partners."

"That's crazy." Black sounded offended by the scenario.

"Maybe. We don't know what happened yet."

"You got that right."

They followed Parker through the house.

He paused beside a door, open to a large room. Unlike the rest of the house, the space looked messy. "What did Chap use this area for?"

"It's his office and workshop. The inner sanctum." Black stepped up for a closer look at the doorframe. "Someone kicked this in. Chap never closed the door, at least that I saw, because he liked the light from the rest of the house to brighten it. But today he, or somebody, not only closed it but locked it. I didn't even know it locked."

The room had a big table in the center with a rolling stool next to it. A large microscope occupied one corner. There seemed to be rocks everywhere, along with white powder and lots of rock dust. Chee saw a large gun safe that appeared undisturbed. Books, models of dinosaurs, stuffed birds, preserved lizards, plastic buckets, photographs, pages ripped from magazines, brushes, a few empty beer bottles, and other clutter filled the space. The floor was littered with papers and tools that seemed to have been tossed from the worktable. The disorder here provided an interesting contrast to the neatness of the rest of the house.

Chee and Parker looked at each other, a shared acknowledgment that something suspicious had gone down in that room.

"Black, what's out of sync here?"

The younger man studied the space. "I think whoever broke in went through Chap's things here, and they weren't very careful about it."

"Or Chap staged this himself, quickly, after he killed the guy who tried to break in." Chee sighed. "I know you don't like the idea, Black, but you have to stay open to possibilities."

"What does Chap do in this office?" Parker wrinkled his brow.

"This is where he worked with fossils, made the casts and replicas, took photos of the specimens, and created his reports."

Chee noticed that Black had switched to speaking of Chapman Dulles using the past tense.

"See these?" Black moved his hand over a pile of small rocks. "Chap explained to me that they are actually fossilized teeth. He said the shape of the teeth influenced the way they worked. He figured out how they changed from tearing the meat off bones to grinding plants, and how some animals had different types of teeth so they could eat all kinds of food. He told me changes in teeth helped mammals to take over from the dinos. Cool, huh?"

Chee nodded. "Heard anything from Chap yet?"

"No." He pulled his phone out. "I'll call him again."

"Never mind," Parker said. "Is it like him to ignore you?"

"Sometimes. I can't blame him. When I called, it was usually bad news, a problem to be solved. After all, that's why people have security, right?"

Parker took more photos from the workshop doorway, capturing the disorder.

Chee squatted. "You'll want a shot of the yellow dirt here. It's the same as we saw in the hallway. Not as thick."

"Good catch."

Parker finished and put the camera down. Then, on his signal, they entered the room slowly. Chee squatted again to study the floor. "Did Chap use a wheelchair?"

"Not at all." Black's answer held the unspoken question.

"Well, something with wheels moved along the floor here. See these marks in the dirt?"

Parker snapped photos, then straightened up. "My guess is that someone found something they wanted and rolled it out with a dolly. Obviously something heavy. Wc'll follow these tracks in a minute."

They moved on slowly. Chee stopped at an arrangement of rocks sitting near a handheld magnifying glass and wondered what tiny fossil treasures they held. On the shelf above the rocks, he saw a colorful collection of small plastic velociraptor and stegosaur figures.

Black walked to the back wall. "Something is wrong with this closet door. It looks like someone forced it open."

The detective used the toe of his boot to move it. Chee had a momentary vision of the body of Dr. Chapman Dulles tumbling out, but instead an old cardboard box fell off a shelf, making a racket as it spilled rocks onto the painted concrete floor. The cabinet had about a dozen shelves, some empty and some filled with hammers, brushes, picks small and large, magnifiers, work gloves, hand tools, old three-ring binders, and more rocks.

Black exhaled. "Thank God. No body." He walked closer to examine the space. "See the empty area? There's dust around it and then a clear spot in the center."

Chee looked, too. "It's the shape of a box. Eight by ten. What else did he store in here that's gone?"

Black shook his head. "Papers? Files? Chap used this for his older research material. And look at this." He pointed out the dangling cords connected to a large monitor, a pair of speakers, and a printer. "His laptop was here. It's gone."

Parker took more photos. "Roper, walk through this room again with me in case we missed anything. Chee, take a quick look at the rest of the house and let us know if you see anything that needs a second opinion."

Chee felt his phone vibrate and pulled it from his pocket. "Will do. I've gotta take this."

He stepped into the hallway. Bernie got to the point, as usual. "Where are you?"

"Still with Roper Black and a detective from the sheriff's office. We're finishing here at Chap Dulles's house. What's up with you?"

"I saw a car parked on the road that goes past the place where I almost got run over. It bothered me, so I mentioned it to Gillman, and now he wants me to go back and get the VIN, look inside, you know. I told him yes. We can leave after that."

"No worries." He sensed that something else

was on her mind and selected what usually bothered her as his first choice. "Have you heard from
your mother or Darleen?"

"I spoke to Darleen. She said you told her we'd
be there for dinner. You didn't tell me."

"I figured that was OK with you."

He heard her sigh.

"Sorry, honey. I should have asked."

"Mama thinks I'm angry with her, and if we
don't make it tonight, she'll decide that I'm the
world's worst daughter." Bernie took a breath.
"Sometimes I think it would be nice to go home,
to our house, and relax. Put my feet up and not
have to be anyone's daughter, not have to play
nice girl with my mother or problem solver with
Sister."

"Or be a wife, right?" Chee felt her frustration.
"Sweetheart, I can call Darleen and tell her I got
busy helping with a case and that we'll have dinner with her another time." A good excuse and
the truth.

"I already mentioned that, but she's been shopping and everything. Never mind." She sucked in
a breath. "Maybe I'll go myself, and you can figure it out later or . . ."

He waited, but she left the thought dangling.

"Honey, I need to keep going on this investigation so I can get back to the motel and we can
leave. OK?"

"OK." She ended the call before he could say
"I love you."

Chee got to work as requested and searched
each room again, finding nothing unexpected, except stealable things that had not been stolen. In

the bathroom he saw a half-used prescription for a narcotic pain reliever on the counter, something a thief might have found valuable. He discovered none of the yellow dirt they had spotted in the entryway and workshop, no sign that anything else in the house had been disturbed. Whoever did this, Chee thought, knew exactly where to find what they wanted.

The reinspection made him wonder again about the nature of the intrusion. He saved the kitchen for last, not expecting anything. But it held another surprise.

# 14

What Jim Chee found in the kitchen might have had nothing to do with the reason a man was dead. But it caught his attention.

"Hey, Black, Parker. Come look at this."

In contrast to the well-tended shelves of dishes and glassware and the collection of single-estate bottled olive oil in beautiful containers on the counter, a dusting of white powder covered the countertop and the dark wooden floor.

Parker studied it closely.

"Messy housekeeping?" He laughed. "This would be a fortune in cocaine."

Black examined the mess. "This looks like gypsum—you know, plaster. Same as in the workshop." He touched it and held his finger to his nose. "I'm pretty sure that's what it is."

"Maybe he was fixing a crack in the wall here or something." Parker surveyed the room. "But I don't see any holes."

"That's right," said Black. "Detective, sometimes people interested in fossils use plaster to stabilize them. They can be fragile. Chap says this keeps them from breaking while they are being moved. He wraps them in burlap and coats them with plaster."

"Interesting."

"Do you know how much longer you'll need me here?" Black said. "I have to—"

Parker cut him off. "You'll stay as long as this takes."

Chee squatted to look at the kitchen floor more closely. "Here are the wheel marks again, like the tracks in the office." He followed them to a door. "What's beyond this?"

Black moved toward it. "The garage. Like I said, this looks like the plaster Chap uses to protect his specimens. It can get heavy."

"What does 'protect his specimens' mean?" Parker frowned. "Speak simple English, man."

"OK. If Chap has discovered a large fossil, say a leg bone or a big claw or something, he uses a plaster jacket to help keep it from fracturing while he's moving it." Black put his gloved hand on the doorknob from the kitchen to the garage. "This should be locked. It's not."

"Open it." Parker exhaled. "Open it now."

The first thing Chee noticed was soft gray light from the winter sky, and then a blast of air hit him like a frozen slap. The sense of neatness that filled most of the house was obvious in the garage too. He appreciated the well-organized shelves, labeled boxes, tools hung in order. He noticed a telescope along with an unopened jug of laundry soap, new rolls of paper towels—and a two-wheeled trolley cart.

Parker stepped into the big, mostly empty room, and the others followed. He paused, surveying the scene, then walked out to the concrete driveway, paused again, and came back into the garage. "Did Chap park his cars in here?"

"Yeah. His car is in the shop but his loaner is gone." Black glanced at his phone and frowned. "I have to be with my wife and baby. I can't stay much longer."

"What was he driving?"

"I can't tell you." Black hesitated. "His Lexus SUV was out of commission, and the dealer in Salt Lake couldn't get the part to fix it. So they gave him a loaner. He didn't say what it was, and I never saw it." He repeated the denial for emphasis. "Chap said Lexus wanted to loan him one of those new RZs something or other, an electric car, but he didn't take it because he thought charging out here could be a problem. I didn't ask him what he got instead."

Chee remembered Bernie's call and told them about the car she'd seen in Valley of the Gods.

"Roper," Parker said, "get the information on Chap's loaner so we can cross-check with what Bernie saw. Either he drove it out there or it was stolen."

"Or he could have abandoned it and taken off for somewhere he doesn't think you can find him," Chee said.

"I need to go home to Hannah and the baby," Black said again. "Someone else can make that call. I wasn't even scheduled to work for Chap today, except for escorting Chee."

"Hold on. I'm in charge here."

Chee noticed Parker's hardened attitude and saw Black stiffen at the tone of voice the detective used.

"You're running the investigation, but I don't work for you, remember?"

Parker paused a moment. "OK, Roper. Sorry if I came on too strong. Here's what's happening. After you get the car information, go through the workshop again, more carefully this time, and let me know if anything else is missing. Then you can leave."

"I *was* careful. Here and in the rest of the house. I told you, all the electronics, guns, jewelry, the good stuff that usually gets taken, all that is untouched."

Chee noticed that Black kept his cool but didn't back down. Both good qualities in a guy who wanted to be a cop.

"You must have forgotten. There's another thing that seems to be missing—the man himself, the guy who hired you to protect him."

Black's jaw tightened, and he clenched his fists.

Chee spoke to break the tension. "Based on where the disturbance was, I think the break-in is connected to Chap's work with fossils." He nodded toward the abandoned two-wheeler. "Someone used this dolly to move what they took from the house. And whatever they hauled out was bulky. The white powder is all over this. And that yellow sand we saw in the hallway? It's here too."

"Right." Parker turned to Black. "I noticed it in the kitchen as well. Have you seen it here before?"

"No. Maybe Chap had it on his boots. Maybe the home invader or invaders brought it in."

"Whatever was hauled away on that dolly might be some kind of specimen," Chee said, "a fossil linked to the research on the missing computer and the files."

Parker nodded. "So, Lieutenant Chee, what's your theory about the dead man?"

"Well, he may have worked for Chap, like Black said, and had a grudge against him. Let's say that he broke down the door but started to run when Chap came out with a gun. Chap shot him."

"No. In that case, his body would be facing away from the house, not toward it."

Chee conceded the point. "What if the dead guy was an employee who came to talk to Chap about something? He had the bad luck to arrive just as the burglars were leaving with whatever was on that dolly. They shot him when he realized what was up. Or the victim was a disgruntled worker in on the burglary plan, but he got cold feet." Chee pictured the body. "They shot him before he got away to rat on them."

Black jumped in. "I don't know everyone who works here, but that guy didn't look familiar. He could have picked up that company sweatshirt at a thrift store somewhere."

"You didn't examine him very closely," Parker snapped back.

Chee cringed at his tone.

"I got close enough to know I hadn't seen him before." Black pushed his shoulders back and stood a little taller. "Everyone who works for Chap gets a photo ID. I already plan to check the records if we need to for the ID."

Like most white detectives Chee had worked

with, Parker had studied the body with no hesitation about confronting the dead. In contrast, Black had acted with appropriate Diné respect for the chindi.

"Let's see what the fingerprints say, and let's bring Chap in to make sure he's safe and to ask him some questions. Black, tell me again why you quit as security up here."

"With the baby, I wanted something full-time."

"Did Chap try to get you to stay on? Or did he fire you?"

"What business is this of yours, Parker?"

"Motivation to disrupt his life with this break-in? Maybe even do him harm? I've got to turn over every rock."

"Well, Chap and I had our differences, but I would never harm him."

Parker turned to Chee. "You got anything else?"

"Yeah. What about this? Chap returned from wherever he was just as the break-in began. He shot the man we found and then drove off quickly with the laptop and the files and whatever he wrapped in plaster in the vehicle, before the bad guys could retaliate."

"Or what if he knew someone planned to steal his favorite fossil," Black said, "so he moved it to his car this morning. He was outside, getting ready to leave, when he heard a car pull up. He went to the front of the house and shot the victim."

Parker shook his head. "Lots of theories. If they took the fossil he protected with that plaster cast, Chap might be looking for them, looking for revenge and to get it back. Was the gun safe locked?"

"Yes." Chee shifted his weight from foot to foot. "No one tried to break into it."

"Chap kept a gun in the car," Black said. "I'll call for information about the vehicle and let you know what I find out. Give Chee a ride. I'm heading home."

Parker glared at the young man.

"Roper, before you go, I have a question." Chee paused, wanting Black's full attention.

"Go ahead."

"What about that dirt in the hallway?"

"Well, it reminds me of dirt from a site Chap worked with a couple other paleontologists last year. His last job with those guys. They are probably still working up there. It's just dirt, you know, and dirt is everywhere out here. Hard to prove exactly where it came from." Black walked away.

Parker turned to Chee. "Thanks for your ideas and help with this. If you ever find yourself bored in Navajo land, we can use a skilled hand out here."

"Appreciate it." Chee thought of Bernie, wishing she had been the one to get the compliment. "Could you take me back to the Bluff Inn?"

"Not a problem. After I talk to the ME and make sure the scene is secure."

They found the medical examiner as she leaned over the body, now lying with his face collecting snowflakes. Carson straightened up. "I was just getting ready to look for you, Detective. I'm done. I can tell you he has a gunshot wound in the chest and what appears to be a fractured skull. As of now, I'm assuming he bashed his head on the concrete as a result of the impact of the shot. It's hard to tell with the cold out here, but I would guess that he died early this morning."

"What else?"

"I didn't find a weapon on him. No wallet either, no cell phone. The only guy in America without either one of those. Just these car keys." She handed them to the detective.

"When will the van be here for the body?"

"Maybe ten minutes."

"Good."

"I bagged his hands. He's missing some fingers, not related to this. Something might turn up under the fingernails, but I didn't see any defensive wounds or signs of a struggle before he died. I think the bullet caught him by surprise."

And that, Chee thought, was a statement that could be said of most shooting victims.

Parker looked at the key ring. "I didn't see a car."

Chee looked toward where he'd noticed the rusted sedan. "Remember the old car I mentioned? The junker parked on the other side of the house."

Parker looked at the keys again. "Let's check it out."

They trotted around the building to the access road. Parker used his gloved hand to put the key in the door handle. It fit, but the car was unlocked.

They noticed that the sedan stank of cigarette smoke and old food. So much trash covered the floor on the passenger side that Chee couldn't see the floor mat. When they dusted the vehicle for fingerprints, the technicians might also need to plow through the garbage for credit card receipts or something else that could identify the driver. The driver who, Chee guessed, could be the dead man.

Parker opened the glove box. Proof of insurance was missing, but the detective found the registration. The paperwork had expired, but the car had been registered in a woman's name. He took photos of everything, just as Chee would have done, locked the vehicle, and called in the plate number.

The van to remove the body arrived as they hiked back toward the house. Parker kept quiet and, Chee thought, looked grumpy. He knew the feeling from his own experience. This case had too many what-ifs.

Parker started the motorcycle.

"OK, buddy, hop on. Let's get outta here."

The frigid air made it a less-than-perfect time to be on a motorcycle, but Chee was glad for the ride. He climbed on the back. "What's with you and Black? Some bad blood?"

Parker spit on the ground. "If he'd been doing his job, keeping Chap's place safe, me and you would probably be sipping a latte or something stronger somewhere instead of freezing our balls off."

There was more to it, Chee figured. "You seemed surprised that the dead man wasn't Chap."

"You know that's the most common thing in an incident like this. The homeowner tries some defense and gets blasted." He stopped a moment. "And despite what Black wants you to believe, his boss isn't exactly Mr. Perfect. The feds have asked us to help with some discreet surveillance on a business he was involved with. Black defends the guy like he is a saint or something. Chap probably should have fired him. Black gets on my nerves. Let's leave it at that."

"What kind of shady deal was Chapman in?"

Parker snorted. "You try getting that information from the agency. I figured Chap for a decent guy. When he reported the vandalism, he apologized for bothering us."

"Do you think the slashed tires, the harassing calls, and what happened here are connected?" It was an obvious question, but Chee needed Parker's view.

"Of course. Before you ask, I think Black is right to be worried about his old boss. The idea that the man is just off somewhere looking at rocks is malarky. I think Chap is dead. And it's on Black."

Chee said, "Black mentioned an ex-girlfriend. Do you know anything about that?"

"I heard she was married to someone else and kind of forgot to tell Chap about him. I'll get her name from Black. Can't hurt to check."

# 15

Roper Black drove away from Chapman Dulles's home, out the private drive, onto the county road, and finally on US 191 toward the little town of Bluff. Last week's snow still covered the mountains. Looking at it made him colder and accentuated his worry. He waited for the gauge on his dash to tick up from below the "C" to closer to midline and finally turned on the heater.

As soon as he had cell service, he called for the vehicle information on the loaned vehicle his boss drove. It should have been an easy ask, but the dealership's computers were down. The manager remembered Chap, however, and said they had provided him with a new Lexus LS in a color called Eminent White Pearl. They offered to give him the plate number and VIN as soon as their system was back online. He left them Gillman's number for the follow-up, then sent a message with the info he had to Parker. Job done.

Of all the women and men he'd worked for, Black had a special fondness for Chapman Dulles,

PhD. Chap never talked down to him, even though he'd had only a year of college. Not only did he treat him with respect, but Chap also paid well. And like Black's own Diné ancestors, Chap appreciated and respected this open, vibrant, and intimidating landscape called Bears Ears, of which Valley of the Gods' thirty-two thousand acres was a tiny slice. Chap called it a terrain of naked geology.

Then Black called Hannah, thinking of her and the sweet, sweet baby. The phone went straight to voice mail. Good, he thought. He had asked her to turn it off so she and their daughter could sleep. He hung up without leaving a message, and images of Chap returned to fill his mind. As he drove, he realized that he knew where Dr. Chapman Dulles was—or at least where he might be.

Even in the winter, Chap was an early riser. On the shortest days of the year, Black sometimes would catch his boss outdoors walking along the road just before sunrise. He'd be standing in the blessed light of early dawn among the oranges and golden tans that glowed softly in the sandstone. In the fall and winter Chap always wore what they called his lumberjack hat.

Black had teased Chap about being part Native. "We Navajos have a tradition of saying our prayers at sunrise, when the gods aren't worn out from all the requests of the day. Guess you're one of us."

Chap had smiled. "Lots of humans, ancient and modern, believe in morning prayer. I'm not religious, but seeing the sunrise gives me hope."

Over the last weeks, as fall turned to early winter, Chap had grown quieter and spent more

time alone in Valley of the Gods. The change
had started when his boss mentioned that he was
receiving threatening anonymous phone calls.
The calls came late at night or early in the morning, Chap said, and concerned his research. He
didn't want to talk about the harassment, Black
remembered. But when Chap went outside one
afternoon and found all his tires slashed, he followed Black's advice, changed his phone number,
and started parking in the locked garage, even
during the day.

The month before, his boss's business partners
from New Mexico had shown up unexpectedly for
several meetings. Black overheard raised voices
when the four people met in Chap's workshop.
Afterward, a dark mood had shadowed his boss.

He'd asked about that. "The partner problem is
a professional disagreement," Chap had said. "But
no worries. I've resigned from Dinostar."

Dinostar, Black knew, was the name of the fossil business Chap contracted with. "Resigned, is
that good?"

"Yes, but I'm disappointed that it came to this.
My partners asked my opinion whenever they discovered something unusual, but I realized they
really didn't want to hear what I had to say or do
what I recommended. Not even Jessica."

Black had taken note of Jessica months before.
He had shown up for work as usual and seen an
attractive woman in a fluffy bathrobe sitting with
Chap at the breakfast table. His boss looked happier and more energized. He'd found things Chap
never bought before, like diet cola bottles and
cottage cheese containers, in the garbage when

he did his auxiliary job as handyman and janitor. He saw a car with New Mexico license plates parked in the driveway for a while. When he asked, Chap volunteered that the woman's name was Jessica, she was a divorced archaeologist who also worked in Bears Ears, and she had an interest in paleontology.

But after Chap left Dinostar, Black hadn't seen the car, the diet soda cans, or the woman at Chap's house again. He'd asked about it.

"I told her to leave after I found out she was married to a man I worked with and respected," Chap said, "and she hadn't even started divorce proceedings. Her husband is a paleontologist and one of the partners in Dinostar. The lie didn't seem to bother her, but it really troubled me. I loved her, but I didn't appreciate being deceived."

The loss of the Dinostar contract and his lover had left his boss quieter and more focused on time in the bone shop. Black reminded himself again that it wasn't unusual for Chap to take off without telling him and to come back with a story of something he'd discovered, or rediscovered, among the spires and buttes. After resigning from Dinostar and splitting up with Jessica, his boss did a lot more hiking. He said it helped him think. He mentioned that his favorite places were the spots where he'd found fossils, and that of all those, Valley of the Gods was closest to his heart.

Chap kept Edward Abbey's description of the place on the wall in his bone shop: "Ahead a group of monoliths loomed against the sky, eroded remnants of naked rock with the profiles of Egyptian deities. Beyond stood the red wall of the plateau, rising fifteen hundred feet above the desert in straight, unscaled, perhaps unscalable cliffs."

Normally, Chap was home and working by 10:00 a.m. If he had left the house before the break-in to visit one of the sites where he found fossilized teeth or old bones, he might have returned, seen the crime in progress, and then driven off to hide. Black held that hopeful scenario in his mind. He couldn't picture Chap shooting anyone, but he knew his boss had several guns and could use one if he had to.

As he drove, Black noticed a group of ravens soaring, then swooping in what seemed to be a coordinated hunt or perhaps avian curiosity. The birds reminded him of something Chap had said once. He was talking about birds as avian dinosaurs, and the conversation morphed to dinosaur carnivores. Chap had mentioned new research that indicated that *Tyrannosaurus rex* may have sometimes traveled in packs and hunted as a group. He'd asked Chap how he knew that, and his boss explained about a recently discovered *T. rex* graveyard and how finding so many of the giants together had added to the scientific knowledge about them.

"Is that one of the projects you're working on, sir?"

"No. I'm focusing on climate change and the resilience of life and what the fossil record has to say about that. If you know where to look, you can see evidence of creatures large and small here in abundance dating to two hundred and fifty million years ago. I'm not big on politics, but this place is a treasure worth protecting."

Finally the comfort of the warm air on his feet and torso, along with the expansive views, began to soothe Black's worry. It had started snowing again, but he knew his boss was tough. He understood the man well enough to have a good idea of where to find him. Black would go to the place they had visited together last week, a spot in Valley of the Gods where Chap had shown him something special, and look for him there.

He remembered the day well. His boss had picked up a rock, turned it over in his hand, and passed it to him. "Look closely."

Roper examined it. It reminded him of something else he'd seen, but he couldn't find a name for it.

Chap must have seen the curiosity in his eyes. "It's a turtle carapace. More than a million years old. Turned to stone."

"Wow."

"Think of this: water-loving creatures in what is now the desert. They died and turned to rock slowly, slowly, slowly over the millennia. And the seacoast itself became sandstone. Amazing, isn't it?"

Black agreed. He enjoyed the way Chap could spot fossils—worm casings, leaf imprints, even dinosaur tracks—in strata where his eyes recorded only weathered stone. Chap told him of the jawbone of an ancient creature that had lived in what was now Valley of the Gods, an ancestor of both mammals and dinosaurs.

"Around here is where I found my first dinosaur bone, a rib of a diplodocus. I'll never forget that." He heard the delight in Chap's voice. "I was a student then, an intern working for peanuts to get an idea of what paleontology was all about. It was literally the opportunity of a lifetime, and it changed my life forever."

It dawned on Roper Black, again, that he had failed Chap by not giving him the protection he deserved. He had to find him and do what he could to help.

He stayed on US 191, heading south as his wipers kept pace with the snow striking his windshield, creating a frozen white ridge on either side of where the swipe ended. The sacred San Juan River ran south of the highway, its cottonwoods leafless in the winter cold. He cruised past the junction for the road to Sand Island, a spot known for its panels of petroglyphs and as a departure point for rafters who planned a journey down to Mexican Hat. Roper's clan brother Dylan had been a guide on many of the trips and took pleasure in infusing tidbits of Navajo culture into the lessons about geology and archaeology the visitors received.

At the junction, he took 163 winding west and north. He sped over Butler Wash, another area known for its early Native settlements and rock art, and then through the multilayered sandstone of Comb Ridge.

Even though he had lived in this landscape his whole life—with the exception of his year at the university in Logan—this wild, harsh country still took his breath away. Nizhoni. It was beautiful, an area blessed with space and color and clouds and quiet. He considered it a gift from the Holy People to remind the five-fingered ones not to get too focused on their particular tiny slivers of life. To think big. To go in beauty because in truth, beauty was all around them.

But despite the beauty that surrounded him, Black drove with two heavy ideas cycling back and forth in his brain: his duty to keep his precious new daughter safe, and his colossal failure to do the same for Chap.

He now thought of the little one as he drove. He pictured the tiny hands, ten perfect fingers with soft baby nails. His heart had filled to over-flowing last night at her birth, and he missed her and his sweet, brave wife all the more with each passing hour.

Black had reached the turnoff for the Valley of the Gods road when his phone buzzed. He was surprised; service here was marginal at best. The call came from his home number. His wife never called when she knew he was at work, but Hannah had never been a mother before either. She kept a level head, that lady of his. He was full of questions about the baby, about Hannah and her day.

Everything must be OK. That was what he told himself when he answered.

"Hi there. How's our—"

"Oh, Roper. I need you. She's so . . ." He heard anguish in Hannah's voice and the crying of his daughter in the background. Then, as happens too often in the hinterlands, the call vanished.

He thought about it for a split second, the length of time it took for him to move his foot from the gas to the brake. He found the first space on the road wide enough to pull off safely and wheeled the green sedan into a U-turn. He didn't bother trying to call back, just sped up and headed home.

His heart overflowed with the special kind of fear born from love.

Chap would be OK, he told himself. Chap would be just fine. He'd call Chee as soon as he could and ask him to go to the place where Chap might be hiding.

As he raced for home, the snow was falling more heavily. And instead of melting, it had started to stick on the road.

# 16

As a girl, Bernadette Manuelito had been taught the danger of feeling sorry for herself. No time for that, Mama always told her. You have other, better things to do. Her mother's advice, of course, had always been solid. She'd internalized it long ago.

But this time, things were different. The good advice she gave herself seemed pointless, and the "better things to do" trivial. She felt adrift. Profoundly disappointed and exhausted. And concerned that her bad attitude was contagious and had lapped over onto her husband.

The sheriff had asked her to give him information on the car she saw. She needed to get going. She had a long to-do list: finish packing, tell Chee she planned to leave for Mama's house without him, do the job for the sheriff, and then head to Toadlena to talk to Darleen.

She looked at the empty suitcase, but instead of putting her clothes inside, she lay on the bed next to it, making sure her shoes hung over the edge.

She stretched from the tips of her fingers to her toes. Relax, she told herself. She stretched again. It felt good.

When she was nearly asleep, her phone rang, and she reached for it and saw an unknown number from Utah. She often ignored calls like this, but she had relatives everywhere. And besides, she gave her cell number only to people she trusted. She swiped to answer as she sat up. After this conversation, she would do what she had to at the motel, and then head out to Valley of the Gods.

"Yá'át'ééh, Ms. Bernie. It's Lilakai."

"Yá'át'ééh."

"I'm on my way home. It's exciting to think about the party. Will I see you there?"

"Sorry, but I can't make it. I have to check on something for the sheriff, and then I need to get back to New Mexico."

"Well, darn it. I really hoped you could join us. Will you tell the woman who was with you?"

"Yes. But Pam already invited her when we dropped off the food. Pam said she had worked for Jessica, but Jessica didn't remember her."

"Jessica Johnson?"

"Yes."

"Oh, that one."

Bernie heard Lilakai's voice change. "I worked for her too, although I mostly helped the two men who ran the company. Ah, don't worry about inviting her."

"It sounds like you didn't get along well."

"I don't wanna say anything negative about her. I quit that job. I really liked her husband. He's a

gentleman. He knows a lot about dinosaurs."
Lilakai paused. "Is he there with her?"

"Jessica's husband died."

"He passed away?" Lilakai sounded shocked. "I
hadn't heard that. I just saw him. Are you sure?"

"Yes."

"What happened? He wasn't that old."

"He's the one a sheriff's deputy discovered in the
cold outside the car on the way from Blanding. I
guess you didn't know about that."

"Oh, I heard that someone had died out there,
but not who it was. How sad." Lilakai stopped
talking for a moment. "Her husband was kind."

"Did you know him from his work out here?"

"Everyone knew him. My sister helped clean his
house a time or two. Jessica wasn't there much."

"Pam drove all the way to Santa Fe?"

"Silly. Why would she do that? No, she cleaned
their house here. The one with the big views of
Shash Jáá."

Bernie raised an eyebrow. "Jessica told me she
lived in Santa Fe. She has to drive back there to
arrange the funeral."

"Maybe they have two houses, like some rich
people."

She didn't like saying the name of the dead, but
she had to ask. "The man who froze out there was
Kyle Johnson. Is that the man Pam worked for?"

"No, not at all." Even over the phone, Bernie
sensed the woman's relief. "I'm talking about Jessica's husband. I'm talking about Chapman Dulles.
They kept their different names. He's a good man."
Lilakai stopped talking for a moment and then

said, "That man who died, the one with the same last name. He must have been her brother."

Bernie knew that Jessica had called Kyle her husband and mentioned Chap as a business consultant. "Are you sure Chap is Jessica's husband?"

Lilakai laughed. "You sound shocked. Well, now that you mention it, I never saw the marriage license hanging on the wall and no rings. But they shared his bedroom."

"I am shocked. Even if Chap wasn't exactly her husband, it sounds like she wasn't especially devoted to Kyle."

"To tell you the truth, I always thought she was primarily devoted to Jessica." Then Lilakai grew serious. "I need to tell you something else. My brother, Ranger Becenti, said that he checked the permits for that site where you had trouble with the men in that truck, and there's a problem. Two problems, actually. They had a permit for archaeology, not paleontology. And the permit had expired. He told me to tell you to be careful if you're driving or walking around out here."

"Sure." After the encounter she'd had, she didn't need to be told to act with caution. "Did he say why?"

Lilakai laughed again. "He wasn't specific, but he always tells me the same thing: Be careful. I tell him if I was as careful as he wants, I'd never get anything done."

The way Lilakai said it reminded Bernie of her aunt Maggie, her Little Mother, her shimá yazhí. She always told Bernie to be brave, smart, strong, and happy. She never said, "Be careful." As a youngster, Bernie hadn't appreciated it, but she wished she could thank her Little Mother now for nurturing her courage.

Then Lilakai surprised her. "What my clan brother is talking about out there, I take seriously. Especially after what happened to our little girl. And now you've had a problem too. That's a bad place." She cleared her throat. "You know, Chris and Chap both asked me to keep an eye on things out here for their company, Dinostar. Then Chap called and told me he'd given Chris his resignation, that he was done with Dinostar. Chris never got around to paying me. So I guess I'm not on the payroll anymore."

Bernie remembered the story of how the family had received the picture with the witchcraft warning. "Did you save that picture?"

"Yes. It's on my phone. I don't like keeping it, but I thought it might be proof of something in case . . . Well, you know."

"Could you please send me the photo?"

"I will."

When the call ended, Bernie finished packing and switched into her hiking boots. Then she called Chee and got voice mail again.

"Hey, there. I'm heading to Valley of the Gods to recheck that car for the sheriff." She realized something and put it into words before she talked herself out of the idea. "I'd like to drive back with you if you can finish in time. Call me, OK? Maybe we can go together."

She put on her cap and gloves, made sure she had water, an energy bar, and other supplies in her backpack, grabbed her Glock, locked the motel room, loaded her suitcase into the truck, and drove off.

A few minutes later her phone dinged with a message, and she pulled over to check. It was the photo from Lilakai, and it made her blood boil. No one should intimidate a child. She thought about the witchcraft warning, the threat on her life, and especially the way the men had treated Crystal, and grew angrier as Bluff and the motel faded into the distance.

Bernie pictured the man behind the wheel of the black pickup, the man with the gold tooth, the bully who had tried to scare and hurt her—Donray something, or maybe something Donray. She remembered that he had an unusual skull tattoo on his arm. She used her phone to quickly send the name and description to Sheriff Gillman, along with the reason she suspected that he was behind the assault on her and the threatening photograph of little Crystal. She shared a copy with Becenti and with Chee.

The snow fell steadily now, sticking to the bushes and the dirt along the side of the road in a thin, soft-looking dusting. Bernie slowed when a green sedan pulled out in front of her. It made a U-turn into the opposite lane and headed back toward Bluff. The car looked familiar, but she didn't focus on it. Lots of old cars in this part of the world.

Just before the road dropped into Valley of the Gods, her phone buzzed with a call. Because it was Darleen, she pulled the truck onto the shoulder, hoping to preserve the signal.

"What's the story? Are you coming?"

"Ah, I hope so. I've got one more thing to do before I can leave, but my suitcase is in the truck."

"What about Chee?"

"He's tied up with something, but I hope so. I can't say yet."

"Sister, you've been acting weirder than usual. Is something bothering you?"

Before she could stop herself, she said "Yes" and felt a wave of relief. Maybe it was time to share her disappointment.

"Gosh, I apologize if I did something stupid. You know I've been upset ever since I told Mama I wanted to go back to school again, and she got all strange on me. But I didn't mean to . . ." And then to her surprise, Darleen, her wild, crazy little sister, started to cry.

"Oh no, dear one. It's not you or Mama. It's my own issue. You have nothing to apologize for."

Darleen took a moment to regain her composure. "It's Mama, too. She said I shouldn't make any plans. She's telling me that when you and Cheeseburger have a baby, I'll be the auntie and that's a big responsibility and I won't have time to go to school or have a job."

"That's just wrong."

"Do you think I'm a selfish jerk?"

"No. Not at all. I think you're smart to want to be a nurse. And you don't have to worry about being an aunt for a while. I thought Mama was happy about you going to school."

"Yeah, that was yesterday. Now she's on to this. You know I'd do anything for you and your husband, but I have to get on with my own life.

Especially now that Slim and I are kinda serious. You know, I'm not getting any younger."

The idea that her little sister was thinking about aging while her mother focused on babies made Bernie smile.

"I'd like to talk to you and the Cheeseburger about this stuff before Mama drives me totally crazy. Can we talk after dinner?"

"Sure." Bernie reminded her about Chee's possible absence and the delay that could come from snow on the road.

"I get it. Can I ask you something?"

"Of course."

"You mentioned that something was bothering you, but it isn't anything Mama or I did. And it's not just the job you lost, is it?"

"No."

"So are you getting divorced?"

"No, no. I'm lucky Chee puts up with me."

"Tell me what's going on. Maybe I can help. That's what families are for, you know? I'm worried about you, Sister. If you just . . ."

Bernie felt unwanted tears rising, and her throat started to tighten. "I've got to go." She could barely choke out the words before she tossed the phone onto the passenger seat. She clenched the steering wheel, closed her eyes, took a breath or two, and then pulled back to the highway.

Bernie drove past a herd of cattle picking out a meal from the dried grass, the snow dampening their coats. The sight of the hardy longhorns increased her anxiety. She realized that Gillman's simple assignment, the chance to examine the car—if it was still there—could lead to an encounter with Donray. This time, she knew what to ask him. And the tattoo on his lower arm could match the one in the photo with the little girl that Lilakai had sent her. And Crystal's mention of the man who was missing fingers was a link to another suspect.

She contacted the sheriff and Becenti again, and left messages for each one about her mission and pending location just in case of trouble with the weather or with Donray if she encountered him. She hoped to never see Donray, but if she did, she was prepared.

The storm had lightened for the moment, and its moisture seemed to evaporate before even leaving a damp spot. The truck now showed the temperature outside at a mild thirty-five, warmer than it had been. She noticed towering sandstone, the almost empty road, and the silent grace of the falling white flakes.

As she drove closer to the valley, she began to feel more at peace. If she encountered Donray, so be it. She could resolve the incident with the truck both for herself and for the possible link to the little girl who had been threatened. No one, no man, no truck, had a right to do that, and the warrior in her wanted to set things straight. She was glad Gillman had given her this task. Focusing on the case felt better by far than focusing on herself.

When she turned onto the Valley of the Gods road, she drove until she found the rocks and wooden sawhorses that blocked it and a note stapled

there: "Road Closed Due to Winter Weather."
She moved the roadblock, drove through, and
then replaced it, with the note attached.

Bernie assumed that the smallish white car
would either be parked where she'd first seen it,
moved to another scenic location along the vista
trail, or gone altogether. She hoped the owner
had decided to drive away from the approaching
blizzard. But when she came to where she'd discovered it, there the car sat. Only now, a BLM
vehicle was parked behind it. She expected Becenti, investigating the car on this closed road after
her message. But Cassidy Kingsley stepped into
the middle of the road to block Bernie's approach.
Bernie pulled to the side and got out of her truck.

Kingsley didn't smile. "Officer Manuelito, didn't
you see the roadblock?"

"I saw it. The sheriff asked me to come check
on this car. He wants the VIN."

"I can get that to him. No need for you to be
freezing here in the snow." Kingsley fiddled with
the zipper on her jacket. "I'll text it. Weren't you
and Chee wanting to get back to Shiprock? The
weather isn't getting any better. That's why the
roadblock was up."

Kingsley was talking too fast, Bernie thought.
"We planned to head back this afternoon, but he's
involved with something here. I don't know for
sure when we can leave."

"Why is Sheriff Gillman interested in this car?"

Bernie wondered what caused Kingsley's ner-
vousness. "Evidently there was a shooting, and he
thinks the vehicle is somehow related to it."

"No kidding. What happened?" As she spoke,

the ranger switched her attention to the road, as though she was looking for someone.

"I don't know many details. Talk to Gillman about that. But because he asked me to send him the VIN, I will. You must have plenty to do without that."

"No, you get going. Getting this car out of here is my job. You need to head on."

Kingsley's attitude irritated Bernie. "What's the deal? This isn't a big ask. Plus it's one less thing for you to do. We're sisters in law enforcement, remember?"

Now she saw anger in the woman's eyes. Ranger Kingsley held her ground in the middle of the road, as if she were contemplating a decision. Then she yelled at Bernie. "Get in your truck and get out of the area, right now. Listen to me. It's for your own good."

And then Bernie heard the rumble of another approaching vehicle, a dark pickup with something unusual mounted on the grille. A cylinder, all right, and one with points on both ends. It was, she realized, an ornament made from the horns of a Texas longhorn.

If she had followed Kingsley's advice, the day might have had a very different ending.

# 17

As Bernie watched the truck draw closer, several things clarified themselves.

She realized why the longhorn cattle trying to graze in the snowstorm had bothered her. Although southeastern Utah was a haven for black pickups, she'd seen only one with real horns from a longhorn affixed to the grille: the truck that had tried to kill her. This one.

She assumed that Donray was in the truck, and that he had seen her and the ranger standing in the road. Bring it on, she thought. Now was the time to find out why he wanted her dead and why he had terrified a harmless girl. Now was the time to make sure he got called into account for his bad behavior.

Bernie studied Kingsley's tight face, worry written all over it. And something else. "You're angry."

"Right," Kingsley said. "And I'm figuring out a complication I didn't anticipate."

"What complication?" Bernie saw the truck slow as it drew near.

"You'll see. I tried to get you to leave." Kingsley shook her head. "Remember that."

"I'm not leaving. Donray and whoever was with him in the truck almost killed me. That's not happening again. Do you know about that?"

Kingsley nodded.

"Do you know that before that, they threatened little Crystal, one of the Zonnie kids? They talked adilgashii." She saw the ranger's blank look. "Witchcraft. We need to take charge. You and me, Kingsley, sister cops. We need to stop this jerk. I'm glad you're out here. We can do this together. This isn't my jurisdiction, but it is yours."

Kingsley shook her head. "Manuelito, you have a knack for being in the wrong place at the wrong time."

"You don't look to me like the sort of woman who gives up." Bernie tried a positive approach.

"I'm not." Kingsley turned away from her, watching the truck approach.

The black pickup inched past the BLM vehicle, Bernie's truck, and the women. It came to a stop in front of the abandoned white sedan.

As soon as the driver emerged, Bernie recognized Donray. She was glad she had her Glock in her coat pocket, and that he was alone.

He walked toward them with a swagger and scowled at Bernie. "What are you doing here? You sure are a slow learner."

"I'm a Navajo cop. The sheriff asked me to check on a vehicle. That car you just passed."

Donray smirked. "Ranger Kingsley wants that thing out of here before the storm comes, and she and I have an agreement. I'm going to tow it out. Tell the sheriff he doesn't need to worry. I've done this dozens of times. Now, run along. It's not your bother."

Bernie put her hand on her gun, ready to defend herself if the situation escalated. "It is my bother. Sheriff Gillman asked me to get some information for him, the VIN, registration, whatever. You can't tow this car."

Donray spat. "You really a cop?"

"Yes."

Kingsley spoke for the first time. "Get busy, Donray. Leave Bernie alone. You're lucky she didn't shoot you. It took you too long to get here. We need to move this thing off the road before the blizzard really hits. I told her I'd deal with Gillman."

The ranger turned to Bernie. "This is my turf. Get out of here. I'll handle the sheriff."

"That Donray is bad news. I'm surprised you couldn't find someone else to help you with this." Bernie swallowed her aggravation and took a step toward Donray. "You can't tow this car away until I'm done with it."

"Watch me." Donray walked to the dolly tow attached to the horned truck and pulled out the ramps.

Kingsley turned to Bernie. "It's an abandoned vehicle on a closed BLM road in a popular visitor area. I'm authorized to remove it."

"Abandoned," Donray said. "That's the same as lost. Finders keepers."

Bernie spoke to Kingsley, raising her voice. "What about Donray and his buddy trying to kill me? Grow a backbone. Arrest him for assaulting me."

"Take that up with the sheriff. You're not wanted here."

Bernie felt her anger boil. "I'll get the VIN and leave it to you. I'm sure the sheriff will want to talk to you both about what's going on out here."

Bernie trotted to the white car, photographed the license plate with her phone camera, and brushed the snow off the driver's-side windshield and photographed the metal tag with the VIN. She looked inside. The interior was spacious, with leather seats in a warm hue. Despite everything going on, she couldn't help but admire the vehicle. Then she spotted the books and what looked like unopened mail. Several envelopes and advertisements were faceup, all addressed to Dr. Chapman Dulles. Either the car was his, or it belonged to someone who had been at his house. Bingo.

Donray was walking toward the white car, prepared to load it up.

"Donray, stop."

He ignored her.

"Get away from there!" Bernie yelled at him.

He swore at her. "You need to learn to mind your own business. Kingsley's the boss here."

Bernie drew her gun and pointed it at his chest. "You're under arrest."

Donray seemed startled. "What? Come on. We can work this out. I like a woman with a good head on her pretty shoulders."

"But you especially like young girls, don't you?

Little ones like that Zonnie child who had trouble with her horse. The one you took out to the witchcraft place."

"I didn't do nothin' to that kid."

"What about trying to kill me with that truck while your buddy took a shot with that rifle hanging there?"

"You got no proof of that." Donray kept his eyes on Bernie. "You don't have a video to show who tried to run you over. Your word against mine."

"Who does a prosecutor or a judge believe? On one side, a smallish woman police officer who says she was harassed and nearly killed by a lunatic in a big truck? Or a guy with a bad attitude, a gold tooth, and a skull tattoo? And especially when that man is the main suspect in the death of Jessica's husband and a man killed at Chap's house."

Donray grunted. "I had nothin' to do with Kyle being shot. Get that straight. And someone got killed at Chap's place? I don't know squat about that. News to me." For the first time, however, he looked worried.

Either Donray ranked as one of the best liars she'd ever heard or, unexpectedly, he was telling the truth. His body language underlined the fact that the news about the shooting had caught him by surprise.

"Do you have a weapon?"

He didn't answer. She shouted the question at him again, wondering where Ranger Kingsley was and when she'd come to assist with the arrest.

"No gun." Donray raised his hands and shook his head in confirmation. "Don't shoot me."

"We're going to the sheriff." She wished she'd had her handcuffs, but Kingsley probably had some. If not, she had zip ties in the truck. They'd work.

Donray stood. "You've got this all wrong. I only scared you, and I didn't hurt that girl."

Bernie took advantage of that partial confession. "She has nightmares now about giant creatures with square bodies and sticks for arms and legs. And holes where their eyes should be. I found some drawings on the rocks, old pictures that had been vandalized, you know? Someone had scratched out the faces. Near there I found a little turquoise bear on a pink ribbon. It looks exactly like the necklace the girl, Crystal, is wearing in the photo you sent to her family."

"It's just a picture."

"In that photo, there's an arm across the little girl's shoulder. If you enlarge it, it's easy to see the skull tattoo. Exactly like yours. Start walking toward my truck, Donray."

He looked at the gun and then at her, and Bernie saw something real in his hard face, something she read as shock and maybe even a whiff of shame.

"Donray, walk toward my truck. You're in this deep. Attempted murder of a police officer and child predator. But that's not all."

Bernie let the idea sink in as Donray moved in front of her. She noticed that his shoulders slumped a bit.

"The worst for you is the murder of Kyle Johnson. And then there's a question about that second victim, shot to death at Chap's house. Chap's car was missing, and it's this one, the one you're try-ing to tow."

When Donray stopped and turned toward her, Bernie held her breath for a split second, expect-ing the worst. She would kill this man rather than let him kill her. She braced for an assault.

But instead of attacking, he raised his hands even higher in a surrender position, took a step back, and looked her in the eye. "I don't know what went down with Kyle or the other dead guy. I swear it. Don't shoot me."

"Donray, come on, you clown," Kingsley yelled from behind Bernie. "Let's move this car out of here. Get on with it. We've got to get going. You towing that car or not?"

"Ranger, Donray is under arrest," Bernie yelled back over her shoulder. "He and I are having a conversation."

Bernie gave the man a piercing look. "The Zonnies are good people. I can help you make restitution for what happened to the little girl. Maybe, maybe, if you cooperate with me, I can work with them not to press child predator charges against you. To let you make this right the Navajo way."

Kingsley hollered again, her voice full of anger now. "Hey, stop talking to that woman and get back in your truck."

Bernie kept her eye on him as she shouted, "Kingsley, I repeat: he's under arrest. Think straight. You can't move this car until the sheriff authorizes it. It could be part of a murder inves-tigation."

She heard the ranger approach from behind.

Good, she thought. Kingsley had come to her senses. She would welcome the backup.

But then Donray's face softened, and he said, "Oh, man." And Kingsley said, "Donray, you bozo."

Bernie felt the blow to the back of her head. And everything went black.

# 18

After years of exploration, Chapman Dulles knew the nooks and crannies of Bears Ears like his own kitchen. He could find the mounds that covered ancient Indian sites. He understood the strata of the geological layers, arranged on top of each other like a fancy baker's cake. He could find the fossil-rich layers of shale and sandstone. What he loved the most were the places where the dinosaurs and their ancestors had become part of the fabric of the earth itself.

When something bothered him, he came to Valley of the Gods for clarity. And he was deeply bothered now. He wondered about the man who had stood in his driveway ringing the doorbell, about the gunshots, about the threat to his life and to his work, his precious Mary.

Despite what had happened, he felt safe here in the rocks. He had hiked in with deliberation, sticking to stone as much as possible, careful to avoid leaving footprints. The only thing he hadn't planned on was the snow. He berated himself for the oversight, even though he'd fled the house quickly. He had lived in the high country long enough to know how fast the weather could change. But the look in the eyes of the man at the front door had panicked him.

Worse than the threat of a blizzard, in his rush to a place of safety he'd lost his balance and injured his ankle. He'd climbed up to this refuge before the swelling started. Now the pain made it hard to focus on anything else.

Roper Black knew the cave, knew his habits. Roper had his trust. When he showed up, Roper would tell him the story of what had happened after he left the house. Chap knew his security guy would get here eventually, and they would hike back to the road and drive to the sheriff's office. He knew that Roper would have been to the house and discovered that he was gone. The only other person who knew of this place was his former girlfriend.

Chap looked out from the cave entrance at the feathery white flakes and zipped his jacket up to his chin. He pulled his laptop from his backpack to continue his notes on the extinction of the non-avian dinosaurs, climate change, and the effect it had on the evolution of premammalian creatures like Mary. He focused especially on the change in teeth to accommodate a more varied diet. The work absorbed him, distracting him from thinking about the dead man, his throbbing ankle, and the woman who had left him.

Paleontology was a science of big theories and big personalities. Chap's belief, supported by years of research in the field, in the lab, and in the library closely reading the work of those who had explored the issue before, was that a combination of factors had led to the rise of mammals. Ever since he'd seen the famous jawbone of *Shashajaia bermani*, he'd realized that life had its own intriguingly complex and unexpected ways of changing, adapting, surviving. And what was true of the big picture was true in the microcosm of his own life.

He looked out toward the pair of flat buttes, the Bears Ears Buttes standing deep blue against the ominous gray winter sky, and reminded himself that his work mattered. He couldn't allow even a home invasion and a dead man to stop his progress.

This landscape was so rich in multilayered fossils that it inspired him to write. When the weather cooperated, he liked writing outside even more than working in the bone shop, despite the time he'd spent making that room special. Nothing could compete with nature itself at Bears Ears.

But he couldn't forget what had happened at his house. He knew he had detractors, but he'd never seen them as life-threatening. He hadn't taken the ugly phone calls, or even the slashed tires, as putting his life in jeopardy. Until now. Until they came for his dear Mary.

Chap considered Bears Ears a treasure trove for fossils, especially from the final stages of the late Paleozoic ice age. The area reminded him of a great library, a library not of books and papers but of bones, teeth, scales, and claws preserved in stone, an archive of animals and plants that had been alive during the final stages of the late Paleozoic era.

Chap typed until his fingers grew too cold to function, then closed the laptop. He shoved his hands into his pockets and hobbled carefully along

the rocks to get his blood and brain stirring again.
The air smelled of cold moisture. He was glad he
had his favorite hat with the warm furry flaps that
tied under his chin. He wondered what was taking
Roper so long. His ankle ached, and every unexpected sound made him wonder if whoever broke
into his home had, by some fluke, tracked him to
the cave. When his hands had warmed enough, he
went back to writing.

After two hours the battery died, and Chapman
Dulles put the laptop away. Roper Black had not
arrived, and his ankle looked like a bizarre sau-
sage. Even though Roper had given him notice,
the man was on the payroll for another week or
so, and was relentlessly reliable. Chap still hoped
he might be able to persuade the young man to
continue working for him.

He studied the overcast sky. If Roper hadn't
shown up by sunset, he would decide if he should
try to return to the car alone or hunker down to
spend the night in the cave. He had extra water,
more warm clothes, and food in his pack, and he
had done more than his share of winter camping.
His decision would depend on the severity of the
storm and his pain level. In any case, he would
eventually drive to an area with phone service, call
Roper to learn what had delayed him, and then
head to the sheriff's office to straighten things out.

## 19

Jim Chee was irritated.

He'd gotten Bernie's message about how she might postpone leaving for her mother's place until he returned. Now he was back at the motel, and she was gone. He knew Gillman had asked her to drive to Valley of the Gods to check on the parked vehicle. But honestly, how long could that take?

Detective Parker had dropped him at the Bluff Inn after a chilly and chilling motorcycle ride. He quickly packed his things and was ready to go. All he needed was his wife and their truck. He sat on the bed. Turned on the TV. Turned it off again. He paced to the window and looked out at the nearly deserted parking lot, noting the absence of Jessica's van. He returned and sat again, bored and frustrated.

After a few moments, he smiled at himself. After all the silent grousing and complaining he had done about his lack of quiet time to think, to figure out his future, now here he sat with unplanned spare moments—and he didn't know what to do with them.

He took a deep breath and then another. He remembered the initial reason, the real reason, he'd come to Bears Ears. The yearning for peace and a renewed spiritual connection had driven him here. That was before his new police captain provided the incentive of fundraising work to make it a business trip, too.

He'd received an invitation from Desmond Grayhair, a real letter in an envelope with a stamp. Hosteen Grayhair had asked him to join a sweat bath and then assist with gathering sacred items for a jish, the leather medicine bundle that was a source of protection and a repository of some of a healer's tools.

Chee viewed his jish in a way vaguely parallel to how some of his school friends from their days at St. Michael's thought of St. Christopher medals. One boy told him the medal reminded the saint to ask God to keep him safe while traveling. For Chee, the jish served a related purpose, invoking the help of the Diyin Diné. As a policeman, he always had his medicine bundle. Bernie and most of the officers he served with did too.

Now that he had no excuses for not contemplating his future, he considered what had happened since he and Bernie had come to Bears Ears:

He joined a sweat lodge with a well-respected hatáálii and leader in the Navajo Mountain community, an area known for its medicine people.

His wife went for a hike in an area the
hatáálii suggested she visit.

She could have been killed by a person in a
truck who shot a hole in her jacket. But she
escaped unharmed.

On her way back to the motel, Bernie delivered a baby.

The husband of the woman in the adjoin-
ing motel room was found dead along the
highway.

An incident at the home of a paleontologist
who wanted to help with a memorial for
slain Navajo police officers left an unknown man dead there.

The paleontologist seemed to have disappeared.

Bernie had found a car that might belong to
the missing man.

And now, she who is never late was late.

He walked to the window again, as if looking
into the parking lot would make his sweet wife
appear. Hosteen Grayhair had suggested that
because Bernie was a major part of his life, she
played a role in his decision about taking Chee on
as an apprentice. So when Chee planned the trip
to Bears Ears, he'd encouraged Bernie to come,
reminding her of Grayhair's request. It pleased
Chee that the healer had asked to speak to Bernie,
but he was disappointed that they chatted only
briefly before the old man nudged her toward a
sunset hike in Valley of the Gods. And that, of
course, was where the trip had switched from
mini vacation to attempted murder. The next

morning he'd met Roper Black, encountered the body of a man shot in the back, and then put on his investigator hat.

It gave him a sense of deep satisfaction to use his knowledge of crime solving to help with a case and to mentor a potential officer. He could see Black's enormous potential.

He'd asked Black to call him when he heard from Chap so they could talk before he and Bernie left for Shiprock. But Black hadn't called. Chee wanted to make good use of his time while waiting for Bernie, so he dialed Black. No answer. He left a message.

A seed of worry for Roper Black and Chap planted itself in his brain. And still no Bernie; her absence was his biggest concern. Then his phone rang.

"Hey there, Cheeseburger. How's it going?"

"Fine. I'm waiting for your sister to show up." And getting anxious about that, he thought, but he switched to Darleen herself. "How's life with you?"

"Oh, OK, I guess." But his sister-in-law sounded unsettled, which had been less common after Slim had reentered her life and she'd decided, again, to change career plans.

"Come on. What's up?"

"Well, you know, this is none of my business, but Sister just told me you might not be coming for dinner."

This was news to him. He listened.

"I know something's been bothering her," Darleen said, "but she said it isn't anything Mama or I said, and she was practically crying, and she got so upset she hung up. So, ah . . ." The phone went quiet, then Darleen sounded subdued. "Never mind. This is too dumb and awkward. I'm just trying to figure things out, you know?"

"I know. Me too."

"She's really upset. Something major. I'm worried. Did she tell you what it is? Am I driving her crazy?"

"No." He had his suspicions, but Bernie hadn't spoken to him about the issue. He was tempted to add, "No more than you ever do," but Darleen seemed more serious than usual. "Your sister worries about you and your mother, but we all know that's who she is. Nothing new in that."

"And Mama and I worry about her. And where does it get us, bro? Nowhere. Sister worries about you, too, Cheeseburger." She waited a beat. "Is everything OK between you two?"

"Yes." He said it with conviction, knowing that even a solid marriage was subject to an occasional tremor. "From what I can tell, she's reevaluating a lot of things. She'll share what she's comfortable sharing when she's ready. Give her some space." Chee took a breath. "How is your mother today?"

"Oh, she's more Mama than usual. Asking me if Slim and I are going to get married. Asking me to tell Bernie she should have a baby." Darleen chuckled. "I don't know why Mama thinks any of this is her business."

"What's this about you getting married?"

Darleen was speechless for a moment. "It's complicated, just an idea. But thank goodness we wouldn't have to deal with any of that clan stuff."

Chee knew what "clan stuff" meant: in the traditional Navajo way of thinking, marriage or sexual relations among people who shared the same clan or clans was highly discouraged.

Darleen diverted the conversation to a safer, less personal topic. "What's the storm doing out that way?"

"The snow is sticking here, and coming down hard. It's gorgeous, but I would have preferred that it waited until we were back home." Chee heard a ruckus in the background.

"Hold on." Darleen clanked the phone down.

She was back more quickly than he'd expected. "Bidziil is barking like crazy. That's Mrs. Darkwater's dog. She and Mama . . . Oh, it's complicated."

"Bidziil?"

"Yeah. That's what Mrs. Darkwater calls him after he saved her life. I've got to go. Don't worry, OK?"

"You either. We'll talk later."

And Darleen was gone.

He still held the phone in his hand, and with a fresh tidbit of news, he called Bernie's number again. Nothing.

Out of frustration, he called Gillman.

"Chee? You still helping Parker? Or are you back in Shiprock?"

"Here, waiting for my wife to drive up with the truck. She copied me on a group text. Evidently you asked her to check on a suspicious vehicle?"

"That's right. I haven't heard from her yet." Gillman paused. "Are you still at Chap's place?"

"No. I left with Parker."

"And no Chap by the time you guys headed out?"

"Right. Black went to look for him. Evidently he knows his boss's favorite hideout."

"Hideout, huh?" Gillman chuckled. "Good choice of word."

"Based on what Black said, it's a place where he's found some fossils, a place he goes to concentrate, you know, to hide out from the world so he can do his work."

"Right." Gillman made a sound between a laugh and a snort. "I think either Chap is dead because he confronted those guys who broke in, or he's on the run because he shot an unarmed man. Or maybe he's hunkered down somewhere. Hiding from the law or the bad guys, if there are any, and waiting for the storm to pass. And maybe Roper is helping. Too many maybes."

"Confusing. Complicated. Lots of scenarios. Seems about right to me for this stage in the investigation." Chee chuckled. "Sounds like you've got the bases covered."

The sheriff cleared his throat. "Unless I hear from Chap, we'll put out a BOLO when we get the info on the car from Bernie. And before you ask, we're busy with the storm—the roads in the northern part of the county are already a mess."

Chee said, "She identified a guy named Donray with a skull tattoo as the man who drove the truck that tried to kill her and threatened a little girl. What do you know about that Donray guy?"

"Officer Manuelito mentioned the name to

me, too. It's not familiar. That's a good thing. Means we haven't arrested him, or at least not very often."

"Where was the car?"

Gillman told him. "That road into Valley of the Gods can get tricky with snow, and it's coming down pretty good now. Sometimes the BLM closes it so they don't have to haul cars out of the drifts. What is she driving?"

"Our truck. It's solid, and she's a good driver. Ask her to text me when you hear from her, OK?"

"Sure thing." Gillman changed the subject. "Did you and Detective Parker come to any conclusions about what happened out there?"

"Parker can speak for himself. There was a break-in, and it looks to me like whoever did it wanted something very specific. As you saw, the only real disturbance was in Dulles's workshop."

"I heard that a laptop and some files are missing."

"Black thinks so. And something else, bones or other fossils encased in plaster, was hauled away. This wasn't a random crime."

"Agreed. And before you ask, no ID yet on the dead guy and no results yet on the fingerprints."

Chee forced himself to picture the body sprawled in the driveway beyond the porch. "As I remember, the dead man didn't have a skull tattoo. Is that right?"

The sheriff seemed to be thinking. "I don't remember any tattoos, old scars, anything like that that could help identify him except for some missing fingers."

"Will you follow up on Donray?"

"Already in the works. I've been doing this job awhile, Lieutenant. I know my way around the block. You can relax, OK?"

But Chee couldn't. He paced outside in the snow for a few minutes, thinking. When he figured out a plan, he went back in to warm up and called Roper Black again. It was a long shot, but he had nothing to lose and time on his hands.

Black answered on the second ring. Chee heard a baby crying in the background.

"Hey, there. I just talked to Gillman, and we were wondering about Chap. Any news?"

"No. But I had my phone off because of the baby. Just turned it on to call the midwife, and there you were."

"Did you see an abandoned car along the road to Valley of the Gods?"

"No."

Chee heard a deep exhale.

"I haven't looked for Chap yet."

Chee knew more than an hour had passed since Black had zoomed away from his boss's house. "Why? What's the matter?"

It took Black a few moments to answer. "Everything. Something's wrong with the baby. She's crying and then falls asleep and then wakes up crying. She won't nurse. Hannah is weak from the delivery. She looks so tired. It breaks my heart."

Chee hadn't expected Black's vulnerability. It left him speechless for a moment, and Black filled in the space.

"And I let Chap down. I need to find him, to help him, but I can't leave my wife and my daughter. My mother-in-law, Hannah's mom, is coming, but she can't make it until tomorrow. I've got to talk to our midwife. This all happened so quickly."

"I don't know anything much about babies, but I know a little bit about being married. You're where you need to be, and help is on the way. Call the midwife as soon as I hang up."

"I really blew it. I should have been here with Hannah instead of at Chap's house. I never should have left her alone so soon after the baby came. And I blew it with Chap too. I should have found a substitute to fill in for me. I mentioned it, and he said no. I should have insisted."

Chee said, "I can't help with your daughter, but I can help with Chap. Just tell me where to look."

And he did.

"There's one more thing." Black paused a moment. "Chap thought this was unnecessary, but we set up a safe word, in case he ever got kidnapped or who knows what. One of us says 'Rambo,' like in a sentence, and if the other says 'Right,' that means there's a dangerous situation."

"Rambo?"

"Yes. Rambo and right. We never used it. If you need it, I hope Chap remembers. I'll call Gillman and tell him you're headed out that way to look for Chap."

"Thanks. And good luck with the little one."

Chee was painfully aware that Bernie had the truck, and he had no transportation. He was stranded at the motel.

After he ended the call, he phoned the BLM and learned that Becenti and Kingsley were both out. Then he bundled up and headed to the motel office. He'd seen the owner's vehicle, a 2016 Ford F-150, parked beside the building, a reliable truck for rough roads and bad weather. Walter, the owner, had given him the motel's military discount when Chee told him he was a cop. He was hoping he could appeal to the gentleman's generous nature again.

The man looked puzzled. "Why? What happened to your truck?"

Chee explained.

"Maybe Jessica can help."

"She's not around now. I'm worried about a person who likes to hike in Valley of the Gods and seems to have disappeared there. You know, with the weather changing, that could be dangerous."

"Why don't you ask the sheriff or the BLM dudes to go out there?"

"I couldn't reach anyone at the BLM, and the sheriff is busy with snowy roads in the north part of the county. I'd be glad to pay you a rental fee for the Ford."

He could see Walter thinking about it.

"If this is too much of an inconvenience, is there another place I could get a car right now? You know, we police are reputable." Usually, at least, he thought. He had worked with surprisingly few lemons. "My wife is out there, too. I want to check on her."

"Well, OK. You can use the truck, although I haven't gotten around to giving it snow tires yet. Look at how the storm is settling in. I bet your honey is already on the way back."

Walter took the truck key out of his pocket and

studied it. "I should show you a few things about Harrison. That's what I call him, you know? Driving someone else's vehicle can be kinda tricky if you aren't used to it."

"Thanks for loaning it to me. I'm sure I can figure it out."

Instead of sensing Chee's urgency, Walter seemed to be settling in for car talk. "Now, Harrison looks good, but he isn't totally new, 67,345 miles. He's yours this afternoon because I like to do my part to keep America safe. I'm a big supporter of you guys. You policemen and the lady cops. My ex-brother-in-law is a highway patrol officer out in Grand Junction. You know where that is?"

"Colorado."

"Right. Well, anyway, he always says—"

Chee, who hated to interrupt, interrupted. "Can we walk to the truck while you tell the story? I need to start looking for Bernie before the weather gets worse."

"Sure thing, Officer. That's a good idea."

Even with Chee's prodding, it took Walter five minutes to explain Harrison's inner workings. Not a lot of time in the average day, but an eternity for a man in a hurry.

"If you see my wife and our truck pull in here, will you tell her to stay here until I get back?"

"Sure. When will that be?"

Chee shrugged. "I don't know. As soon as I can."

Walter grinned. "You know, I saw your lady. She looks strong and smart, and you told me she's a cop. I don't think you have to worry about her."

Chee hoped Walter was right about that. He

drove faster than he normally would have in a
vehicle that was new to him and with the snow
limiting visibility. He watched for Bernie approaching from the other direction, but there was
no traffic. The frosting of pure white made the
deep red color of the stone more dramatic, the
formations even more formidable. Chee focused
on the road and thought about Chap, and then
about Bernie and what could have caused the delay. She was a good driver, and their truck was well
maintained. He knew he probably didn't need to
be concerned, but he worried anyway. Perhaps
something beyond her control had happened—a
collision with a deer, an obstacle in the road she
couldn't avoid that damaged the truck, a blowout?
Or worse, perhaps she'd run into the two guys
who had tried to kill her.

The Valley of the Gods road was a loop of
seventeen miles, with two entrances. She could
be leaving at one end while he was entering the
other. After about ten miles of driving Harrison,
he spotted their truck parked just off the Valley
of the Gods road. He exhaled with relief. This
was roughly the same place Black had told him
Chap liked to park and hike to look for fossils.
Interesting, Chee thought, and convenient that
Bernie would have parked here, but where was
she now?

He was relieved not to see Chap's car. The
man must have gone somewhere else, he thought,
perhaps back to his house, where he was dealing
with the damaged door and the mess in the bone
shop.

He parked the Ford behind their truck. All its

tires were inflated, and he saw no damage that indicated an accident. He wondered if the truck had died, and that was why Bernie abandoned it. He had his keys, but it wasn't locked. He climbed in, his concern for Bernie escalating. He knew his wife never left a vehicle unlocked. He started the engine with no problem. No worrisome dash lights came on. He looked around and saw that she hadn't left a note or her backpack.

There was barely any snow on the road's shoulder in front of the truck. Whatever vehicle had been there—perhaps the car she'd come to investigate—was gone. If the vehicle was Chap's, perhaps Bernie had driven him to the sheriff's office to talk about the incident that left a man dead. Or to the hospital, if necessary.

He liked that scenario, although it didn't explain why Bernie would have taken Chap's cold car instead of their warm truck, and why she'd left the truck unlocked.

He shouted her name. Waited. Called again. And again. If she had walked from the truck for a closer look at the stone monuments here, the snow now covered her tracks. He moved away from the truck in a direction he thought most logical and called again. Walked another few minutes and called again. With each lack of response, his worry increased. He didn't understand what prompted evil, despite his experience with it as a cop, but he had seen enough of it to know it was both real and pervasive. Bernie was strong and smart, but she wasn't invincible.

The fifth time he yelled out, he heard a voice call back from the rocky hillside. "Hey, whoever you are! I'm not Bernie, but I'm freezing my como se llama off. I could use some help."

"I'm Jim Chee, Navajo Police. If you're Chap, Roper Black asked me to come look for you. If you're not Chap, you're one lucky joker, because a big storm is headed this way."

When the man didn't respond, it dawned on Chee that this might be a trap. The people who invaded Chap's house could have found him here. They could be threatening him for whatever reason had prompted them to break down Chap's front door.

Finding Bernie and protecting his own life were Chee's main jobs. But if the person who called out to him was in jeopardy, he couldn't just walk away.

"Sir? I need directions if you want me to help you."

"You in uniform, Chee?"

"No. But I've got ID." Then the idea came to him. "I'm not Rambo, you know."

The man's voice changed. "OK, then, come ahead. I'm not saying 'right' because I'm not in danger from anything except my own poor balance. Follow the ridge until you see the greenish sandstone ledge. I'll be able to spot you from there. Be careful. The snow makes things slicker."

"Have you seen a woman in a red cap hiking out here?"

"No way. Bad day for a hike."

Chee had to watch his footing, which gave him more appreciation for Chap's strength, agility, and sense of balance. He stopped when he reached what he thought was the ledge the man had mentioned and called again. "Now what?"

"Where are you?"

"I'm standing at the ledge you mentioned. Who are you?"

"Chapman Dulles, at your service. I think you've figured that out. Why didn't Roper come?"

"There's a problem at home. He asked me to drive out here and make sure you were OK." Chee considered giving Chap the story of the baby and Bernie's role in the delivery, but he decided that could wait until they were both sitting in the warm truck.

"I'm mostly all right. But I tweaked an ankle on the way up, and now it's the size of my calf and still swelling. I don't think I can climb down without help." Chap's voice sounded scratchy. "And I'm nervous. Terrified, actually. Do you know about the dead man at my house?"

"Yes. Who is he?"

"A man who used to work for me."

"Did you shoot him?"

"No." Chap answered without hesitation. "I assume whoever broke into my home killed the poor man. That's why I'm here, and why I'm still shaky."

Chee waited for him to say more.

"But you weren't calling for me, you were calling for Bernie. Who is he?"

"Well, he's a she."

Chap laughed. "Sorry. So who is Bernie?"

"Bernadette. My wife. Our truck is down there, but she's not." He wasn't inclined to say more.

"Why didn't you go to the police after that incident at your house?"

"I knew Roper's 911 system would notify them. There's more to it. A long story. But you're concerned about your wife. Go look for her. Then come back and help me hike out. We can talk then."

"Are you sure?"

"Yes. I'm fine here, enjoying the view and not in immediate danger. I've got plenty of food and water."

"Promise you won't try to climb down without me."

"I promise. Don't worry. I'm not going down to my car or anywhere else on this ankle, and my heart has been feeling the stress too."

"I'll get back as soon as I can. Where is your car?"

"It's in the shop. I had to get some loaner wheels, the little white Lexus on the road down there. Go to your wife." Chap's voice had faded into a hoarse croak. "And call Roper for me."

"OK, then. I'll be back before dark." Chee decided not to tell Chap that the white Lexus he'd left on the road was gone. That bad news could wait. He had another thought. "Is that a burial cave?"

"No, nothing like that."

For the first time since he'd climbed the ridge, Chee noticed how lovely it was, even in a snowstorm. Beauty surrounded him. He thought about the protective spirit of the bears and the idea that the bones of their long, long, long ago ancestors slept in these rocks. He let the cold air fill his lungs and smiled. He envisioned Bernie with a bit of time to relax, also breathing in the peace of this fine country.

On the way back down, he noticed that new snow had nearly buried his tracks. He crossed the road and began yelling for Bernie, again with silence as the only response. Finally he climbed into Harrison, silently thanking Walter for the loan of his vehicle, and drove down the road, stopping to shout and then driving on, continuing his search for Bernie.

# 20

The darkness and lack of fresh air grabbed Bernie's attention first. Then came the pain as her head hit the floor and bounced up again. She braced her legs against something hard to keep her skull from another bump and stop herself getting tossed sideways. She could see light seeping in from the outside. Then she noticed the smell of rubber and new carpet. For a split second she thought she might be having a scary na'iidzeeł, a dream so disturbing she would call it a nightmare. But then she remembered holding Donray at gunpoint and hearing Kingsley come up behind her. To help her, she'd thought. But she'd read the situation wrong.

She was locked in the trunk of a car, she realized. Since Donray and Kingsley drove trucks, it had to be Chap's Lexus loaner that was being towed. They hadn't bound her hands or feet. Maybe Kingsley thought the blow had killed her.

Bernie couldn't tug her jacket—Chee's extra jacket, which she'd borrowed from the truck—up close enough to insulate her torso against the frigid draft coming through the trunk's floor. It seemed to be stuck on something. One good thing about being short was that she had a bit of room to readjust herself in a tight spot. She maneuvered until she figured out that the trunk lid had come down on the bottom of the jacket. The more she squirmed, the tighter it grew around her, restricting the movement of her arms.

She hoped the coat stuck out of the trunk, and someone like Chee or Gillman or Becenti would see it flapping like a flag and get curious enough to ask Donray about it. But would they even notice it in a snowstorm?

The effort of reaching the bottom of the jacket, along with the car's motion and the pain in her upper body, had made her nauseous. No use wasting energy. She lay as still as possible.

Her head ached, and she closed her eyes. She could use this time while the car was in motion to come up with a plan. If she could think clearly, she might be able to save her own life.

She heard the sound of a truck approaching, then pulling up alongside the towed Lexus. A horn blasted, and she heard Donray swearing loudly out the window and finally rolling to a stop. She listened to the doors opening and footsteps squeaking in the snow.

Then voices. One sounded like Jim Chee's, hot with anger. Good, she thought. Amazing.

"What do you mean, you haven't seen her? That's our truck parked right where you towed this car from."

She heard Kingsley's lie. "I haven't seen her. I don't know what you're talking about. Her truck wasn't there when we came down here to tow out the Lexus." Kingsley's voice sounded close, and Bernie realized that she was standing next to the car being towed—the car that had the trunk that contained her. "Isn't that right, Donray?"

Donray laughed. "That little gal is something else. You ought to keep a better eye on her. She likes to poke around in things that aren't her business, and she's got a mouth on her, too."

"Don't talk about my wife like that. Tell me where she is."

"Your wife, huh? Well, since no one made you God, I'll say what I want, Indian. Move that truck so we can get this car outta here before I push you off the road."

She expected Chee's response, but instead she heard Kingsley's voice, a touch of the peacemaker in it. "Chee, do what he wants. This is a safety procedure and official BLM business. I have to make sure this vehicle gets towed off this road before the weather gets any worse."

Her husband's voice was firm. "No. This is the car Sheriff Gillman asked Bernie to check on. Ranger Kingsley, you realize you have to cooperate. Where's Officer Manuelito?"

Bernie started to make noise, shouting for help, kicking the inside of the well-insulated trunk with the hard soles of her shoes.

"No idea. I'm not her keeper, you know?" Kingsley sounded put out. "I'm in charge here, and Donray works for the BLM as a towing service. If you understood what was good for you, you'd shut up and drive off."

"Ranger, here's what's going to happen. Donray

will tow this car to that pullout and leave it and the dolly off the main road until Gillman gets here. That satisfies the safety issue. And then you both will help me find Officer Manuelito."

Bernie realized that Chee couldn't hear the racket she made. Maybe the truck engines were idling. The gusty wind carried off the others' voices now; they were too far away for her to overhear the conversation. She stopped, saving her percussion for when someone moved closer. Then she heard Kingsley shout, "Donray, you deal with this. I'm checking the vehicle to make sure it's secure." Then came the sound of Kingsley's footsteps walking away.

Now only the cold howl of the wind penetrated her cage. When the gusts stopped for a moment, she picked out Donray's voice, less confrontational. "OK, Chee, here's the deal. I'll tell you where your wife is if you promise that nothing serious will come down on me."

"What do you mean?"

"I'm just the hired help, you know? Things got out of hand."

"Donray, what are you doing?" Kingsley yelled at him. "I told you to take care of this."

Chee said, "Where's Bernie?"

"First a deal, then my information. You know, Kingsley has—"

A gunshot cut off his words. It was followed quickly by another. She heard someone tumble into the fresh snow.

Then, to her relief, she heard Chee's voice from behind the car. "Kingsley, drop your weapon."

Silence again, and then two more shots in quick

succession. Bernie felt the impact as a bullet struck the car, and then a rush of gratitude that it hadn't found her in the trunk.

She heard a deep moan and hoped with all her heart that it wasn't Chee. Then silence outside.

She knew there should be a lever to open the trunk from inside, but the way the trunk lid had come down on the coat made it impossible for her to lift her hands. She made the biggest ruckus she could, and waited for someone to find her.

If Kingsley opened the trunk, she would face the woman head-on and fight as hard as she could for her life. If it came to defeat, she would die bravely, a warrior.

She wasn't afraid anymore, she realized. The injustice of being knocked out by a bad woman and locked in a trunk made her furious. And she had more reasons to be angry. She started to yell, to rage against the life-changing loss of innocence of Crystal, the Zonnie girl. She raged against Mama's diminished capacity, against her sweet sister's ongoing struggles, and finally against her own deeply personal loss.

Her yells moved into a fierce wail. She felt like a bear in a cage, desperate to escape.

She became aware of a noise outside the car. She stopped to listen.

The sound was Chee's voice, deep and gentle above the trunk lid.

"Sweetheart, I'm going to get you out of there. Are you hurt?"

"Not much. How about you? Did you get shot?"

"No. I'm OK. Better now that I've found you."

She listened as he walked toward the front of

the car and heard the door open. Then came a clicking sound, and she realized the trunk lid had unlatched. It rose toward the sky, letting in light and a swirl of snowflakes. The fresh, cold air was a tonic for her body and brain. She moved her legs to the edge of the trunk, and then Chee was back, smiling at her, touching her ankle. "Would you like a hand to sit up?"

"Yes." It had always been hard for her to ask for help, but now the words came easily. "I'd like to get out of here and into the fresh air. Ahéhee."

"Before you get out, you see that handle?"

It was bright yellow and had been out of her reach. "Yes."

"If this ever happens again, that's the interior trunk lid release. Newer cars all have them." He smiled at her. "I heard you yelling. You saved your own life."

When she stood, she began to shake, and he wrapped his strong arms around her. She would not fall, she told herself. And in her love, this good man wouldn't fall either.

After a while, Chee asked her what had happened. She gave him a fortune-cookie version.

"The man driving the truck towing this car, Donray, is the same man who tried to run over me yesterday. Kingsley was working with him, and she seemed to be in charge. I should have—"

He put a finger to her lips. "You don't have to worry about them now. The woman ranger is dead. I had to shoot her before she killed me."

They stood together in the cold while she absorbed the news. When he spoke again, his voice was softer.

"I checked to make sure and then moved her body off the road and covered it. When I lifted the ranger, I noticed some yellow sand on her boots. I could barely see it because of the snow. It might tie her to the break-in at Chap's place."

"She's dead?" As much death as she'd seen as a police officer, it never sat well with Bernie, and she knew each death left a scar on the officer involved in the situation.

Chee nodded. "She shot the man who drove the truck because he was about to tell me where you were and what had happened to you. He's alive but bleeding. The bullet hit him in the shoulder. Come with me to check on him."

"Give me a minute to collect my thoughts."

Bernie watched the lightly falling snow and took several breaths of fresh December air, all the way to the bottom pockets of her lungs. The wind was calm now.

Chee kept his arm around her as they walked down the dirt road toward Donray and the truck. "Officer Manuelito, what have we gotten ourselves into? What happened that was worth two deaths?"

"I can't figure it out either, but I do know it's bigger than the woman you shot or Donray. They are a piece of the puzzle, but that ranger is new here. She wouldn't understand the way witchcraft can terrify people."

Bernie noticed that her stiffness from being locked in the trunk was fading as they moved, and she could think past the headache Kingsley had left when she hit her from behind. "What's the update on the break-in at Chapman Dulles's house and the dead man there?"

"Nothing much yet. I spoke to Roper Black, who told me where to find his boss. I found Chap hiding in the rocks. They had a safe word in case something terrible happened, and Black shared that with me."

Bernie stood a little taller. "Did Roper mention how the baby is doing?"

Chee nodded and squeezed her a little tighter. "He said she was crying, and he was calling the midwife to help. I think babies do a lot of crying, especially early on, but I'm glad he's calling in reinforcements."

They found Donray on the ground near his truck. Bernie noticed blood on his jacket. He looked cold, she thought. His eyes were closed.

Chee nudged the sole of one of Donray's boots; he flinched and looked up. Snow had accumulated on his jacket.

"So you're still alive."

The man groaned. Chee noticed him pawing the snow. "If you're worried about your gun, I've got it, unloaded and secured. Let me look at the place where the ranger shot you. I want to see how bad it is."

Donray cooperated. Chee pushed his jacket and shirt aside to look at the wound. He motioned to Bernie. "Can you bring the first-aid kit from the truck?"

When Bernie returned, Chee used gauze with pressure to stop the bleeding. "Take a look at this. Is it as serious as I think it is?" He winked at her.

She wasn't an expert, but it seemed as though the bullet had penetrated a fleshy part of Donray's torso near the armpit and passed through the flesh and his coat without doing serious harm. Painful, but not life-threatening.

"I see." She hoped she sounded concerned. "Wow."

"What? How bad is it?" Donray's voice was worried.

Bernie just shook her head. The wound needed medical attention, but the treatment they had provided sufficed for now. "I'd rather not talk about it."

Donray swore as he pushed himself to sitting, leaning against a truck tire. He gave Bernie a hard look. "I thought Kingsley hurt you so bad you'd still be in that trunk. Not standing here."

"I'm tough. I'm surprised the BLM officer shot you. Sounded to me like you two were a team."

"She wanted to shoot you, too, after she hit you on the head. But I knew it would be harder for us to clean and sell the car with your blood in the trunk. So I told her I'd handle it, that I'd take care of you." Donray looked at her. "I would have let you live so you could have kept your word about helping me with that girl's family. With the restitution. You meant that, right?"

"Right. But you have to cooperate now."

"I am. I already saved your life."

Bernie saw that the bloodstain on Donray's jacket had grown no larger, and that Chee had secured his hands with the zip ties she'd seen in the truck.

"You're lucky she wasn't a better shot, Donray. Kingsley could have killed you."

"Yeah. Now I get to freeze here while I bleed to death. Lucky, right?"

"I call that bad luck." Bernie noticed that his face looked a bit grayer. "But it doesn't have to be that way."

"You and I need to talk." Chee sounded commanding, serious. "So here's the deal. We can take you now and get treatment for that wound, and some of those meds that make the pain go away. Or Bernie and I can hike back into the hills and rescue Chap first. We can't leave him up in that cave to die of exposure. The temperature is dropping, the snow is piling up. The ground isn't getting any warmer. What happens next is up to you and the information you give us."

"What kinda information?"

"Let's start with who you and Kingsley work for."

He shrugged. "I worked for Kingsley, and she paid me cash for each job. I thought you already knew that she worked for the BLM."

"Come on. What else?" Bernie jumped in. "Who pays you to drive around an excavation and scare people?"

"I get a check from Dinostar for doing security, if that's what you mean."

"Dinostar?" Chee wrinkled his forehead. "What's that?"

Donray shrugged. "The company that pays me to guard the place they are digging. They've got a permit or something."

"Who's they?"

"The honcho is a tall guy named Chris." He

winced as he adjusted himself. "It's cold out here, man, and where she shot me hurts bad."

"What's going on out here that's so secret?" Bernie asked.

"I don't know. They don't pay me to be nosy."

Donray had begun shivering, Bernie noticed. "Earlier today, you told me you worked for Chap. Which is it?"

"Chap hired me. But then he left Dinostar, so now they pay me, not him. Kingsley has used BLM money for me to tow a car out here now and then. That's all I've got."

Chee examined Donray's bound wrists and then squatted down close to his face. "If you'd like to stay alive, you ought to talk to us. Your fingernails have turned blue with cold. As the temperature drops and the snow gets heavier, in about an hour you'll be too cold to talk, too cold to think. They call that hypothermia. It's a slow way to die."

"But better than being knocked unconscious and trapped in the trunk of a car." Bernie's voice was deadly calm. "You've probably lost enough blood now that you'll freeze pretty quick. Time to talk while you still can. Wanna try again?"

Donray said nothing.

Bernie opened the door to the truck. "I'm cold. I ought to start this truck. I bet you've got a good heater in here. I might take this bad boy for a drive in the snow. Glad you left the keys in here, buddy."

Chee noticed the man's new tension. "Let's talk. If you tell me what's going on with Dinostar and why they need you to keep people away, I might ask Bernie not to drive off in your truck."

"I swear they don't tell me nothin'. I figured it had something to do with mining, some kind of cover-up for illegal exploration. There's uranium all around out here. My old man worked in the mines."

Bernie returned. "Nice truck. I'm letting it warm up before I take it for a spin."

Chee continued to his questioning. "What do you know about the incident today at Chap's house?"

"Kingsley told me somebody got killed out there." Donray shivered again. "I got no beef with Chap. He treated me fair. What's all this about, man? You gonna just let me freeze to death?"

"What else about Dinostar?"

"OK. Chris said Dinostar fired Chap. He told me to keep Chap away from the site because he was mad and might try stuff to get even. Not to let him in, no matter what bull he gave me." Donray made a snorting sound and then grimaced with pain. "Chap knows this country like the back of his hand. He'll go where he wants."

"Chris mentioned that Chap wasn't with Dinostar anymore," Bernie said, "but he made it sound like a mutual thing. He never mentioned firing him."

"I'm saying what I heard."

"I haven't met Chris." Chee brushed the snow off his shoulder, noticing that the flakes were melting on Donray's pants, making damp spots that would eventually freeze. "Tell me more about this guy you work for."

"Dinostar, that's who writes the checks. Chris works for them, along with Kyle and Jessica. But he's the boss out here."

Bernie jumped in. "So did Chris tell you to damage those petroglyphs?"

"Yeah, but he said it was Jessica's idea, to keep Navajos like you guys away. It bothered me, but a job's a job."

"Did Chris tell you and Kingsley to steal Chap's car?"

"Huh?"

"The expensive-looking white sedan you were towing."

Donray shrugged. "Kingsley said we should take it. That's all I know. Let me sit in the truck, for God's sake. I saved your wife's life."

Bernie spoke up. "How did she know that car was here?"

"I told her. I saw it parked when I drove by this morning, checking things out. I figured it musta broke down or somethin', so I called Kingsley and said I'd tow it for the regular fee."

Bernie raised her voice. "You're dying, and you're still lying. You were stealing that car."

Chee stood and motioned to Bernie. "Let's go find Chap." They started to walk away.

"Wait. I'll talk. Just let me warm up in the truck."

"After you tell the truth."

"Better hurry." Bernie tugged her hat over her ears. "It's getting colder. Snowing harder too."

Donray quivered with the cold.

By the look on his face and the tone of his voice, Chee sensed that Donray was telling the truth. Bernie felt a drop of sympathy for him because he had left her alive, but she soaked it up with the memory of Lilakai's terrified niece.

Donray shivered again. It was time to move him into the cab of his warmer truck.

After she'd helped Chee bring the injured man inside, Bernie slid behind the truck's steering wheel. Chee used the zip ties to bind Donray's ankles and fastened his wrists to the doorframe. The man slumped against the seat.

The truck had a high-powered heater, and Chee stood close for a moment, enjoying the warmth. Bernie could tell from her husband's posture that something bothered him.

"What's on your mind?"

He smiled. "It's something good, actually. I really do have to help Chap climb down from the cliffs. I need to do that now so we can leave."

"Did Chap shoot the dead man at his house?"

"He says no. And he believes whoever killed that guy probably would have killed him too. That's why he's hiding. He's back up the road about a mile and hunkered down in a cave. I have to hike in and help him because he injured his ankle. If all goes well, I'll be back in an hour. We'll come back in our truck where you left it."

"You go. I'll stay with Donray and the dead one out there until you get back, and then we can drive to Bluff together. But if it looks like Donray needs immediate care, I'll need to risk heading out in this truck."

Chee nodded. "I saw those bald tires. If you have to leave, when you have phone service, tell Becenti and Gillman about the dead ranger."

"Sure."

"And keep an eye on the weather. And be extra careful."

"I will." An idea occurred to her. "Kingsley's phone is in the car. I want to secure it for Gillman in case it has evidence his investigation might need." They both knew extended freezing temperature didn't work well with electronics. "Stay here with Donray, and warm up a little before you go into the cold."

Chee climbed in.

Bernie trudged back through the snow to the fancy new sedan attached to Donray's truck. She saw Kingsley's phone on the leather passenger seat. She took a picture of it in place, then tried the doors and found them unlocked.

Once she had the door open, Bernie used her gloved hand to pick up the phone. She put it in her pocket and closed the door again. If the storm lived up to predictions, she knew it could take twenty-four hours or more for the sheriff's office to get around to removing the rental car. The phone might have evidence on it, photos of Donray, texts between them, and more.

On the way back, she noticed that Chee had borrowed the truck she'd seen at the motel and cleared the windshield.

She kissed him gently. "Be careful. Be brave." She glanced at the monoliths. "Let the spirit of those stone warriors here go with you." She took her warm red hat off and handed it to him. "Wear this. You'll need it."

"Thanks. It will come in handy even though I'll be moving, working up a sweat." He gave her a quick hug. "How do you feel?"

"Almost good as new." Her head ached severely from Kingsley's blow. Her back and hip felt bruised, probably from when the ranger and Donray had shoved her into the trunk. But she was glad to be alive.

He smiled. "We'll caravan out as soon as I return with our truck and Chap. If Gillman or Becenti show up in the meantime, don't wait for me."

"Great. I really don't want to find out how well this beast does in the snow with those smooth tires."

"Hey." Donray had been so quiet they'd almost forgotten about him. "This truck deserves some respect, OK? Lady, you are the only one who has been in the driver's seat except me and my brother. You might not realize it, but that's an honor."

# 21

Chee watched closely for a safe place to turn off the main dirt road and park. The developing blizzard made the roadbed hard to distinguish from the shoulders and the land beyond. He crept along and kept looking until he saw three juniper trees that seemed to be growing right out of the red rock—he'd used them for his guideposts. Then he saw their truck, parked near a spot where he and Chap, with his damaged ankle, could hike out.

He locked Harrison, grabbed the emergency backpack from behind his truck seat, pulled Bernie's borrowed hat closer over his ears, and headed off. He found something sweet about wearing Bernie's hat, a closeness to her he had missed over the past few weeks.

At first, memory of the trail served him well, even though the falling snow blurred the landscape and subtly altered the appearance of the landmarks he had memorized. After a few minutes, he began calling for Chap. The lack of response bothered him. Had he taken a wrong turn? He began to no-

tice a bit of numbness in his face, but his toes and
fingers still felt fine. If it came to huddling inside
a cave in freezing darkness because Chap's ankle
was too weak to hike safely, he was prepared. And
Bernie's smile had reassured him.

Chap had seemed to be prepared too. He'd told
Chee he had plenty of food and water, and he was
dressed in enough layers to prevent frostbite. And
although he didn't know the guy, Chee had heard
a note of confidence in Chap's voice that made
him trust the man's attitude, a key survival skill.
Chap had sounded like a winner, not a victim.

December, Nítch'itsoh, brought a progression of
shorter days and longer nights. People Chee knew
celebrated Keshmish whether they were Chris-
tian or not, and most cheered the year's end and
welcomed the fresh start of a new calendar. Today
he wished for July's long evening light, and more
time to get Chap out. The snowfall had lessened
a bit, and if the cloud cover lifted, the full moon
would brighten the night to help with the rescue.
He hoped to be safely on the road again by then.

He called out for Chap more loudly, and again
heard nothing. He continued on, trusting instinct
and perhaps the guidance of the warriors in these
sacred rocks Bernie had mentioned. The guard-
ians were said to watch over those who honored
the old ways.

Chee climbed the ridge where he remembered
the greenish rocks, now covered with accumulat-
ing snow, and stopped to catch his breath. To the
west, he saw a hole in the gray sky, an oblong of
blue. He'd welcome a reprieve from the weather,
even if temporary.

He walked on until he came to a junction he remembered and he heard a voice. Not Chap's. He paused to listen. At first, he couldn't discern what the man was saying. Then as the person raised his voice, Chee's brain deciphered his words.

"Come on, for God's sake. You know it's the right thing to do. Sensible. Just say yes, and we're out of here. It's a small compromise, compared to a huge loss. Don't be so stubborn. You know I value your work. I'm one of the few people who understand how brilliant you are, Chap. Just agree. We don't need to argue anymore. You know it's the best option."

Then Chee heard a groan.

"Chap, for God's sake." The man raised his voice. "Let me see that ankle. Getting angry isn't good for your heart either. I can help you. Jessica is concerned about you, too. Is that skull with the jawbone worth your freezing to death out here?"

Chee heard an obscenity. Time to make himself known. "Hello up there. It's Jim Chee. You guys all right?"

Silence for a moment. Then, "Jim Chee? I don't know who you are or how you got here in a blizzard, but thank God for you. We could use some assistance. There's two of us in here. Chap, the older man, is having some trouble walking."

Chap mumbled something.

The man spoke louder. "Poor soul is delirious with pain and cold and, um, dehydration. No water or food up here all day for him."

Chee now knew that the person with Chap was lying. Along with Chap's silence, it set him on alert.

"What's your name, man?"

"Chris. Chap and I used to work together. We're old friends."

Chee heard Chap say something that sounded like "Stinking bastard."

"I'm climbing toward you. Chap, are you feeling all right?"

No response.

"Chris, what brought you up here in weather like this?"

"I heard that there was a break-in and a shooting at Chap's place, and that Chap was missing. I remembered this cave as his safe haven, you know. I got up here to him right before visibility dropped and it started snowing like crazy. How did you find us?"

Chee ignored the question. "We all need to head out of here. The trail is slick and getting slicker. I'm struggling even with my hiking boots."

"Don't worry about me." Chris's voice dripped with bravado. "I'm part mountain goat. But I will need your help with Chap. He damaged an ankle, and now he says he's having chest pains."

He heard Chap mumble something, and Chris responded, more loudly than necessary, "It's OK, my friend. I'm here to help you. Just rest. Don't try to talk. I can see you're in agony."

Chee moved toward the cave, noticing that two inches of fresh snow, maybe more, had accumulated on the trail since he'd last been there. The air was colder, and the light had begun to fade the way it does in late afternoons in mid-December. He could barely see his earlier footprints.

He talked as he climbed. "Chris, I know cops

try to keep stuff like this quiet. How did you hear about what happened?"

"Chap called me after he ran out of the house. I could hear how frightened he was. Poor old soul. It's no wonder his heart is acting up. How terrifying to experience something like that. To listen to all that noise and not be able to see what was going on."

"What do you mean, listen to it?"

"Chap was in his office at the time of the shooting, and I know it doesn't have windows. I always complained about that when we worked together, but he said it was less distracting and better for the computers. He told me he heard the noise, you know, the gunshot and then the door coming down, and made a run for it."

Chee recalled the security camera with its exact view of the door. For a split second, he wondered why Chap hadn't told Chris the truth, and then he gave the injured man credit. He brushed the snow off a flat stone and sat to consider his course of action. In a few more yards, he'd be able to see the cave, and then Chris and Chap could see him.

"You know, Sheriff Gillman is puzzled by what went down at that place. Chap, can you give us any more details?"

Silence. Then Chris answered.

"Ah, no. He told me he got out as quickly as he could. The poor man should not have had to go through all this."

"From what I've heard, he's not exactly Rambo." Chee hoped Chap would hear and could respond.

"Right!" Chap yelled. His voice carried both fear and pain.

And now Chee knew he had to solve a problem even more complicated than rescuing an injured man from a barely accessible place in a blizzard.

Bernie had watched Chee drive away from inside Donray's truck. When it had warmed to almost tolerable, she turned off the engine to save gas. She closed her eyes and listened to Donray's steady breathing. It felt good to rest—the energy she'd spent struggling in the trunk left her exhausted. Chee should be back in an hour. Plenty of time to move Donray into their reliable vehicle, to get out of here safely and find some medical help. His wound wasn't life-threatening, but he'd lost some blood, and the cold was taking a toll on them all.

If Gillman, one of his deputies, or Becenti came to the scene before Chee returned, she would happily turn Donray over to them and let them do the work.

She had grown cool enough to consider starting the truck again when she heard a chiming noise. Rhythmic. Like an alarm. She opened her eyes. She heard it again and realized the sound was coming from her jacket pocket, from Kingsley's phone.

An incoming call. She picked up the phone and said hello, skeptical that the signal would hold for more than a few seconds.

"Kingsley, where are you? You know it won't be a party without you."

The screen said "Cleaner," and it took her a split second to connect the nickname to Ajax Becenti.

"The ranger is dead. Valley of the Gods. It's Bernie. You'll see Donray's pickup, and . . ." But even as she spoke, the signal faded, and she realized Ranger Kingsley's phone had died too.

She put the phone down, restarted the engine, and used a few swipes of the windshield wipers to clear the snow. While she waited, she decided to consider the good in this unsettling situation.

First, Chee not only had rescued her but also had solved the mysterious disappearance of Dr. Chapman Dulles.

Second, Donray remained well restrained, and Kingsley's bullet hadn't done serious damage. He could be brought to justice, and if she had her way, he wouldn't threaten anyone again.

Third, thanks to Chee's conversation with Roper Black, she knew husband, wife, and daughter were together. A tiny worry about the new baby poked up, but she put it to rest. Every new parent she had known worried about every possible problem with an infant. Most of that worry came to nothing.

It had been a remarkable day, a mostly good day, except for Kingsley. The ranger's involvement in towing Chap's car and her attempted murder of Donray, Chee, and herself left Bernie unsettled and deeply uneasy. She had met cops-gone-bad before, but Kingsley didn't fit the mold. The ranger seemed too smart to risk her career to team up with Donray to steal a vehicle. Kingsley must have played a bigger role, but what had motivated her? Maybe she had been with Donray the night before when he had attempted to kill her with the truck. But why? Bernie tried to reason out the answer, but the bugaboo remained, an irritation just beyond her reach.

Back at the Shiprock police station or at home when she was helping Darleen handle an issue with Mama, physical motion often stirred her brain to life. She noticed that the snow had stopped momentarily. With Donray safely restrained in the truck, his wrists and ankles bound, and help on the way, she'd take a quick walk among the snow-dusted stone shapes. Maybe that would help her figure out why Kingsley had tried to kill her.

The wind blew her long midnight-black hair into her eyes as she headed down the road. The day felt colder. She stopped for a moment, thinking about the area, about Big Snake, who was preserved at what maps called Comb Ridge. She pictured the San Juan River that flowed nearby, the sacred male waterway that also ran past her home in Shiprock.

She bent down and used her gloved hand to sweep away the snow as she searched for the most appropriate rocks. She created a small stone offering, building it thoughtfully, as a shrine at the base of a red sandstone formation. She added a prayer for Chee's safety, and for herself and everyone else at risk. She was thankful that her own drought of the spirit had lifted with this gift of the snow's light, cold moisture and of work that released her from her worries.

After ten minutes she walked back to Donray's truck, shook the snowflakes from her hair, and opened the door. It was cold enough inside the truck to let her see her breath. She immediately smelled the cigarette smoke that seemed embedded in the upholstery. She started the engine and let it idle for a while to warm the cab. Except for

the tread-free tires, the truck was in great condition, a classic.

Donray looked pale and tired. As she observed
him, he opened his eyes. "Manny, can we talk?"

"My name's Bernie."

"Bernie. Are you really a cop?"

"Yes."

"OK. Is the woman who shot me dead?"

"Yes."

He was quiet again for a while.

"She was bad news. I know I'm not perfect, but
I appreciate what I've got, you know. That woman
always wanted more. Kingsley thought money
would solve her problems. I wouldn't mind giving
it a try, but I think the more money she got, well,
the more money she wanted. Can I ask you something else?"

"Go ahead."

"If I go to jail, what'll happen to my truck?"

"I don't know." As she enjoyed the warmth that
had begun to spread through the cab, she realized
she was tired, bone-tired, exhausted. The contrast
between the cold outside and the warmth inside
began to make her drowsy.

Then Donray's irritating voice intruded.
"Manny—I mean, Bernie—come on. Just tell me
what usually happens, you know, with vehicles
like this if someone's in lockup."

"If I do, will you answer a question for me?"

"Yeah. I guess."

"You guess?"

"Yeah, I will."

"OK, then. The truck will be towed and im-
pounded somewhere. It will run up a bill for stor-

age that's probably more than it's worth while you're incarcerated, you know, in jail somewhere waiting to be brought to justice as accessory to the attempted murder of a law officer. Then the truck will be auctioned with other unclaimed vehicles. If no one bids on it, it will be sold to a wholesaler or to a scrapyard."

Donray erupted with a string of swear words. "No, that's not right. This truck is special."

"Really?"

If he heard the sarcasm in her tone, he ignored it.

"I'll tell you about it. OK?"

"Sure. Go ahead."

"To start with, it was my brother William's. He died fighting in Afghanistan. This is all I have left of him, ya know? His spirit rides with me."

"Oh, I'm sorry he's gone."

"Him and me was the only two of us left in the family. Daddy brought us all out here because he had that job in the Moab mines and died in an accident before the bad juju from uranium could kill him. After that, Ma stayed drunk until she passed. Me and William stuck together till he got in trouble and had a choice of joining the army or, you know . . ."

She did know. She'd seen many young people heading down the wrong path and selecting a stint in the service as a way out. Sometimes it worked. Sometimes they came home with more troubles.

"So you two grew up out here."

He nodded. "It was OK, I figure, if you don't mind livin' with Indians and Mormons. You see them horns on the grille?"

"Yes."

"William put those on there. That's another thing that makes this special. That's the story."

Bernie watched the snow fall for a few moments. "Something's been puzzling me. Maybe you can clear it up. I figure you tried to run me down last night out here because it came with your security job."

"We thought you were a guy. I was just messin' with you, but Kingsley wanted to take a shot."

"Not Dev?"

"Nope."

"Why was she with you?"

"She said her partner didn't think I was doin' enough to keep the place safe."

"Ranger Becenti?"

"Not that dude. He's a straight arrow. The one she freelances with."

Bernie had been groggy, but now she was wide awake. "Freelances?"

"Money on the side. Usually Dev rides with me, but she told me to give him last night off."

"So why wasn't he with you today?"

"The dude never showed up. He had a gig early, but after that he said he'd come tow the car. He didn't bother."

"What kind of a gig?"

"Do I look like his mother?"

Bernie frowned.

"It was some job for Chris where he had to wear that sweatshirt that didn't fit me. That's all I got."

"Go back to last night with you and Kingsley. Why was she shooting at me?"

"She didn't know it was you. I don't think she

was trying to hit you. Just scare you off. But she told me she'd killed a guy earlier that night."

"You're serious?"

"Yeah." And Bernie could tell by the tone of his voice that Cassie Kingsley was nothing to joke about.

"Did she say who?"

"No." Bernie knew of only one person who had been killed last night—Jessica's husband, Kyle Johnson.

After a while Bernie turned off the engine, and they sat, thinking and getting colder.

"Hey, Manny, I mean Bernie, can you get me that hat back there behind the seat?"

She looked and found a cowboy hat and a ball cap.

"You want them both?"

"Yeah. Wait. Do you have a hat?"

"I gave mine to my husband."

"You take the ball cap then. You can adjust it to fit."

The restraints made it hard for him to reach his head, so she put the cowboy hat on him and wore the other. It helped a little with the cold.

"Do you have some gloves in here?"

"Yeah. Work gloves. They're under the driver's seat."

She found a pair of heavy-duty leather gloves and slipped them over his hands and put her own hands, already gloved, in her pockets. She felt the turquoise bear in the right pocket and squeezed it in her palm.

"Bernie?"

"Yes."

"I'm glad we didn't hurt you. That jacket Kingsley shot, it's behind my seat. We could tell you weren't wearing it when she put a hole in it. We were just trying to run you off. We went back for it when we filled in the trench. It's a mess. Sorry about that."

"Why did you fill in the trench?"

"Chris and Kyle had been working there, looking for some kind of old bones, but evidently Jessica had the permit, and it was just for pots. They didn't want anyone catching on and finding them. I should have done it that day, I mean before you found it, but I forgot."

The answer made sense to her. She had another question. "How come you're playing nice now?"

"I got to thinking that you are the only other person to drive Bill—that's what we call the truck—except me and William. That's a bond, ya know, a connection like you're a part of the family."

The connection she'd like, Bernie thought, was a connection to a steaming hot cup of coffee and a hamburger. That led to thoughts of dinner and, of course, to the situation with Darleen and Mama. Chee had been gone about an hour. And where were Gillman and Becenti?

Donray continued. "And I got to thinking about Kingsley getting shot and how Dinostar used me to scare that girl. To scare you. I could go to prison while they get rich. It's not fair."

"You're right about that."

"Can you turn the heat back on?"

"In a few minutes. We don't want Bill to run out of gas." According to the gauge, the truck had about an eighth of a tank of fuel. She figured she could run the engine for ten minutes every fifteen minutes or so until Chee returned with Chap. Surely it wouldn't be more than another half hour.

Snow had collected on the windshield and the side windows in a layer thick enough to block the view, so Bernie climbed out to check the weather. From both her police training and growing up in a rural area on the Navajo Nation with a self-sufficient mother, she knew not to panic as the blizzard worsened. She knew about checking the tailpipe to make sure it was clear of snow so that carbon monoxide wasn't coming into the cab. She'd do it again soon because of the rising snow level.

She came back in the cab and started the engine.

"You're quiet, Donray. What's up?"

"I don't feel so good. Can't think straight."

She studied his face. His skin had taken on a gray cast. She might have to risk driving in the storm if Chee didn't return soon.

"I never knew a Donray. Where did you get that name?"

"My mama was Donna; Daddy was Big Raymond."

"I get it."

"I hate the name."

"So change it. What do you wanna be called?"

"Just Ray." He took a deep breath. "After my old man."

"OK, Ray."

"Thanks. I'm too tired to talk."

She turned on the wipers to clear the windshield and then watched the snow fall. It came down with so much enthusiasm that she couldn't see the white car behind Donray's truck. To match the changing weather and Ray's downturn, she needed to consider plan B. She might have to leave before she knew what had happened with her husband and Chap.

She looked at her phone, which clearly showed no service, and at Kingsley's, which was dead. She tried calling Gillman and Becenti anyway. Then she attempted to send them, and Chee, a group text that she was leaving soon in Donray's truck with the injured man, heading to the closest place where he could get medical treatment.

She waited another five minutes. No Chee, but heavier snow.

"Ray, I'm going to drive us out of here. Any quirks to Bill?"

"What? I don't . . ."

She remembered the tow dolly and climbed out to detach it from the truck.

The hitch seemed frozen solid, caked with ice and snow. The cold made her gloved fingers too stiff to move fast. After some effort, she freed it and began to trudge to the white car. The accumulated snow had filled the tire tracks on the road and blown into drifts along the shoulder. She pushed through, glad for the ball cap and glad that the snow was still feather-light, even as it grew deeper.

She appreciated the way the flakes now made it impossible to see Kingsley's body and the blood where she had fallen. The storm had cloaked the sedan's side windows and windshield with a thick, protective snow blanket.

Then she struggled her way back to Bill the truck.

She brushed the fresh flakes off her shoulders and shook the snow off the cap and out of her hair before she climbed back into the driver's seat. She turned on the engine, offered Ray some water, and took a sip herself.

"You have a windshield scraper?" The wipers now revealed a layer of ice beneath the snow. She'd left the one she'd used on their truck in that vehicle.

"Ah, I don't remember . . ."

She looked in the glove box and found an old plastic CD case. It might work. She used the hard plastic to clear a path of vision in the front, on both sides, and to the back. Then she moved the truck seat closer so her shorter legs could reach the gas and brake pedals. She had just started the engine and turned on the wipers when she heard a vehicle approaching from behind. She rejoiced. Chee? Sheriff Gillman or a deputy?

No, but it was a vehicle suited for this road, a Jeep. She waited for it to inch past, glad she didn't have to worry about it getting stuck. But instead it stopped next to Donray's truck. She recognized it, but instead of Chris at the wheel, she heard a woman's voice. "Cassie? Donray?"

Bernie rolled down the window. "Jessica? What are you doing out here?"

"Who's speaking?"

"It's Bernie."

"Why are you in Donray's truck? I thought you were heading back to Shiprock."

"I was. It's a long story. Why are you out in

the storm? You shouldn't have come through the Road Closed signs."

"Where's Donray?"

"He's here. He's hurt. We need to get out of here now." She expected Jessica to ask what had happened, but she didn't.

"Bernie, you can't go. I need your help. Remember my business partner, Chris? The guy with the birthmark on his neck?"

"I remember Chris." She hadn't noticed the birthmark.

"He's lost in this blizzard."

"What happened?"

"He wanted to take a final look at a site he was studying before we left for New Mexico, so I dropped him off while I finished packing." Jessica sighed. "I told him to hurry. I'd be back in an hour. I've been waiting thirty minutes. There's no phone service out here, of course, so I was driving back to town for help."

"Chee is rescuing someone out there, so if Chris is in trouble, Chee may find him. And Sheriff Gillman is on the way."

"No, Gillman's slammed. There's a bad accident on the highway because of the weather. He let me through the roadblock only because I told him Chris needed me to pick him up and because this thing has four-wheel drive." She laughed. "The so-called sheriff won't be here until he's done with that crisis. He's barely competent. Like most of the local yokels out here who are willing to work for peanuts."

Bernie thought about the Zonnies, about Becenti. People with big hearts doing their best with intelligence, skill, and grace. "You're wrong about that. I've met lots of great people, Navajo and otherwise, at Bears Ears."

"Whatever. How come you're driving that ugly thing instead of your truck?"

Bernie thought of the simplest answer. "I came across an attempted vehicle theft. I've got to go into town now with Ray."

"Who?"

"You know him as Donray. The man with the gold tooth."

"Oh, that loser. I thought that truck looked familiar. What an eyesore."

Donray shouted a chilling collection of four-letter words and ended with, "You don't know nothin' about it."

"The beast suits you. You're a misfit, a dumb jerk. I bet that Crystal was just your type."

Bernie gave an order. "Jessica, stop. We have to get off this road while we still can. Let's go."

"Why is that white car here? Where's Cassie?"

"It's complicated. I'll explain later. I have to get help for Ray."

"No. You have to help me find Chris. Or don't you care if he freezes out there?"

"Shut up, witch," Donray yelled at Jessica. "I'm shot, and she's gonna save my life." Anger seemed to have strengthened him. "Believe it or not, you don't always get your own way. Just like that Kingsley bitch got what she deserved."

"Don't you dare call her that."

Bernie's patience frayed. "We're leaving." She closed the window, shifted the truck into drive, and eased down the road, wipers doing their best, defroster blasting. The truck's tires weren't suited for these conditions, but she'd had plenty of experience in marginal situations. She focused on the road in front of her, though she noticed Jessica's car following.

The snowy loop road from Valley of the Gods to the more traveled pavement was about sixteen miles. If she drove carefully, she ought to make it to Bluff before the truck ran out of gas. Once on the pavement, even if they had to stop, the odds that someone would come along to help, or that her phone would work, improved dramatically.

"Manny—I mean, Bernie—you know about the picture of that girl at the witching place?"

"Yes, I saw it."

"That was Jessica's idea. Her and Chris wanted to keep the Zonnie family away. I didn't do nothin' to that girl except squeeze her arm and take that photo with the bad things in the background."

"You don't have to lie anymore, Ray."

"This is honest." Ray coughed and then groaned. "Like Jessica said, I've got a thing for young women, but not girls."

"I don't want to hear it. Get some rest. My driving might make you nervous, but I'm good at this."

"Jessica gave the orders, but Kingsley made sure the work got done. That Chris seemed numb to the whole game."

Bernie felt her chest tighten. She realized now that more pieces of the mystery of her near death, of the photo, of Kyle's murder, had fallen into place. Her challenge was to get out alive and give the sheriff what she knew. "Tell me again, what were they doing at the site that was so secret?"

"Looking for something, not archaeology. But I dunno what."

The snow that had accumulated on the truck bed helped with the traction, but she wished she were driving the pickup, or even her trusty old Tercel.

She glanced at Ray and noticed that his eyes were closed. Good, she thought, she didn't need any unsolicited advice about how to deal with the road. She gripped the steering wheel tightly and kept the truck moving through the deep snow on the road and the avalanche of thickly falling flakes. Minute by minute, breath by breath, she rolled forward, Jessica's car following. As soon as she had cell service, she'd call 911.

Then she heard a horn blast behind her. She took her foot off the accelerator and looked in the rearview mirror. The Jeep had slid off the road, emergency lights flashing.

Bernie brought the truck to a careful stop and shut off the engine.

Donray woke up. "Are we there?"

"No. Jessica's in trouble. I'll be right back."

"Let her be. That's what she'd do for us. Nothin' but leave us to freeze here."

Bernie opened the door and started to slide out.

"Wait." Donray wiggled his handcuffed hands. "Take these gloves. Please. And there's a warmer hat in the glove box."

She put on the hat, a dirty wool cap with a fierce-looking cardinal logo. She tucked her hair inside for extra warmth. The gloves could have used a good cleaning, but she put them on, too. They were far too big, but that meant they fit over the ones she already wore.

She hiked through the snowdrifts to see what had happened to Jessica, bringing anger and resentment with her as well as a bit of worry.

Jessica watched her approach. "Donray. Help me with this mess." She sounded frantic.

"Not Donray. It's Bernie."

"Bernie? OK, I recognize the voice now. I slid off the road, but the Jeep isn't damaged. Can you help me move it?"

"No. The Jeep can wait. Climb in the truck with us. Let's get out of here."

"Not on your life. I can't leave this vehicle here. We can push it back to the road."

Bernie raised her voice. "I'm not arguing. Donray's truck is low on fuel, and he's hurt. Come with me now."

"You're heartless. Come on." Jessica's voice broke. "Please. Please. Kyle bought this car for me. Now that he's dead, I can't leave it. It means a lot."

"You told me it was Chris's car, and I saw him sitting in it."

"Well . . ." The pause told Bernie that Jessica was stirring up a lie. "There is no rule that you can't have more than one vehicle, is there? I loaned it to Chris."

Bernie turned toward Donray and his truck.

"You can't leave me."

"I can, but there's room in the cab for you." And, she thought, I still have some zip ties if I need them.

"At least help me get something from the hatch. I really need it. It's important."

"What is it?" Bernie spoke quickly, hoping that Jessica would pick up on the urgency and cooperate.

Jessica hesitated again. "It's a collection of old bones Kyle used for his research on evolution. It has crucial scientific significance. And it was part of his legacy."

"Old bones will keep until the weather is better." Bernie felt like screaming with frustration. "I've had it with you. I'm leaving now."

She noticed vehicle lights on the road behind them, moving faster than she'd expect for the conditions. From the height of the lights, she figured it was a large pickup. She hoped it was Chee, that he was safe, and that Chap was with him.

# 22

Jim Chee considered the situation he'd just en-
dured and the animosity between the men with
him now, finally, in the warm truck.

He remembered how the temperature dropped
and the snowfall increased as the afternoon light
faded. He recalled his decision to head toward the
cave after Chap's warning response to the Rambo
prompt. He remembered what he had said that
started the chain of events that led to the three of
them now sitting exhausted side by side.

"Chris, we have to get Chap out of there. I've
had a lot of emergency medical training. If you
help me, we can get this done."

"I see you now, Chee. Navajo, right? Same as
the woman who was in the room next to Jessica. I
know she was a cop, and you're a cop."

Chee kept moving, watching his footing on the
steep terrain. "Why does that matter?"

Chris ignored the question. "Did the sheriff
send you to find Chap?"

"He knows I'm here. Too bad you didn't know I

was on my way. That would have saved you a cold, hard trip."

"Chap is my buddy. I don't mind the weather." Chris fell silent for a few beats. "He seems to be having some heart trouble."

Chee reached the cave, and a tall white man gave him a hand up. Like Chap, Chris had the appearance of a person who had spent considerable time outdoors.

Chap sat on a rock with his head in his hands, looking older than Chee pictured from his voice. Chee put a hand on Chap's shoulder. "How are you doing?"

The man squeezed Chee's hand with an ice-cold grip and stared into his eyes. "I've had some heart issues, and this is making it worse. This man, who I thought was my friend, came to threaten and intimidate me."

Chris laughed. "My old pal is delirious. I'm a fellow paleontologist. We're colleagues. I'm here to help."

"Mary is my life's work," Chap said. "I've kept quiet about her until I knew all her secrets. I'm just about to release my report to the scientific community, and now this interloper—"

Chris laughed again. "Interloper? Dr. Dulles, we were in business together, the fossil business up at Hell Creek, remember? I respect you and your work. That's why I'm here to help you. This cold isn't good for you, buddy, and neither is the stress." He nodded to Chee. "You're absolutely right about hustling out of here. I'll gather up his stuff."

Chee looked at Chris. "Wait a minute. Chap, what's this about being intimidated?"

"That's what I call it when someone threatens to steal a rare skull I've researched extensively. Dinostar wanted to sell it for me. I said no, so Chris decided to stalk me and take it. I think he'd kill me if it came to that."

Chris took a step close to where Chap sat. "Bull. I came here because a terrified old man, a fellow scientist whose work I've long admired, called for my help."

"Liar."

"Argue later. We need to move." Chee offered Chap a hand up from the rock he was sitting on. "Can you stand on that ankle?"

"Maybe. My heart is racing so much I'm not focused on the pain."

Chap tested the injured joint with his weight, and Chee grabbed him to keep him from collapsing in agony. Chap leaned against him, off balance. "Come on," Chee called to the other man. "It will take both of us to help him out of the cave safely."

"Hold on. Chap and I have something to discuss privately first." Chris smiled. "Tell you what, Chee, why don't you go down and warm up your vehicle, and the two of us will start down after you in a minute or so."

"No. That's not gonna happen. Let's go together before we all end up spending the night in this cave." Chee felt Chap tremble and focused on changing position. When he looked up, Chris had a gun in his hand, pointed at Chee's chest.

"Let go of Chap, and put your hands up."

"He'll fall."

"Let him." He stared Chee in the eye.

Chee released Chap as gradually as he could. The older man sank with a grunt. "What's going on? Why the gun?" He kept his voice level.

"Shut up." Chris's voice had a higher pitch. "Your meddling made this more complicated than it should have been. Get out of here. I don't want to hurt you. Chap and I have to talk."

Chee stayed calm, assessing the situation.

"He's a lunatic." Chap spat out the words. "He wants me to give him credit for the work I've done on Mary."

"Half the credit. I made you a good offer. Share the honor with me, because you wouldn't have found her if you hadn't been a consultant on contract with Dinostar. I hired you and helped you find her. It's fair."

"It's bull."

Chris kept his eyes and the gun on Chee as he spoke. "OK. I'll tell Jessica that the item she has, the thing she thinks is Mary that was on your worktable, is actually the replica."

"Tell her. So what?"

"So I know where you hide the real Mary. Work with me, Chap, or I'll let Jessica sell your pride and joy."

"You're bluffing. You both can screw in a bolt. The contract allowed me to do scientific research. Mary belongs to the public."

"Jessica wants your laptop and files so she can change the location of your discovery to private land and make it legal to sell the skull. Move the site from Bear Ears to your property. Work with me, and we'll hold her off."

Chap was screaming now. "You and that harlot!

You call yourself a paleontologist, but you've de-
volved into a pathetic lapdog on her leash."

"Shut up." Chris kept the gun pointed at Chee.

"No. I admired you and your work, but now
you're a pathetic con man with a college degree
who sold out for profit. Working with you and
Dinostar was the worst decision of my life."

Chee focused on staying calm, waiting for
Chris to give in to a moment of distraction.

"You're wrong, Chap. The worst decision you
made was luring Jessica away from me. That's no
way to treat a friend."

"Lure her away?" Chap chortled. "You're a fool
to believe that. I didn't pursue her. She seduced
me. Never told me that she was romantically involved with you. Or that she was still married to
Kyle. I loved her, and I guess I still do."

"She never . . ." Chris slumped, and he let the
gun drop a bit.

It was the break Chee needed. He grabbed
Chris's hand and pushed against the gun barrel,
pointing it to the ground. Before the next breath,
Chee twisted Chris's arm hard, feeling his resistance until the weapon fell onto the cave's sandy
floor. He kicked the handgun away just before
he shoved Chris to the ground. The momentum
meant that Chee fell too, on top of the white man.
Chris grabbed for Chee's head, pulling off the
red hat, and Chee used the move to jab an elbow
forcefully in the soft part of the man's exposed
throat. Chris raised his arms to defend himself,
but Chee had more leverage and more experience.
They struggled on the cold sand until Chee was
able to stand and draw his weapon.

"Roll onto your belly. Move a muscle, and you're a dead man." Then Chee spoke to Chap. "You OK?" Chee reached down and pocketed Chris's gun, keeping his eyes on the man.

"Yeah. Right where you left me. How about you, Officer?"

"No serious damage."

"I'm hurt." Chris's voice was muffled. "I think you broke a rib and dislocated my shoulder."

"Serves you right." Chap seemed invigorated. "What happens now?"

Chee thought about it. "Well, it's snowing hard out there. If we don't get going, we could end up spending the night here. Cozy, huh? You, me, and a guy who wants us both dead. And my wife will be forced to drive an old truck with bald tires through a blizzard to get help for a man with a bullet wound."

"I don't want either of you dead," Chris said. "I'd never shoot anybody. I just needed to get Chap's attention. You're overreacting."

"This is how I react when someone pulls a gun on me."

"I didn't mean it, Chee. You're a good guy to come up here for Chap." Chris winced. "Can I try to sit up?"

"Not yet. We have to get a few things straight."

The climb from the cave to the truck had several complications: Chap's painful swollen ankle, Chris's fractured rib, and Chee's need to keep his gun at the ready while helping both men. Chris had started to cough and moan with pain. And because of Chap's pleading, Chee's emergency backpack had the additional weight of his laptop and his files.

As they slowly made their way down, Chee noticed that Chris seemed to treat Chap with actual kindness, helping him when he couldn't negotiate the rocks, and that Chap accepted and thanked the man for his help. They kept moving, supporting each other as best they could. The snow had piled higher than the top of Chee's hiking boots but was low in moisture content, as December storms often are. The feathery lightness was deceiving; Chee knew that driving on it turned the light flakes into treacherous ice.

The men moved away from the rock face, down the challenging slope, and toward the road without conversation, using their breath to maintain the exertion and to keep pain somewhat at bay. While they hiked, Chee came up with dozens of questions for both of them. By the time they reached the truck, Chap and Chris looked depleted. Chee's own exhaustion was as deep as the snow they had trudged through.

It was nearly dark, but Chee noticed that someone had driven on the road after he had parked. The fresh tire tracks were partly buried in fallen snow.

Chee had led the two men back to the road on a route straight to his truck. Harrison would have to be left until the storm cleared.

Chap leaned against the truck. "I thought we'd never get here. I'm freezing."

Chee unlocked the truck and started the engine with new urgency. He put the pack with the laptop behind the driver's seat, all the while keeping an eye on the two men. He helped Chap into the truck.

"Thanks. I could kick myself for twisting that damn ankle."

Before Chee could respond, Chris said, "Don't do it. We've had enough trouble, buddy."

It was good to hear Chap's laugh.

"Speaking of trouble, you both need to quickly tell me the truth about what happened at Chap's house. Chap, you first."

"I already did."

"This time I want the whole story, no omissions. Start at the beginning, but make it fast."

"OK. I figure Kyle set it up when he came to see me last night. He wanted to talk to me about my research with Mary. I welcomed him because I thought we were friends and professional colleagues, not expecting his bad attitude. He came close to threatening me when I wouldn't let him see the files. He yelled at me, arguing that my work was not only pointless but would limit Dinostar's commercial fossil operations. And then he played his ace in the hole: Did I want his wife, Jessica—the woman he knew I had once loved—to suffer financially because of a theory? I told him to get out, and when he wouldn't leave, I threatened to call Roper and the sheriff."

Chap took a deep breath.

"I think Kyle hired Dev to do the break-in and try to steal Mary. Maybe he was there himself this morning, too."

"Who's Dev?" Chee asked.

"The one who got shot. I think he came to warn me."

"Did you shoot him?"

"Of course not. I liked him. When I saw the terror in his face, I knew something bad was happening. I looked for the gun I always kept in the bone shop. That's when I realized it was gone."

Chris spoke for the first time. "Jessica took it. I bet it's the gun she gave me. The one I pulled on Chee."

"Who shot the man found dead at your house?"

"I don't know. I couldn't see who did it. If I had to guess, I'd say Kyle. He must be the mastermind. He knew that there were only two things in the house worth stealing: Mary and my research supporting her uniqueness."

Chris said, "Are you going to tell him about Kyle?"

Chee ignored the question. "So why was all that white plaster on the kitchen floor?"

In the darkness of the cab, he could see Chap shrug his shoulders. "I didn't want to take a chance on anything happening to the fossil, so recently I made a replica. Plaster and modeling clay. Messy. I kept it for reference on my worktable. But Mary herself is sequestered away in a safe place. Eventually Mary and her replica will go to the Natural History Museum in Salt Lake. They'll never be for sale like the stuff Dinostar sells."

Chee waited, but Chap stopped talking.

"Are you going to tell him about Kyle?" Chris asked again. "Come on, Chee, this is pointless. Kyle couldn't have been involved in the home invasion because he was dead before this went down."

"Dead? Kyle's dead?" Chap took in a sharp breath. "No. What happened?"

Chee drove in silence for a moment, focusing on the slick challenge of winter driving. "The officer who found the body thought he'd died of exposure, but it turns out he was shot. It happened last night." Then he turned to Chris. "Did you kill Jessica's husband?"

"No, no. Jessica asked me to shoot Kyle, but I couldn't. She said she asked Chap to do it, too, and he told her to get lost. That was earlier, before they broke up."

"That's right." Chap exhaled and shook his head. "She hadn't even told me she was married. That's when I knew she was evil."

"Evil?" Chris spoke with a jolt of energy. "Now, wait—"

"Talk about that later," Chee said. "Were you involved in what happened at Chap's?"

"No, I wasn't there. I don't even know exactly what happened. I just know Jessica told me to come up here and get the laptop and Chap's notes as part of her plan."

"Did you kill the man who was breaking in?"

"No. Like I just said, I wasn't there."

"Tell me more about the plan."

"The plan?"

Chee stopped the truck and leveled the gun at Chris. "Talk fast, or hypothermia is around the corner when I leave you on the side of the road so you can take that long, cold walk back to town."

"OK. OK. Jessica told me she'd hired someone to go to Chap's house and reason with him about how the skull belonged to Dinostar, that is, to me and her. She said that she'd need a second person with some muscle because Mary could be heavy. I thought about asking Donray, but Jessica had this sweatshirt she wanted the helper to wear. Donray was too big, but it fit his buddy. That's all I know."

Chee continued the slow drive toward the paved road, both hands on the wheel, wipers at top speed, the defroster losing the fight to keep the warm breath of three men from fogging the windshield. He hoped Bernie had left and, with her skill as a driver, managed to handle the snowy road and lack of visibility. He was glad to be in his own safe truck.

They had been creeping along for about ten minutes, although it seemed longer, when he saw the emergency lights flashing from a car off the road. Then he noticed two people outside the car in the near darkness. They were struggling to walk in the deep snow and seemed to be arguing.

Chee slowed even more, and then saw the headlights of the Jeep and an old pickup truck. From her size and posture, he realized one of the two on the road near it was Bernie. The scene began to make sense.

He got the attention of his passengers. "Hey. You guys. Do either of you recognize that car in the ditch or those people?"

Chap said, "I don't."

Chris shifted for a better view out the window. "It's my Jeep. Jessica drove it out here."

"Why?"

Chris took his time answering. "She dropped me off so I could look for Chap, see if given everything that went down at his house, I could persuade him to let me have the paperwork connected to the fossil she thought belonged to Dinostar. She didn't want that Jeep out here in case the sheriff came looking for Chap. She thought that would be suspicious." He kept looking out the window. "That's Jessica standing by the car. I recognize her coat. I guess the weather forced her off the road."

Chee kept silent, but he sensed a dangerous, complicated situation. He knew Bernie had recognized their vehicle, and he didn't want to do anything to put her in further danger.

Chee rolled down the window and yelled to the women, "Hello out there. The weather is getting worse. Leave that stuck car. Get back in the truck and get off the road now, or you'll be in serious trouble."

"Who are you," Jessica snapped at him, "and who put you in charge? I'm not leaving my car. We'll get this done quicker with your help. Get out here and give us a hand."

Before Chee had decided how to reply, Chris yelled out the open window, "Jessica, honey, it's Chris. Listen to this good advice. Do this now. It's just a car. Not a reason to risk your life."

"Chris? Thank goodness. Did you take care of Chap?"

He looked at Chee. Chee nodded yes.

"I did." Not even a fib. Chris had helped Chap survive.

Jessica looked at Chee's truck. "I didn't know Chap owned a big hauler like that. Must be new. The old goat had good taste."

"Donray's truck slips in the snow," Bernie said, "so this other truck needs to follow me out. Jessica, you can stay here with that precious car or you can do the smart thing. Come with me."

"And leave it? Like hell. Chris, get off your butt and help me. We can use the truck you're in, because this pathetic excuse for a woman is scared of a little snow."

Then Jessica extended her arm, near the level of her waist, and held out her hand to catch the big white flakes as they fell. "This blasted weather sure complicates our plan."

Bernie cringed. The old Diné stories said that a hand extended during a blizzard set the level of how much snow would fall, and they strongly advised against it. Too much deep snow caused trouble for livestock and people.

In the truck, Chris leaned toward Chee and spoke softly. "I can calm her down, but I need to go out there. She's not thinking straight, and she'll die if she stays here."

"Why does that Jeep matter so much?"

"I don't know," Chris said.

"You're lying."

"Let me go out there to handle this. You've got to trust me."

"I don't trust you. You tried to kill me, remember?"

"That was a mistake, and the gun wasn't loaded or anything."

"Save your breath. Does Jessica have a weapon?"

"I don't know." Chris exhaled. "Probably."

Chee considered the options. "OK. We're both going."

"Here." Chap took off his green hat with the

furry ear flaps and reached across Chris to hand it to Chee. "Wear this, best hat ever. Bring it back. Do you need my gloves too?"

"No, thanks." Chee looked at Chap. "Hunker down low in the seat in case of gunfire."

"Got it." Chap pulled the hood of his coat over his head for warmth and snapped the closing flaps beneath his chin.

Chee opened the door to the frigid night and steady snowfall. The bitterly cold air tightened his throat. He felt instantly grateful for the lumberjack hat's practical warmth. He heard the fresh snow compress beneath his boots as he walked from the truck. Chris, walking in front of Chee, joined him, moving toward the disabled Jeep. The way Chris hunched as he walked reminded Chee of the man's injured rib.

The women looked up at the sound of the truck door slamming, and Chee saw the accumulation of snow on Bernie's hat and the tension in her body. She'd been standing in the blizzard for a while. Jessica watched them approach, hands on her slim hips and her chin thrust forward. He'd seen that pose too often. She was ready for a fight. He put his hand on his weapon.

"It's about time," she yelled to them. "Get over here and . . ." She fell silent, and seemed to see Chee for the first time. "Chap? I'd recognize that hat anywhere."

Chee didn't answer, watching the woman's agitation.

"Honey," Chris said, "that's not—"

She yelled over his voice. "You stupid jerk. I

can't count on you either, just like the other men in my life. If I need anything done, I have to do it myself. Or have Kingsley handle it."

Jessica slipped a hand from her hip to her pocket. In the combination of filtered moonlight and his truck's headlights, Chee saw her draw a gun and point it at him. He held his own service weapon at his side. "I should have killed you myself, you traitor. You abandoned Dinostar for your stupid research. And you know that skull you found—a twelve-million-dollar ticket—belongs to us. If you'd listened to Kyle and changed the location of your own damn discovery, you could have avoided all this. One little change, Chap, and we all could have been rich. But you were too dumb to negotiate with Kyle, so we have to handle you this way. Chris, walk over to him and make sure he doesn't have a gun."

"Jessica, honey—"

"Wait!" Bernie shouted. "You're making a mistake." There was authority in her voice. Chee watched her move smoothly toward Jessica, her gun drawn and steady in her hand.

"That's not Chap, it's Jim Chee, wearing a hat you recognize. You don't have a grudge against Chee. I'm standing behind you, with my loaded gun pointed at your back. I'll kill you if I have to." Bernie gave the words a moment to sink in. "Jessica, put your weapon on the snow and then turn to face me. Do it now."

Jessica didn't move. "Chris? You coward. Shoot her. You know we're in this together."

"No. Listen to what she says. Put the gun down. Stay alive."

"You're an idiot. The same as Kyle and Chap."

"Jessica!" Bernie was shouting. "This is over."

Jessica turned quickly, gun in hand, changing her focus from Chee to Bernie. Bernie shot, and the woman tottered backward and then collapsed onto the snow. Chee ran toward Jessica, kicking her gun away. Then he went to Bernie.

They stood together, noticing a flickering of light down the road, coming from the opposite direction.

"Gillman?"

Chee nodded. "Better late than not at all. Thanks for saving my life."

"Anytime." Chee heard new tenderness in her voice.

"You played it just right out there."

She sighed. "My biggest worry was what the woman might do to you."

Now they could hear the vehicle approach through the falling snow, and see the lights flashing blue and red.

Chris knelt in the snow and took Jessica in his arms.

# 23

Chris looked at Jessica's body. "I loved her, you know. I would have done almost anything for her. Almost anything, but I couldn't kill for her."

Bernie, Chee, and Chris stood awhile watching the snow drift down, gently sparkling in the on-coming headlights.

"So who killed Kyle? And why?" Bernie asked.

"All I can tell you is that Jessica asked me to do it last week. I thought she was joking. The three of us—me, Chap, and Kyle—were buddies, you know, drawn to each other by our fascination with dinosaurs. And, I guess, by our love for Jessica. We called ourselves the Triceraguys." He rubbed his nose with his gloved hand. "Anyway, I told her to lighten up. Divorce Kyle and marry me. No need for such drastic action. I can see now that wasn't her style."

"So who killed him?" Bernie asked again, but she thought she knew the answer.

Chee said, "I'd suspect Jessica herself after this,

but the manager at the motel told me he and Jessica were playing chess that night. She had an alibi."

Bernie realized she couldn't feel her toes. "Guys, I need to warm up. Until that vehicle gets here and someone needs to talk to me, I'm heading to the truck. Donray needs the heat, too."

Chee nodded. "Is he doing all right?"

"Yeah. I found a blanket for him. As soon as I've talked to whoever is in that cop car, we need to get out of here."

Chee walked to the truck with her and checked on Donray.

"How are you feeling?" Chee asked.

"I've been better."

Bernie had snugged the blanket around him up to the armpits and down to his calves.

"Did Jessica get the Jeep unstuck?" Donray said.

Chee shook his head. "Nope."

"What was all that shooting?"

"Oh, nothing you need to worry about."

"I'm not worried about anything except somebody driving me out of this blizzard to someplace where I can get something for pain. And maybe a steak and a beer." He looked Chee in the eye. "I told Bernie and I'll tell you too. I'm sorry about what happened out there, with your good woman here and with that girl. I was flat wrong."

"Got it. Good luck to you." Chee walked away, back toward the site of the shooting.

Bernie climbed into the cab. "I'm soaking up the heat here for a minute or two, Ray, and then we'll go."

* * *

Chee found Chris still standing near Jessica's body, looking toward the flashing lights. The dim glow of the full moon through the clouds reflected on the snow where the woman had fallen. He noticed Chris shivering, and the icy tears on his cheeks.

"Come on. It's over. Let's warm up."

Chee put a hand on Chris's shoulder and walked with him to the truck.

By the time the vehicle with the flashing lights crawled to where she was parked, Bernie had warmed to almost human again. It turned out that the man behind the lights was Ajax Becenti. The Cleaner had come to clean up the mess.

Because Ray's truck was the closest vehicle, Becenti pulled up next to it. Bernie lowered the window. "Work never ends, does it?"

"That's the truth. Gillman and all the deputies are tied up with traffic accidents until the highway patrol can get here. So the BLM to the rescue. Gillman wouldn't have reached me at the birthday party, but Chatterbox got a network extender for phone service at her house, and his call made it." Becenti grinned. "I'd had more than enough cake anyway. What's up?"

After all she'd witnessed, Bernie hardly knew where to begin. "I'll start with Ranger Kingsley. She shot Donray and tried to kill me and Chee." She explained, careful to stick with the facts. Noticing Becenti's growing emotion, she gave him time to deal with the immediate shock, grief, and rage at his partner's betrayal.

"What about that car in the ditch?"

So she told him of Jessica's death, and explained that Chap and Chris were with Chee in the other truck. "I have the ranger's phone. I'll make sure the sheriff gets it. Chee can tell you more. Ray and I have to go."

"Sure. I thought his name was Donray."

"It was," Ray said. "Folks, I hurt like a son of a gun. Can you guys talk later?"

Bernie put the truck in gear and eased the vehicle onward as Becenti drove toward Chee.

Chee introduced Becenti to Chris; he already knew Chap. Becenti questioned Chee about the events and Kingsley's and Jessica's deaths. His details meshed with Bernie's.

"I'll get some pictures of the scene tonight and secure the bodies," Becenti said. "I'll do what I can to preserve evidence for the sheriff's investigation."

Chee nodded. "The woman ranger can be left where she is until the weather calms down. I covered the body and moved it off the road. She's buried beneath the snow by now. The other dead person, the bilagáana, will need your attention." He felt bone-tired, the result of a long, stressful day. "Anything else from me?"

"I don't understand what happened with my partner. I knew she was unhappy out here, but that shouldn't have made her a . . ." Becenti shook his head.

"A killer?"

"Right. You or your wife could have been the one dead here. She was a good shot."

Chee stayed quiet, giving Becenti time to say what he had to.

"That ranger was always complaining about Bears Ears, about not making enough money, about how she missed California. Why didn't she just quit if she didn't want to be here?" Becenti fell silent for a moment. "I know life can be hard on people who are, you know, different. On women like her who love other women."

Chee said, "I didn't know that about her. Did she have someone here?"

"Yeah. She let it slip that they'd meet privately. She never said who it was. But I think I know now. That part I can understand, but I don't know why she went bad as a cop."

"I think it was money." Chee shook his head. "They all said the skull Chap was studying would have been worth millions on the black market. The ranger and her lover both loved money the best."

As Bernie eased the truck and its questionable tires away from the deadly spot, she told herself to relax. Ray was silent as she headed out from Valley of the Gods toward the pavement and then whatever came first, a gas station or a hospital. Her experience from years of driving unpaved roads in slick, muddy, and all breeds of other impassable conditions helped, too. She turned the wipers on full force, kept the truck on the road with skill and some good luck, and hoped they didn't run out of gas. The few times Ray tried to give her advice on driving, she told him to zip it. He shut up.

When she finally reached the blacktop of Utah 163, she found it had been sanded and plowed. The truck was running on fumes, but at least it was still moving and the going was easier. She took a deep breath.

"Bernie, you drive good."

"Thanks."

Ray groaned. "You know, that Kingsley was the only woman who scared the stuffing out of me, but I never thought she'd shoot me. No, I take that back. Jessica scared me, too. They were alike in some ways."

"What do you mean?"

"Both of them were good liars. Kingsley told me that Jessica promised her she'd buy a beach house somewhere for just the two of them. I told her that Jessica had been sweet to Kyle, and then to Chap, and then to Chris. She said this was different. This was the real deal. And now they're both real dead."

Bernie focused on driving, willing the vehicle to not run out of gas quite yet.

Ray stretched his legs under the blanket. "What happened to Dev?"

"I wasn't there, but I can tell you what Chee told me."

Ray listened without interrupting. "That guy was always after the extra buck, kind of like those women, but he wasn't a bad dude. I told him some jobs weren't worth the money. He never listened to my jive, but I didn't take his advice neither. Anyway, I'll miss the jerk."

They watched the wipers fighting the snow-flakes.

"Dev told me he liked Chap," Ray added. "Thought the man was a stand-up dude. It's weird that he'd get tangled up in something that would do the guy harm."

"Chee said it looked like the bullet entered from the back, and that he died quickly. Do you know who would have killed him?"

"My money's on Kingsley. She was a good shot." Ray shifted in his seat and fell silent for a few moments. "You know, Bernie, death happens to everybody. Can't avoid it. I'm glad my number wasn't up tonight."

Death. The trip had started with Bernie's own near-death experience, thanks in part to a man whose life she was now saving, and then segued into the surprise birth of a baby. Positive and negative dancing together. The news of Jessica's husband's death had been followed by the trip to the Zonnie place to share food for a celebration of life. Then the discovery of a dead man at Chap's house, followed by the revelation that Chap, a missing person, was alive.

Bernie realized that Chee would talk to Hosteen Grayhair about a ceremony and perhaps Becenti would join them. All three had seen too much death, and she knew this would happen again. It was part of their calling as protectors and defenders in a profession she loved—a calling that might not agree with motherhood. It hadn't so far, she thought.

She glanced at her passenger prisoner. He looked pale. "You doing OK, Ray?"

"It sucks to get shot. I'm not feelin' so great."

"How long can Bill keep going with the gas gauge on E?"

"Maybe another five miles."

She focused on driving. Just about the time Bill couldn't have rolled forward another mile, three fine things happened. In retrospect, she considered them gifts from Valley of the Gods, now beautifully blanketed under fresh snow.

First, she came to a roadblock where a sheriff's deputy was waiting to discourage traffic. When she explained the situation, the deputy radioed for an ambulance to take Ray to the hospital. They were in luck; an emergency medical crew was minutes away.

Second, just after the ambulance arrived, Chee pulled up in their own familiar truck. Chap declined the ride in the ambulance, arguing that ice for the swelling, compression, and a pain-killer he took for his arthritis would work just fine. Chee arranged for Chris to be transported, because of his broken ribs and cough, and Chris happily agreed.

Which led to the third good thing. Bernie could leave Ray's truck for the sheriff to deal with.

As she parked and locked Bill, for the first time in a long time, Bernie realized, she was at peace. Unborn babies and mothers-to-be shouldn't witness death, especially violent death. Her miscarriage, she knew now with absolute certainty, was appropriate. Everything in life had two sides, positive and negative, good and evil. Maybe someday she would be able to see the loss of what might have been as a blessing. And she knew she would always wonder about her precious baby, who was not meant for this world.

# 24

Bernie left Ray's vehicle on the side of the road, happy that there was room in their own warm truck for her. And happy, finally, to meet the legendary Chapman Dulles and learn his version of why people who had been his friends wanted to do him harm over an old skull turned to stone.

The snow plows had partially cleared the road to Bluff. Visibility was still marginal because of the falling snow, but she saw Chee relax a few degrees. Bernie sat close to him, typing a quick text to Darleen, explaining that work and the storm had delayed them.

"OK, Chap," Chee said. "Now that my wife is here, fill in the blanks."

Bernie put the phone aside and looked up.

"Officer Manuelito, we haven't met, but I've heard your husband sing your praises. I'm Dr. Chapman Dulles."

"Chee told me something about what happened at your house. That's terrible. I'm curious to learn your take on it."

Chap sighed. "Sure, but first, I'd like my hat back."

Chee slipped it off. "Nice and warm. It almost got me shot, you know. She recognized this unusual headgear and thought I was you."

"That face blindness is a strange thing, isn't it?" Chap took a breath. "I'm sorry it ended that way for Jessica. She wasn't totally bad, just enormously insecure in her financial life. I'll miss her."

Bernie heard the sadness in his voice. She didn't want to discuss the dead.

Chee turned the wipers down a notch. "Tell my wife what happened at your house."

Chap spared no details as he unspooled the story of his morning, his work with Mary, and how the unexpected visitor had changed everything.

"I checked the security camera when the doorbell rang, and there was Dev. He shouted a warning to me, and I saw the look of pure terror on his face. I'm sorry that he died because of Mary."

"He warned you? Donray told me that Dinostar had hired him, and that Chris asked him to do a special job this morning."

"Well, they picked the wrong guy for the assignment at my house. They didn't realize that I'd saved Dev's arm and at least some of his hand. Probably his life, too."

Bernie's face reflected her surprise.

"Really. He was working with me as a laborer on an excavation in Wyoming. I had a lot of stone to move at that site. A huge rock fell on him, crushed his hand, and pinned his arm at the shoulder. I figured out how to use leverage to move the rock so we could get him out of there. After we got the bleeding stopped, I drove him to the hospital, made sure he got treated fast, and paid the bill. Dev never forgot it. He lost those fingers, but it could have been a lot worse."

"I understand."

Chap shook his head. "I saved his hand, and he saved my life. Mary was at the root of all this. Mary and human greed."

Chee said, "Tell Bernie and me about Mary."

The truck cab was silent for a while except for the beat of the wipers and the hum of the truck's heater.

Then Chap chuckled. "The real answer to that question is a college course, but here's the short version. Mary is more than an ancient skull. She's a rare find, the jewel of my life's work and, I hope, a beacon for the future. She will help unlock the mystery of how, when the great age of dinosaurs came to an end, mammals ultimately rose to dominance. Most importantly, she might offer a clue to how life adapted to survive in a changing climate. Information we will certainly need soon."

"Why did you name her Mary?"

"Glad you asked. Mary was the first name of several wonderful female paleontologists many people have never heard of. For example, Mary Anning, a nineteenth-century pioneer in the field who contributed to huge changes in scientific thinking about life in the Jurassic period. Then there's Mary Dawson, Mary Schweitzer, Mary Leakey. All of them wonderful researchers."

"How old is your Mary?"

"Oh, maybe three hundred and twenty million years or so. The only other example of her kind, *Shashajaia bermani*, was discovered by a brilliant paleontologist from the Carnegie Museum of Natural History. He did lots of work here in Bears Ears. I wish I had met him."

Bernie was quiet for a while, thinking of how to phrase her next question without using the name of the dead woman. Although chindis seemed to only cling to deceased Navajos, she didn't like taking chances. "Your former girlfriend wouldn't tell me what was in the trunk that was so important. I guess she was stealing Mary. Right?"

"That's what Jessica thought. Actually, what's in that Jeep must be the replica." Chap leaned forward. "I left the replica on the table in the bone shop. Whoever took it didn't have time to look at it closely."

"Why would anyone believe they could get away with a theft like that?" Chee asked. "I mean, it seems obvious that your Dinostar colleagues would be the only ones who could steal that fossil. No one else would even know what Mary was, or how valuable she is."

"And here's another question," Bernie said. "Who would buy a stolen skull?"

"Unfortunately there are unscrupulous collectors, people who see these rare fossils as a kind of trophy and pay huge prices for them at auction or on the black market. Mary should be on display in a public collection someday, not on a pedestal in someone's dining room. I found her on public land, so she belongs to the American people, not in some mansion behind a locked gate." Chap moved his hands toward the truck's heater vents.

The snow was abating. Chee turned the wipers a notch lower and remembered something.

"When you get a chance, call Roper Black. He feels responsible for what happened at your place. He worried that you were dead inside the house and helped me find you. He told me he failed at his job because of what happened today."

Chap pursed his lips. "I'll talk to him. I respect the man, but I was surprised that he didn't come for me himself."

Bernie said, "I guess you can give me the credit for that. When his wife gave birth last night, I suggested that he take some time off to enjoy his baby." She told Chap the story of the delivery. "They have a little girl."

Chap chuckled. "Wow. How wonderful. And here I was feeling neglected. Roper is a good man. I regret that he decided to leave me at the end of the month."

"He wants to move to Shiprock and work with the Navajo Police," Chee said. "He'll be a good cop."

They drove in silence, creeping along in the storm. Chee kept his eyes on the road and both hands on the wheel.

Chap's voice grew serious. "How did Kyle die?"

"Someone shot him on the road from Blanding. A deputy sheriff found his body outside the vehicle, so at first the officer assumed he died of exposure."

"I think you'll find he was shot with my gun, the gun that Jessica stole from me. Knowing how her mind worked, I figure she planned for the police to blame his death on me if necessary. After all, my gun was the murder weapon. I'm sure she also wanted Chris to kill me in the cave with that same gun. Leave me for the animals as a suicide."

Bernie had come across women killers before, but Jessica didn't seem to fit the pattern. "Why would she want her husband dead?"

"My theory is that he resisted her plan to steal Mary, and she was tired of him. He wasn't perfect, but he was a solid paleontologist who valued knowledge over everything, including money. He never felt comfortable with Dinostar, but he knew Jessica wanted more financial security, and it seemed like a solution." Chap leaned against the back of the seat. "Jessica had face blindness, but she was an expert at reading people, especially men. Getting us to do what she wanted."

Bernie shifted in her seat when her phone buzzed. She saw who was calling. "Sheriff?"

"Bernie, I just talked to Becenti. What a terrible mess out there. Chris and Donray are at the hospital. Is Chap with you?"

"Yes. In the truck with Chee and me."

"Let me talk to him."

She handed the phone to Chap, whose contribution to the conversation was mostly "Yes, sir" and "I understand" and "I will" and "That long?" and a few times "Thank you."

He gave the phone back to her. "Detective Parker needs to talk to me about the incident, so he's meeting us at the Bluff Inn in a patrol car to give me a ride to the house."

Chee remembered the damaged door. "You might want to stay at the Bluff Inn. With this weather, I'm sure they'll have room."

"OK." Chap pulled out his phone. "I don't have much battery left, but I need to call Roper and Hannah before Parker meets us." The conversation they overheard was brief and touchingly sweet. Chap ended the call with a smile. "I won't need the motel. Roper called the sheriff and got permission to jerry-rig something so I can sleep in my own house tonight."

A San Juan sheriff's unit waited at the Bluff Inn, the only car in the parking lot. Chee pulled their truck in next to it, noticing with relief that Walter, the manager, had closed the office. They could drive back to Valley of the Gods and get Harrison as soon as the roads were passable, and return it before Walter even realized it had spent the night away from home.

Chap opened the truck door to climb out and then reclosed it. "Chee, one more thing. I know you came to Bears Ears in part to talk to me about helping with the Fallen Officers Memorial Fund."

"That's right. I'd almost forgotten."

"Ask the chief to let me know what it costs, and I'm good for half of it."

"Wow. Thank you. All of us officers will appreciate that."

"And tell him that I'd like to contribute that same amount to a fund to help the families of those officers."

"That's wonderful." Chee hadn't expected such generosity.

Bernie took a deep breath. "I need to ask you one more thing before you go. Where is Mary now? I'm worried about her."

"She's fine. Securely stowed in the gun safe. I said goodbye to her before I left."

Parker walked to the truck, and Chee introduced him to Bernie.

"The three of us need to talk about the dead women out there in the snow," Parker said.

Chee gave him a quick briefing, and Bernie reinforced what he said. "Just for the record, that woman by the red Jeep would have killed Chee. And the ranger he killed? She shot a man in the shoulder tonight after she tried to kill me. Becenti has the gun."

"I'll be in touch." Parker paused. "I've been in situations like the one you two are in. Don't quote me, but I know that sometimes it's your life or theirs. I'm glad you survived."

The detective led Chap into the patrol car, and they drove away slowly through the heavy snow of the unplowed parking lot.

Chee locked the truck, and they went into their motel room, where he had already loaded his things in the suitcase. He sat on the bed to take off his boots.

Bernie turned up the heater. "I'm going to finish that note I was typing to Sister and apologize for missing dinner." Bernie sighed. "I should have done this a lot sooner."

"You were kind of busy, sweetheart." Chee stretched out on the bed. "I'm glad we can stay here tonight. I don't feel like socializing, not even with your mother."

After she sent the text, Bernie remembered that her suitcase was in the truck and went back outside to get it. Chee had fallen asleep.

The snow had stopped, and the sky had begun to clear. She watched as the brilliant moon appeared though the clouds, settling into a patch of celestial blackness. And then, slowly, three perfect diamond stars peeked out. The fresh snow caught the subtle glow and reflected a thousand miniature points of light.

She put her hands in her jacket pockets and touched the pink ribbon and the little bear. She knew the storm would cancel school because buses couldn't make it through. Tomorrow, before they drove home, she would stop at the Zonnie place and ask to meet Crystal. She would tell her the story of how the Holy People and bears protected the Diné, in part by teaching Navajos to be strong and brave. She would return the bear on its ribbon, not as a memory of a terrible incident, but now as a symbol of the young woman's own strength.

Her phone chimed. Darleen had texted. No prob. See you soon? Call me, OK? Mama and I are still up.

She dialed her sister and gave her a synopsis of the last few hours and the storm.

"Gosh, Sister. You and Cheeseburger . . . I could have lost you both." Darleen's voice caught in her throat.

"We're fine now. Tired. I'll tell you more about it later. There's nothing to worry about."

The phone was silent for a moment, and then Darleen said, "Guess what?" She never waited for a guess. "Lieutenant Leaphorn called me from Hawaii."

"No kidding."

"And he said Louisa landed a consulting job there with Hawaiian Natives. Remember how she used to do those interviews out here with Utes and Paiutes. Something about cultural differences?"

"Sort of."

"Well, the lieutenant said that's what she'll be doing there. And he'll go with her sometimes, too."

"Cool. Are they heading back to Window Rock?"

"Not yet. He said she wanted to go to the island where the volcano is and take a look at the lava. What a plan!"

"How did he sound?"

"Happy." Darleen paused. "I told him I wondered if they got married. You know, people do that in Hawaii. You know what he said?"

"I bet he said no." Leaphorn had told her and Chee that he'd suggested marriage several times to his housemate. Louisa had consistently reminded him that she had tried it before and wasn't good at it.

Darleen laughed. "You lose that bet. He said, 'Not yet.'"

"Whoa. I'm glad you talked to him. Why did he call you?" She knew chatting never made Leaphorn's list of things to do unless it involved business.

"Oh, that's another good thing. He wants me to do more work on the Missing and Murdered Indigenous Women project. He asked if I could go to a meeting in Window Rock with the rest of the Navajo Nation committee."

"So what did you say?"

"I said yes, silly. I told him I'd be glad to do that. I'll ask Mrs. Darkwater and Bidziil to keep an eye on Mama."

Bernie loved hearing energy in her sister's voice. It cheered her. "How is Mama?"

"About the same."

"Is she in bed now?"

Darleen laughed. "Not at all. She wants me to get off the phone and help her move the furniture so she can sweep the carpet. I'm glad, actually. Maybe she'll sleep better tonight."

"I hope so."

"I've got to go. Love you, Sister."

"You too."

Bernie ended the call and looked at the clearing sky. It reflected her thoughts.

The door to the motel room opened, and she saw Chee at the threshold, looking out toward her.

"Hey there, I just heard from Roper Black. The backup video was working. It shows the man who got shot at Chap's house and the woman ranger. After she killed him, she made a phone call, then went inside. Now we know who stole the Mary wannabe." She heard the relief in his voice. Of all the suspects involved, the ranger was the least likely to notice the difference between a replica and a legitimate fossil.

"What about the baby?"

"Oh, that's good news. The baby is fine. The midwife told them that getting born makes babies sore. It's a tough squeeze. Her crying was a way of saying she needs comforting; she doesn't want to be ignored. Not that Roper and Hannah would let that happen. There's something else. The proud parents asked me to tell you that they've come up with a name for their daughter."

"So, what is it?"

"They are calling her Bernadette."

Bernie grew quiet for a moment, and then she smiled. "Put your boots back on, and come out and look at the moon with me. It's just now peeking through the clouds. I need to tell you something important."

Before she knew it, he had his arms around her, and his words came in a rush. "Just to be clear on this all, I don't care what you decide about the job, or if you need to take time off and help your mother and sister. Really. I mean it." He gave her a tender squeeze. "I'll get that suitcase for you."

She gently pushed away from him so she could look him in the eye. "It's not the job. I'll figure out what comes next for work. I've already got some ideas. It's not that. I need to tell you something else."

She took a deep breath and gave the little bear in her pocket a quick squeeze.

"I know you want to be a father, and I thought I'd have good news for you, but I don't, and I'm so sorry about that . . ." And then, for the first time in a long, long time, she started to cry. She wept with her whole heart.

Chee sang to her, gently at first, and then with more power. He sang a song she recognized as a healing song. The perfect song at the perfect time and in a place perfect for healing. Her tears stopped. She let the words of the song, a gift of such amazing love, fill her to the brim.

She looked at the glorious moon and at the peace in Chee's face.

"I'm glad we aren't driving back to Shiprock tonight. What I'd like to do now is talk to you about what happened and have you, you know, just listen. I need to tell you the story."

"Wonderful." He wrapped her in his arms again. "But first, let's go inside and warm up."

# Acknowledgments

Whether I'm reader or writer, the end of any book I love comes, like many endings, with mixed emotions. That is especially true of *The Way of the Bear*.

It was an honor to set a story in the amazing landscape of the Bears Ears National Monument and, especially, Valley of the Gods. That beautiful area speaks to me, and I hope it will resonate with readers as well. It is a real place, and, as I write this, the newest national monument in the United States. It has another distinction—it's the first national monument created at the request of Indigenous tribes. The 1.36 million acres of Bears Ears National Monument are managed jointly by a tribal coalition of representatives from the Navajo Nation, the Hopi Tribe, the Ute Mountain Ute Tribe, the Ute Indian Tribe of the Uintah and Ouray Reservation, and the Pueblo of Zuni, along with the Forest Service and the US Department of the Interior's Bureau of Land Management.

The area beneath the twin Bears Ears Buttes

shelters more than a hundred thousand Native American cultural sites, ranging from lithic scatter left by early migrating hunters to granaries and complex villages. The region also contains the geological record of a host of significant events in the development of life on our planet. The abundant and extensive paleontological story here offers clues to major extinctions, evolutionary events, and the sustaining power of taxonomic diversity.

The fossil-bearing rock in Bears Ears National Monument comprises a nearly continuous record of changing climates and life's adaptation to those changes from approximately the middle Pennsylvanian period (some 310 million years ago) through the middle of the Cretaceous period (about 115 million years ago). The Bears Ears geological library includes the icehouse-greenhouse transition and the evolution of fully terrestrial tetrapods—four-legged animals, most of which live on land and use lungs to breathe. The fossils document the rise of the dinosaurs following the Triassic mass extinction, and the response of ecosystems in dry climates to the sudden temperature increases that came at the end of the last glacial meltdown.

I could not have invented a more interesting setting.

Besides the setting in which *The Way of the Bear* unfolds, my stories need people, and real people in my life help bring the fictional characters to life.

*Shashajaia bermani*, the unique fossil species that inspired the fictional discovery of my character Chapman Dulles, was named to honor both the Navajo people and the paleontologist who discovered it, Dr. David Berman of the Carnegie Museum of Natural History. The genus name *Shashajaia* comes from the Navajo *shash* (bear) and *ajai* (heart). The fossil's partial jaws, complete with teeth, represent an anatomically primitive branch of animals known as Sphenacodontoidea, a subset that includes the well-known sail-backed dimetrodon, often confused for a dinosaur. The teeth, turned to stone over millions of years, give scientists clues to how the animal's diet changed as mammals became more specialized. As prey moved from the water onto land, *Shashajaia* adapted to life on land, too, and grew larger teeth.

As always, my first acknowledgment is to the men and women who patrol the Navajo Nation as the Nation's law enforcement team. Eighteen officers have died in the line of duty, and I would like to also acknowledge them here:

Esther Charley, Lamar Martin, Michael Lee, Houston James Largo, LeAnder Frank, Alex K. Yazzie, Ernest Jesus Montoya Sr., Darrell Cervandez Curley, Winsonfred A. Filfred, Esther Todecheene, Samuel Anthony Redhouse, Hoskie Allen Gene, Andy Begay, Roy Lee Stanley, Loren Whitehat, Burton Begay, Gordon C. James, and Hoska Thompson.

Next, my sincere appreciation to Dave Tedlock. His fine brain helped me ferret out problems in this novel and move the book forward, all the while also assisting with a variety of promotion and outreach opportunities. This book is better and my life is infinitely richer for his presence.

Arin McKenna has done a wonderful job with my social media postings on Facebook and figured out how to make me look and sound respectable on video. She also gracefully resuscitated a Facebook page in honor of my dad, author Tony Hillerman, to alert viewers of the *Dark Winds* AMC television series based on the novels that he began and I now continue. Kudos to Jonathan Black for his lovely annehillerman.com website design, and to Jean Schaumberg for helping me provide books for talks and signings at library and book club events. And for her abiding friendship.

My steadfast crew of beta readers again generously took the time to review a manuscript with a wide assortment of glitches and help me smooth things out. Any mistakes in *The Way of the Bear* are my responsibility. Huge thanks to Lucy Moore, David Greenberg, Gail Greenberg, Rebecca Carrier, and Benita Budd for their insights and suggestions. After that, Jim Wagner's skilled proofreading rescued me from serious embarrassment. And thanks to Andrew Werling for his help preparing the final manuscript. Because of my team's outstanding efforts, I've had more time for writing, research, and sleep.

Thank you to the folks at HarperCollins for their hard work on my behalf. Editor Sarah Stein, assistants Hayley Salmon and David Howe, cover artist Jerrod Taylor, copy editor Miranda Ottewell, and production editor Nikki Baldauf all helped make this book a reality. And a shout-out to my first editor at HarperCollins, the esteemed Carolyn Marino, for her ongoing support. I appreciate DeLanna Studi for her work on the audio version of this book and others in the series, and

Hosteen Peter MacDonald for his help with the Navajo words and the glossary.

Thanks to Dylan Lansing, a guide with Wild Rivers Expeditions, for sharing his passion for Bears Ears' beauty and stories from the Diné tradition. Thanks to Meghan Wetherell of the University of Arizona Paleontology Department for her insights into the world of fossils large and small and the men and women who devote their lives to studying them. And a tip of the hat to Rachel Wootton, public affairs specialist for the Bureau of Land Management in Moab and Monticello, Utah, for politely answering my questions.

After the quiet months of COVID isolation, I rejoiced in the opportunity to resume in-person events. What a treat to be back in the company of live readers as well as the remote presence of other attendees in little electronic boxes. I am especially grateful to four booksellers who have cheered for me since the debut of *Tony Hillerman's Landscape*: Dorothy Massey of Santa Fe's Collected Works Bookstore & Coffeehouse; Barbara Peters of The Poisoned Pen Bookstore in Scottsdale; John Hoffsis of Treasure House Books and Gifts in Albuquerque; and Susan Lang of Peregrine Book Company in Prescott, Arizona.

I also own a huge debt of gratitude to public libraries and bookstores for extending to me the honor of speaking to their patrons in person or via Zoom and its video cousins. I appreciate the ongoing support of my readers, and hold my Navajo fans close to my heart. I love the stories I hear about the way parents and grandparents have novels by my dad, Tony Hillerman, in their homes, and how they introduce their children and grandkids to this series.

Finally, a warm thank-you to all the fans who responded to the name-the-dog contest and to the booksellers who volunteered to help with the judging. The name I selected is Bidziil, which means "He Is Strong" in Navajo. It was submitted by three astute readers: Gwen Desselle of Georgia, and Gail Greenberg and Nina Wooderson of New Mexico. Thanks to them and to everyone who shared an idea for the name of Mrs. Darkwater's dog.

Until next time,
*Anne*

# Glossary

## A Few Navajo Words

**adilgashii**: Witchcraft

**ahéhee**: Thank you

**awéé' hayiiníłí**: Midwife

**bidziil**: "He is strong"

**bilagáana**: A white person

**Ch`ah Lizhin**: The Black Hat rock formation, also known as Mexican Hat rock

**chindi**: The restless spirit of a dead person

**Dikos Ntsaaígíí**: Coronavirus

**Diné**: The Navajo people

**Diné Bikéyah**: The people's sacred lands. Utah Diné Bikéyah is a Native American–led nonprofit organization dedicated to supporting Indigenous communities and protecting their culturally significant ancestral lands

**Dinétah**: The Navajo homeland

**Diyin Diné**: The Holy People of the Navajo

**hatáálii**: A Navajo singer and traditional healer

**hosteen**: A title of respect for an older man

**hózhó**: A state of peace, balance, beauty, and harmony

**jish**: A small pouch, usually made of deerskin, which contains a few items that have totemic, spiritual, and ceremonial value

**Keshmish**: Christmas

**Lilakai**: A woman's name. Lilakai "Lily" Neil (1900–1961) was the first woman to be elected to the Navajo Tribal Council. The name is perhaps derived from the Navajo words *łįį́*, "horse," and *łigaii*, "white"

**na'iidzeeł**: A dream (during sleep)

**né'èshjaà**: Owl

**Níłch'itsoh**: December

**Shash Jáá**: The Bears Ears Buttes that give Bears Ears National Monument its name

**shimá yazhí**: Maternal aunt; literally, "little mother"

**ta'chééh**: Sweat lodge

**Tséyík'áán**: Comb Ridge

**yá'át'ééh**: It is good; hello